Burning Cold

A Cara Walden Mystery

Books by Lisa Lieberman

Cara Walden Mysteries

All the Wrong Places

Burning Cold

History

Stalin's Boots: In the Footsteps of the Failed 1956 Hungarian Revolution

Dirty War: Terror and Torture in French Algeria

Leaving You: The Cultural Meaning of Suicide

Translations

Simone de Beauvoir, *An Eye for an Eye*

Jean-Paul Sartre, *Paris Under the Occupation*

Burning Cold

Lisa Lieberman

Lisa J. Lieberman

Passport Press

Book design and conversion by Eddie Vincent/Encircle Publications
Cover design by Deirdre Wait/Encircle Publications
Passport Press logo design by Timothy Lang
Author Photo by Sharona Jacobs

Publisher's Cataloging-in-Publication data

Names: Lieberman, Lisa, author.
Title: Burning cold / Lisa Lieberman.
Series: A Cara Walden Mystery.
Description: Amherst, MA: Passport Press, 2017.
Identifiers: ISBN 978-09989837-1-4 (pbk.) | 978-0-9989837-2-1 (e-book) | LCCN 2017907808
Subjects: LCSH Hungary--History--Revolution, 1956--Fiction. | Brothers and sisters--Fiction. | Historical fiction. | Suspense fiction. | Mystery and detective stories. | BISAC FICTION / Mystery & Detective / General. | FICTION / Mystery & Detective / Women Sleuths
Classification: LCC PS3612.I3347 B87 2017 | DDC 813.6--dc23

*This book is dedicated to the Hungarians who died
in the 1956 Revolution*

CHAPTER ONE

Sárvár, Hungary
November 4, 1956

Through me the way to the suffering city;
Through me the way to eternal suffering;
Through me the way among the lost.

Dante, *Inferno*
Canto 3: *The Gates of Hell*

I never saw the newsreel footage of Budapest after the siege of World War II, when the Russians and Germans battled it out and Hungarians hid in their cellars. I was only twelve at the time. But I have no trouble imagining the ruined city as it was then, its buildings ripped open by cannon fire. The grand boulevards strewn with rubble and shattered glass. Charred trees and the eerie silhouettes of metal street lamps twisted in the explosions. Turning a corner, you'd come upon the remains of a burnt-out tank. Abandoned trolley cars stopped in their tracks, cables dangling from the overhead wires. Crumbled barricades blocked your way. And the makeshift morgues, the most terrible sight of all. Bodies spread on the frozen ground awaiting burial. Freedom fighters, a good many of

1

them students, teenagers. Sometimes you'd see people wandering among the rows of corpses, searching for their missing children.

Lost souls, all of them.

We were there in 1956, when the Soviets came back and crushed the Hungarian revolution. Fleeing the country in a borrowed Škoda sedan the color of dried blood, we passed scores of refugees escaping to the West. Some rode in carts piled with belongings but most walked, carrying a suitcase or two, small children trudging alongside the adults on the muddy roads. Hungarians held no illusions about their fate when order was restored. They'd been "liberated" once before by the Russian Army.

"I could have told you it would end like this," said Zoltán. He was pacing the floor while the three of us, Jakub, Gray, and I, sat crammed together on the bottom bunk bed in a basement cell of Sárvár's police station. The building was silent; everyone seemed to have gone home. Or perhaps they'd been waiting until nightfall to join the exodus and were halfway to Vienna by now. Sárvár was a stone's throw from the Austrian border. We ourselves would have crossed into safety hours earlier, had our luck held.

My brother Gray was in no mood to be scolded. "We risked our lives trying to get you out of Budapest. If you had any gratitude, you'd thank us."

"Gratitude," said Zoltán. "From the Medieval Latin *gratitudo*. Gratitude figures in most religious worship, but notice how the word acquires a mercenary flavor in the mouth of an American. We might be bankers tallying accounts on a balance sheet." He stopped pacing and stood over us, menacingly close. "Is that why you came on this ill-conceived mission, to settle our father's debt?"

"Your father had no part in it," said Jakub. "If you need to blame someone, blame me. Rescuing you was my idea."

"Your idea! What were you thinking, bringing your bride into this hell? You've seen war, for God's sake."

In the scant light coming in off the corridor, I couldn't read Jakub's expression, but I didn't need to see his face to gauge the depth of his remorse.

"You're right," he said quietly. "I should have known better. Forgive me, Cara."

He never called me Cara. From the day we met, he'd used a Polish endearment, *najdroższa*, the tenderness in his voice so plain, it hardly mattered that I didn't speak his language. Anyhow, he spoke English beautifully, and several other languages besides.

I took his hand and raised it to my lips. I couldn't bear to see him suffer because of me, and I wasn't being noble or self-sacrificing. Really, it was quite the opposite. I needed Jakub to be strong. Twice before, he'd gotten me out of trouble, and I was counting on him to save me again, to save all of us. Even in jail, not knowing whether we'd been left to rot as Sárvár's population scattered in advance of the Soviet onslaught, even fearing that Russian soldiers might burst in at any moment and shoot us, even so, in Jakub's presence I wasn't afraid.

This makes me sound like the heroine in a melodrama from the silent era, Lillian Gish or some other damsel in distress. I must admit, I watched far too many of those movies growing up. Father specialized in the genre during his early years in Hollywood and the screening room at the lodge was stocked full, reels and reels of long-forgotten pictures from his early years at Famous Players-Lasky. But I felt uncannily like Lillian Gish at that moment: helpless, naïve, and in peril.

The problem was, my savior courted danger as ardently as he'd courted me. Jakub had a reckless streak. During the war he'd been a courier in the French underground, passing messages practically under the nose of the Gestapo. Repeatedly—and unnecessarily, in my opinion—he would go out after curfew. One night he was apprehended near the Sorbonne while disguised as a priest. Some priest! With his dark eyes and that sensuous mouth of his, I can imagine his female parishioners swooning at the communion rail, women lining up ten deep outside the confessional, awaiting their turn to whisper fantasies in the darkness, fabricating sins and revealing their secret desires, all of them vying to be the one who enticed the young cleric to break his vows.

At least I didn't have to invent steamy scenes out of thin air. If I closed my eyes, we were back in our atelier in Paris, undressing one another when we'd scarcely gotten inside the door. Jakub played jazz violin in a trio that also featured a bass player and a pianist. I'd joined them as their vocalist right after our marriage at the end of September, and my renditions of American standards went over pretty well in the touristy Saint-Germain-des-Prés nightclubs that were the trio's bread-and-butter. "Smoke Gets in Your Eyes," "Stardust," "Night and Day," "Ev'ry Time We Say Goodbye." These were the ballads people wanted to hear, and I loved singing them, even if I was no Juliette Gréco. She was all the rage in those days and I adored her; at my urging, the fellows had added "Autumn Leaves" to the repertoire. I'd practiced against the record of her singing the French version, *"Les Feuilles mortes,"* until I could replicate Gréco's phrasing, note by note, breath by breath, including the whispery bits at the end of a stanza. I wore black, of course, and rimmed my eyes with kohl, fully inhabiting the role, and something of the sultry chanteuse I impersonated onstage carried over into our lovemaking.

We couldn't get enough of one another. After our last set, the trio and I would head off to a café in Montparnasse, Chez Lázár, to jam with the house musicians. The sessions were purely instrumental, but I was content to sit off at a side table by myself, smoking and nursing a cognac while I watched Jakub play. The room might be crowded, but I felt as if he were performing just for me, seducing me with the sounds he coaxed from his violin. The soulful vibrato, the virtuosic riffs, bow sliding along the strings, tension mounting steadily, inexorably, to resolve at last in a sensuous purr. He seemed utterly absorbed in the music, but I found ways of distracting him; it was part of the game.

When he finished a solo, I'd toast him with my glass, holding his eyes as I brought the snifter to my lips and drank. The first sip was harsh, but its sweetness would soon spread across my palate, warming and emboldening me. I imagined kissing him, the peppery taste of his tongue in my mouth, the heat of his body as we drew close. Just the thought made me yearn for him, a longing I conveyed through my gaze alone, appraising him from head to toe as I drew languorously on my cigarette. Flustered, Jakub would somehow manage to tear his eyes away from mine and return to his playing, but the awareness we would soon be in bed together lent his performance an exquisite edge. Soon I'd catch him sneaking glances at me, missing cues, pausing to tune his instrument with trembling fingers. Then we'd be hurrying upstairs to our studio, Jakub's mouth on mine, his hand sliding up beneath my dress before we'd reached the attic landing. This was also part of the game, the risqué part, because our landlord, Lázár himself, lived on the floor below.

"Let's not make it too easy for him," I'd say, attempting to pull away. Or half attempting. Father had schooled both Gray and me in old-world manners. Born into a good Jewish family in Hungary during the waning years of the Austro-Hungarian Empire, he had an immoderate respect for the rules of propriety—except when applied to himself. Since emigrating to America in 1918, he'd had three wives, Gray's mother, my mother, with one short-lived marriage in between, and numerous dalliances. Walden Lodge, his Hollywood estate, was notorious for wild parties, champagne flowing morning to night, scantily clad starlets cavorting around the pool. My childhood was quite bohemian, but at the age of twelve I was sent to a snooty boarding school in Connecticut to learn decorum and ladylike subjects such as English literature and art history, along with a smattering of French and Italian. All to no avail; the bohemianism was too deeply instilled. Half of me wanted to be a proper young lady, but the other half didn't care if we made an exhibition of ourselves in the hallway, Lázár be damned.

Our landlord was, in fact, a voyeur who had a habit of letting himself into the studio with his key at random hours, obviously hoping to catch us in the act, and once or twice he'd succeeded. But even without him walking in on us, I always felt as if we were being watched because of the puppets: marionettes dangling from the ceiling, Balinese shadow puppets decorating the walls, elaborate box puppets with mechanisms controlled by keys you played like a piano, hand puppets whose carved and painted faces conveyed distinct personalities. The café downstairs had started as a puppet theater between the wars, the creation of avant-garde artists fleeing fascist regimes in Central and Eastern Europe. They'd formed a little troupe under Lázár's direction, painters, designers, sculptors, writers, and composers experimenting with new forms, new tableaux. The result was Le Théâtre de Minuit. The Midnight Theater. Performances started well past midnight and lasted until the wee hours of the morning, a tradition that carried over into its current incarnation as a jazz club.

Lázár, as it happened, was a Hungarian émigré just like Father—nobody knew whether Lázár was his first name or his last name—and our studio had been his workshop. Tucked away in the cabinets were scraps of fabric, silks and velvet in many hues, starched linen, antique lace, and a treasure trove of notions, from tiny mother-of-pearl buttons, sequins, beads, and feathers to satin ribbons and rickrack. I'd been taught to sew at the Wentworth Academy for Young Ladies. It was my most ladylike skill. Having such luscious materials at hand, and seeing the tattered state of the puppets' garments, I undertook the project of repairing their wardrobes, beginning with the marionettes. I pitied them most of all, hanging over us, dusty and disheveled, heads bowed in shame. They used to be dressed quite grandly, you could tell, and I labored to restore their costumes to their former splendor, attentive to the smallest detail. A satin lapel for the monocled gentleman's tuxedo jacket, a shimmering shawl for the one I called the countess, to cover her décolletage. A silk rose I constructed for Señorita Margarita to wear in her black chignon. When she danced a flamenco, she might clench it between her teeth, or toss it to one of her admirers.

Needlework filled the idle hours when the trio was rehearsing without me, and Lázár was delighted with the results. Soon we were planning a revival that would bring the old Théâtre de Minuit back to life for a single night. Some of the artists who'd comprised the original troupe still resided in Paris. Lázár gathered them together and within a week we had sets and lighting, a sketch commissioned from a Romanian playwright known for his absurdist dramas, with a score composed by a professor at the Paris Conservatoire, who recruited half a dozen musicians virtually overnight to perform the piece. We'd scheduled the event for a Tuesday in late October. There was no need to advertise; the café was barely large enough to accommodate the friends and relatives of all who'd had a hand in putting the show together.

I'd invited Gray, who was living in London at the time. Blacklisted Hollywood people, my brother among them, had flocked to Europe in the early 1950s to avoid testifying before HUAC. Colonies of expatriate Americans were established in England, France, and Italy, each taking on the complexion of the culture in which they found themselves. The Paris contingent had attached themselves to the circle of Left Bank artists and intellectuals surrounding Jean-Paul Sartre. It was from them Gray learned, on the very evening of our performance, that a popular revolt had broken out in Budapest.

"Have you heard? Hungarians have taken to the streets," he proclaimed, bursting in on our dress rehearsal. "They've started a revolution to drive out the Communists!"

"*Qu'est-qu'il y a?*" Lázár shouted in irritation from behind the puppet stage. Jakub was still out on a gig with the trio—I'd begged off that night to help with the last-minute preparations for the show—and my schoolgirl French was not up to the job of conveying Gray's news. The puppeteer was genuinely alarmed, firing off one question after another, not waiting for the answers. His sister and her family lived in Budapest and strongly opposed the current regime.

"Who told you this?" I translated. "He takes *Le Monde*

and saw nothing about a revolution in Hungary in this afternoon's edition."

"It wasn't in *Le Monde*. It was on the radio. They were talking about it at La Coupole."

"La Coupole!" Lázár picked up on the name before I'd rendered the sentence into French. The existentialists' favorite gathering place was right around the corner. The countess, who had been on the verge of lecturing an oafish butler on mollusks, of all subjects, went limp. Draping the controller over her inert body, the puppeteer went dashing out the door, still wearing his long black gloves, to get the story firsthand.

Needless to say, the uprising in Hungary eclipsed our little production. The show went on, but without zest. No scenery, no matter how fabulous, no dialogue, however scintillating, not even an original score performed impeccably by some of Paris's finest musicians could compensate for the listlessness of the marionettes. The countess flubbed her lines in the mollusk monologue, lumping squid in with gastropods such as snails and slugs, ignoring bivalves altogether. Señorita Margarita was supposed to flirt scandalously with the monocled gentleman in the second act, but when the orchestra launched into a spicy paso doble, you'd have thought the couple were dancing a waltz, so chastely did they move around the stage. I felt sorry for the audience, who dutifully stayed until the very end of the play, but more sorry for the people who'd worked so hard behind the scenes to make it happen. I'd experienced that kind of camaraderie when I was touring with a repertory company in England, the director's vision combining with the talent of my fellow actors to inspire everyone's best work. The Théâtre de Minuit must have been magical in its day, judging from the glimpse we'd been given, but there would be no resurrecting it again after this fiasco.

Lázár was too despondent to care. He'd disappeared without taking a curtain call and as soon as we could extricate ourselves politely from the group of well-wishers in the café, the three of us went upstairs and knocked on the door of his apartment. There was no response.

"Try talking to him, *najdroższa*," my husband prompted. "He's fond of you."

"Monsieur Lázár?" Still no answer. Was he okay? I hoped he hadn't harmed himself. Raising my voice, I knocked again. "Monsieur Lázár?"

"J'arrive." We heard the sound of approaching footsteps. *"C'est toi*, Cara?"

"Oui, monsieur. Pouvons-nous entrer?"

"Je vous en prie."

The door opened and a disheveled Lázár appeared in his shirtsleeves, looking as if he'd aged a decade since we'd seen him last. Wearily he ushered us into a room cluttered with broken antiques. He gestured toward a set of more-or-less-intact Louis XV salon chairs, but sitting on the Persian rug on the floor seemed like a safer bet. With Jakub translating for Gray and me, the puppeteer filled us in on the crisis. The police had opened fire on the protesters, he told us, killing hundreds and wounding thousands more. Soviet forces stationed in Hungary had been summoned to the government's aid. The first Russian tanks were already rolling into the city. Russian planes flew overhead.

We all sat there, stunned. Tanks and planes and soldiers, all massed against the people of Budapest. They didn't have a chance.

"What about his family?" I asked. The puppeteer was so downcast I was afraid something terrible had happened to someone he loved.

Jakub explained that Lázár had telephoned his sister in Budapest the minute our production had ended. She and her husband were safe, but their son, a student at the technical university, had been wounded in the battle outside the radio station. His friends had managed to carry him home and his injuries, fortunately, were not fatal, but our landlord was sick with anxiety. I wished there were something I could say to raise his spirits—he was so low—but I'd experienced enough sorrow in my twenty-three years to know there are times when keeping company in silence is the most we can do for one another.

My beautiful mother, Vivien, had drowned when I was ten. The loss of her became part of who I was, tinging even my happiest moments with regret. I'd grown used to her absence, I'd been motherless for so long, but that didn't stop me from wondering what it would have been like to have had Vivien in my life as I was growing up. She would have consoled me, the first time my heart was broken, I was sure of it. Wasn't that what mothers did? Instead, I'd run off to England with Gray, burying my pain inside. I'd tried so hard to convince myself that I didn't need anyone, but it didn't work. I'd plunged into another love affair and was hurt again. Then Jakub came along and I discovered I wanted to be with him every minute of every day. Needing somebody wasn't a bad thing if that person needed you too.

When we got married, I wore the pearls Father had given Vivien on their wedding day. She was already pregnant when she'd walked down the aisle, carrying me. "Imagine that you are carrying her," said Father, fastening them around my neck. He'd loved her dearly and for his sake, I attempted to conjure her presence, but wearing those pearls next to my skin stirred up old feelings of abandonment. *You're missing everything*, I found myself thinking. So many years had passed—and I know this sounds unfair—but I could not bring myself to forgive Vivien for dying and leaving me to grow up without her.

Lázár could not forgive himself for being in Paris, safe and sound, instead of joining the struggle in Budapest. "*J'aurais dû revenir*," he lamented. I should have gone back. Ever since Stalin died there'd been signs of unrest, he told us, some subtle, others too obvious to ignore, indications that his countrymen were uniting to throw off the Soviet yoke. And yet he had ignored all of them.

"Ask him what kind of signs," said Gray. He made a point of being up-to-date on world events, but very little of what went on behind the Iron Curtain was reported in the West.

Jakub reeled off a series of events related to him by the puppeteer. Following Hungary's defeat to West Germany in the 1954 World Cup, hundreds of thousands of disappointed soccer fans protested in the streets. They weren't only upset about their team's loss; they were manifesting their dissatisfaction with the regime. Next came the discontented rumblings of students, artists, and intellectuals, who began holding public forums to air their grievances, meetings that attracted hundreds, then thousands. Soon they were publishing their criticism in pamphlets and underground newspapers that circulated hand-to-hand.

Abruptly, Lázár got up and went to rummage through the drawers of a walnut secretary, returning with a sheaf of mimeographed pages fastened at the corner with a brass rivet. "*Regardez ceci*," he said, thrusting the manuscript at Jakub. It was a copy of a clandestine magazine that published the work of enemies of the Hungarian state. *A Rideg Valóság* was the title. *The Cold Truth*. Lázár's brother-in-law was one of the editors and had smuggled him out a copy of the first issue.

"Does he mean presumed enemies of the Hungarian State, or are we talking about bona fide traitors?" Gray wanted to know. Most of the time he viewed world events with cynical detachment, but I could see he was really wrapped up in this story.

"Presumed enemies," my husband answered after consulting with our landlord, "but in Hungary, you must understand, that meant just about anybody."

Lázár proceeded to explain, via Jakub, how so many Hungarians had come to be branded as enemies. The country's Stalinist leader, Mátyás Rákosi, had jailed thousands in the early 1950s, tyrannizing the population into submission with the help of his ruthless secret police, the ÁVH, who recruited a network of informers. Friends and neighbors betrayed one another at the drop of a hat; people you'd known for years cut you dead, crossing to the other side of the street to avoid you. Nobody was above suspicion and nobody could be trusted. Not even relatives.

Some of the regime's victims had composed poetry while they were in prison, recollections of sunlit days in the past, preserved in words like amber. Lacking pencils or paper, they'd spoken their poetry aloud, committing it to memory. And when one of their fellow inmates died, the others strove to capture his spirit in a poem. Jakub was holding the result of their labors.

The sky outside was lightening with the approach of dawn, and I thought we should all be getting to bed, but now that we'd gotten him going, Lázár seemed to want us to stay. He'd ordered a bottle of whiskey from the bar downstairs and he and my brother were keeping apace with their drinking, sip for sip, glass for glass. Jakub had barely touched his glass, I was glad to see; at the rate Gray was going, it would take the two of us to get him back to his hotel. It seemed like the right moment to interrupt the history lesson.

"Please," I said, "*s'il vous plaît, monsieur, nous lire un poème.*" I wanted to hear the sound of one of those poems, even if I couldn't understand the words.

Lázár leafed through the typewritten pages. He seemed to be looking for one poem in particular. "*Voilà!*" he said when he came upon it. He recited it first in Hungarian, then in French. It was quite short, almost a haiku. Translating it required very little effort on my part.

"Winter death
"Your name is no secret.
"War could not claim him
"Only this: cold despair
"Oh, brave Jónás."

Well before the puppeteer gave us the words in French, Gray's eyes had filled with tears. "Who wrote that?" he asked, setting his glass of whiskey on the rug to fish a handkerchief out of his trouser pocket and blow his nose.

I understood why the poem had affected him so deeply. It moved me too. Three years earlier, racist thugs in England had murdered a man he loved, Dory, a Trinidadian who sang with a calypso band. My brother wrote a play to honor our friend's memory, just as this unknown poet had done for his fellow inmate. "Out of Place" was still playing on the West End. I'd seen it several times, and every time the Dory character died, I grieved for him all over again, so fully had Gray brought the man we knew to life. I envied him his gift, the way he used words to reveal what was in his heart. Nobody who saw his play could fail to emerge from the theater unaffected by the terrible tragedy of Dory's death.

He possessed the power to make people pay attention to what really mattered.

"Szabó Zoltán," Lázár replied when Jakub asked the name of the poet. Then he corrected himself: "Zoltán Szabó." For some reason, Hungarians put the last name first.

"Szabó," I said. "What a funny coincidence." Szabó was Father's name before he changed it to Walden. The word meant tailor, a not uncommon profession for Jews in Europe. The family had been in the clothing business for generations, rising from humble tailors to found a menswear line that was sold in Hungary's finest shops. I'd probably come by my skill with a needle genetically.

Gray was shaking his head in disbelief. "It's more of a coincidence than you realize, Cara. Zoltán Szabó is the name of our Hungarian half brother."

"Half brother! What are you talking about?"

"I didn't think you had any relatives left in Hungary," said Jakub.

"Qu'est-qu'il y a? Savez-vous de lui?"

Jakub turned to Lázár. *"Pas moi, mais ils pensent qu'il est leur frère."*

"Leur frère? C'est incroyable!"

"Unbelievable," I echoed, having gotten the gist of the exchange. Surely I'd have known if I had a brother somewhere in Hungary.

"I didn't say he was actually our brother," corrected Gray in the patronizing tone that used to drive me crazy. "I just said he has the same name as Father's son by his first marriage."

"First marriage! Are you telling me he was married back in Hungary? And there were other children?"

"Just the one child, Zoltán. He was still quite small when Father left his family for another woman. It caused a terrible scandal at the time, his absconding. Come to think of it, I wouldn't be surprised if that's the reason he changed his name."

"How did you find out?" It bugged me, that Gray knew something about our Father that I didn't.

"My mother was the other woman. When he ran off with that Vegas showgirl, she told me everything."

"Out of spite, do you mean?"

My brother shrugged. "Indubitably."

I'd never met Gray's mother, but I had no difficulty believing she had it in her, judging from her onscreen presence. Dark-haired and exotic-looking, she was cast as a vamp at the outset of her Hollywood career, but her strong accent consigned her to dragon lady parts when talkies came in. I found her terrifying in those pictures and couldn't imagine her in the maternal role. Like me, Gray had been shipped off to boarding school at a young age. Unlike me, he still had a mother, although he kept her at a distance.

"Your father certainly buried the past," observed Jakub. "Didn't he ever look back?"

Gray shook his head. "He and my mother spoke Hungarian in the house, and I knew all about her family, parents, grandparents, aunts and uncles, but not his."

"He never talked about his family," I agreed. "The subject was off-limits, especially after the war." Father's parents and all three of his siblings had perished in Auschwitz. He'd kept the terrible information to himself for close to a decade, only revealing it when he learned Jakub's family had met the same fate in Poland. Even then, he'd shared little more than the names and ages of his brother and sisters. He'd never mentioned a Hungarian wife and son. How would Father react to the news that this son had survived, assuming our poet was indeed the same person? We'd want to know for sure before we told him, but I couldn't imagine he'd be anything less than overjoyed.

"What are the odds?" I mused.

"Are you asking how common a name is Zoltán Szabó?" said my husband, preparing to translate the question into French.

"Well, yes. And I'm thinking about his age. He'd have to be a couple of years older than you," I said, turning to Gray.

"That would make him around forty." My brother did the math. "So, he'd have been in his twenties during the war."

"That would fit, because this Zoltán Szabó knew war. It's in the poem, don't you agree?"

"*Je le connais,*" Lázár interrupted.

I looked at Jakub, to confirm that I'd heard correctly. Was the puppeteer saying he knew the poet personally?

"*C'est vrai?*"

"*Oui, oui. Il est le copain de mon beau-frère.*"

The poem's author, we now learned, was also an editor of *The Cold Truth.* He and Lázár's brother-in-law, József, had been inmates together in one of the regime's most notorious prisons, where they'd forged an indelible bond. József would know if this Zoltán Szabó was our relative and, what's more, we could ask him ourselves because he spoke English. They both did. A facility with Western languages was evidently one of the things that got you branded an enemy of the state during the Rákosi era.

"What if he turns out to be our brother?" I asked Gray as we left the apartment. "I'd like to meet him. Wouldn't you?"

"Very much." He grew thoughtful. "I used to feel badly about Zoltán, as if it were my fault that Father abandoned him."

Jakub looked at him in disbelief. "Your fault? Please explain to me how that's even possible."

17

"I'm not saying it makes sense, but you need to remember, I was still a kid when I found out about him. A pretty lonely kid. I'd try to imagine what he looked like, this forgotten sibling in Hungary, whether he shared my interests." My brother paused on the landing and turned to face us. "Pure fantasy, but you know, after hearing his poem, I think we might have been friends. We chose similar paths, he and I, but mine was so much easier."

"Oh, Gray," I said, moving to hug him. "That's the saddest thing I've ever heard."

"It is, isn't it?"

"Budapest isn't all that far from Paris," said Jakub. "If this man is your brother, we ought to go there and bring him out while there's still time."

CHAPTER TWO

En Route to Budapest
October 30, 1956

We hit the first roadblock outside Győr: a barricade constructed of fenceposts, chicken wire, sawn-off tree limbs, and bales of hay, the ramshackle structure manned by a bunch of farmers in rubber boots, some wielding hunting rifles. Next to them stood a run-down tractor draped with a Hungarian flag, the Soviet emblem torn from its center.

"What's this?" said Gray, bringing the Škoda to an abrupt halt that nearly sent me into the windshield. We were all in the front seat, the back given over to an assortment of luxury items impossible to procure behind the Iron Curtain: fashion magazines, perfume, tins of caviar, fancy chocolates, French cigarettes, and a bottle of champagne, along with several pairs of dungarees for Lázár's nephew. Once we'd committed ourselves to making the journey, the puppeteer had enlisted us as emissaries in an effort to entice his sister and her family to leave Hungary by showering them with capitalist goods.

"*Maguk kicsodák? És mit akarnak?*" Two of the farmers had detached themselves from the group and were approaching the car, one covering the other, his rifle pointed in our direction. The one without the rifle mimed pulling something out of his pocket. Gray reached for his wallet and handed him a ten-dollar bill in lieu of relinquishing his passport. He'd only recently had it restored by the State Department, after five years of living on the lam in England, and was understandably reluctant to lose it again. The man scrutinized the bill, eyebrows furrowed in suspicion, before taking it over to show the others, leaving his compatriot alone to guard us.

"I hope they know how to share," my brother quipped. Fine for him to make light of the situation, but I couldn't seem to stop myself from shaking. What were we doing, thrusting ourselves into the middle of a revolution? This wasn't an episode in some swashbuckling adventure serial where you know the characters will survive their various trials to fight on in the sequel. We weren't guaranteed a next scene, let alone a sequel.

Jakub tightened his arm around me. "We're on their side, *najdroższa*. Just don't make any sudden moves and we should be okay."

"How do you know?" I said sharply. From the start, I'd had qualms about the expedition. The stories coming out of Hungary were so scary: reports of peaceful protesters in towns exactly like Győr being machine-gunned by Hungarian soldiers, angry mobs taking the law into their own hands and lynching local officials. I'd wanted to wait until things settled down—even Gray was getting cold feet—but Jakub had argued we were better off going right away, in case things got worse. The chaos would work in our favor. We could slip in and out without attracting attention. The authorities had more important things to worry about.

Maybe I should have stood up to him, but once József confirmed Zoltán's relationship to Father, everything had moved so fast. Lázár threw himself into the preparations, buying gifts, convincing the Romanian playwright to loan us his car, exploiting his Budapest connections to get us rooms in the hotel favored by Western journalists—no easy feat as the city was overrun with newsmen and photographers, all eager to cover the story. We were on our way before I knew it. A night in Zurich, staying with friends of Gray's, a night of luxury in the Sacher Hotel in Vienna, and now here we were, not twenty miles beyond the border crossing and already in trouble.

"*Amerikaiak!*" The farmer had returned with his comrades from the barricade, all smiling, and motioned to the one with the rifle that he should lower his weapon. Remarkably, he also returned Gray's money. The men seemed to be under the impression we were the advance brigade of some larger US government effort to guarantee Hungarian independence and even had we spoken their language, we wouldn't have had the heart to tell them we were traveling without any authorization whatsoever. Not when we were being patted on the back and handed glasses of homemade fruit brandy, accompanied by toasts to President Eisenhower. An hour later, and several packs of cigarettes poorer, we bid our newfound friends farewell and tottered back to the car.

"What did they say that stuff was? Lighter fuel?" Gray asked, fumbling in his pocket for the car keys. He wasn't yet slurring his words, but his coordination was noticeably impaired.

Jakub grimaced. "Pálinka. Our slivovitz is better."

"It would have to be, wouldn't it?" I said. "By definition, I mean."

In response he ruffled my hair, boyishly short in the pixie cut I wore in those days: my Audrey Hepburn phase, Gray called it. Even the smoothest and most delicately flavored of spirits would have failed to measure up to Jakub's very exacting standards. Early in our courtship, I overheard a conversation about vodka in the chic nightclub in Juan-les-Pins where the trio was playing. My soon-to-be-husband was extolling the virtues of some Polish brand over anything produced by the Russians. It was the first display of national pride I'd observed in him and, not being a vodka drinker myself, his vehemence surprised me. I'd since learned Jakub's family had owned a Warsaw distillery whose herb-infused elixirs were highly prized—the first such business in Jewish hands in all of Poland. Only one uncle had survived the war to carry it on. When the Communist regime nationalized the enterprise, he'd emigrated to Israel.

My brother was having difficulty fitting the key into the ignition. He didn't argue when I proposed he and Jakub switch places; the Škoda was not ours, after all, which was actually a good thing. I couldn't understand why the front doors opened backward, for one, but on top of this design flaw, the Romanian playwright hadn't been maintaining the car. It was burning oil and required topping up each time we stopped for gas. We'd purchased a few extra cans before setting off that morning from Vienna on the final leg of the trip. With luck, we could make it to Budapest on a single tank.

"*Viszontlátásra!*" Gray called out the window as we negotiated our way around the barricade.

"What did you say?"

"Huh? What do you mean, what did I say? I said goodbye, Cara."

"Not in English, you didn't." He was tipsier than I thought. Good thing Jakub was driving. Who knew what sort of trouble we'd encounter next? I still wished we hadn't come, but I trusted my husband to keep a cool head in a crisis.

22

Sure enough, a few miles after leaving the farmers, we found ourselves overtaking a convoy of Soviet tanks and armored cars that had halted by the side of the two-lane highway. They paid us scant attention, but it was nerve-racking all the same. A bicyclist approaching from the opposite direction headed straight across the fields at the sight of the heavy vehicles. The best we could do was to cross our fingers and hope some trigger-happy gunner didn't get it into his head to shoot at us just for kicks. We all heaved a sigh of relief when we had the road to ourselves again.

Budapest was a battlefield. Everywhere you looked, you saw the toll of the fighting. The streets and sidewalks were stained with blood. Bodies lay where they'd fallen, Russian soldiers in their greatcoats and fur hats, bare-headed freedom fighters, old women dead on the pavement but still grasping their string shopping bags, caught in the crossfire as they waited in line to buy bread. I didn't want to look, but it would have been cowardly to avert my gaze. The news reports we'd watched on television, the photos that had begun to appear in the daily papers, had hardly prepared us for the horror we were witnessing in the Hungarian capital. Here were people like us, some who were simply going about their business, others who were following orders, but many who believed so strongly in freedom they'd risked their lives in the effort to obtain it. In death they looked ordinary, diminished, but they'd been brave to dream of a better future. Ordinary people made heroic by the sacrifice they were prepared to make: the least I could do was to acknowledge their courage.

Jakub brought me back to the here and now. "*Najdroższa*, can you figure out where we are?"

We'd purchased a map of Hungary in Paris before we

left. One side showed the country, the other featured insets of its major cities. Lázár had marked the location of our hotel on the inset of Budapest. The Duna was located on the right bank of the Danube ("Duna" was the Hungarian name for the river) just south of the Chain Bridge, a major landmark that was impossible to miss, he'd assured us. But we couldn't get there. Crossing over from Buda to Pest further north, on the Margaret Bridge, we'd found our way blocked by an upended tram, leaving us no choice but to enter the labyrinth of narrow streets and alleyways that crisscrossed through the commercial district, each turn taking us farther away from the river. Time and time again we'd been forced to go back the way we'd come, weaving around the destroyed armored cars and artillery pieces left helter-skelter in the road while keeping clear of unexploded mortar shells as we searched for a street that was still passable. But at last we'd reached the junction of two major arteries, Andrássy út and Bajcsy-Zsilinszky út, which I was able to locate on the map, thankfully.

"You'll want to turn left up ahead, onto Attila József út. It's a straight run to the hotel." The way looked clear and I was beginning to relax, confident we would reach our destination, but no sooner had we come to the next intersection than we were met by a crowd of student insurgents, all armed to the teeth. They motioned with their machine guns for Jakub to roll down the window of the Škoda and asked for identification, but their belligerence vanished the minute they realized we were Americans. In exchange for a box of fancy chocolates, we were given a prize souvenir: a chunk of metal from the gargantuan Stalin statue they'd toppled on the first day of the uprising. A gift from the Soviet leader to the Hungarian people on the occasion of his seventieth birthday, it had stood for years at the entrance to Budapest's City Park. Now all that remained were Stalin's boots.

One of the girls, Kati, who spoke a little English, volunteered to ride with us the rest of the way as our escort. She installed herself in a space we cleared for her in the back seat and aimed her machine gun out the window, prepared to shoot any Russian soldiers or renegade secret policemen we might encounter along the way. ÁVH headquarters was situated farther down the block, she explained; the revolutionaries had commandeered it and were in the process of liberating the files housed inside. At any moment, the authorities might try to retake it. That's why she and her fellow freedom fighters were on edge. Wearing a school uniform beneath her wool jacket, an ammunition belt slung across her chest, and a beret perched jauntily on her blond curls, she made an unlikely guerilla. At her age I was swooning over movie stars and memorizing the lyrics to popular songs.

Our guide clearly had more important things on her mind. "Look there!" she'd cried as we detoured around the wreckage at Deák tér. Jakub stopped in the intersection on her instructions, to give us a better view of the action. We saw a tank proceeding slowly along Tanács körút. The next thing we knew, the tank had come to a standstill and two boys were darting out from the shelter of a newspaper kiosk, unobserved by the Russian soldiers in the turret. We saw the first one approach—Kati provided a running commentary, telling us exactly what he was doing as he unscrewed the cap to the gas tank and dashed back to his hiding place—and then the second heaved a Molotov cocktail at the open port.

"Christ! The bloody thing's going to blow up!" Gray exclaimed. "Go, man. Go!"

Jakub floored it and managed to get us beyond the square

and out of range of flying debris in a matter of seconds. We felt the blast at the same time we heard it, the paving stones vibrating beneath our tires with the force of the explosion. The sound was deafening, the boom reverberating off the surrounding buildings as if we were in some kind of echo chamber. I hugged myself and closed my eyes. Was this how I would die, far from home in a sudden explosion?

Gray had trained as a soldier in World War II (although he'd never seen action), and Jakub had his wartime experiences in the French underground, but the closest I'd ever come to a battle was seeing the bombed-out ruins of Italian towns and cities when I was in Sicily for a film shoot the year before. Imagining how the ruins got that way was nothing like witnessing the destruction as it was happening. And yet a strange calm had come over me. Death was arbitrary, and if it came now, there was nothing Jakub, Gray, or I could do to stop it. Why had I assumed that it would mean something? I realized in that moment that the way you lived your life mattered more than the way you died. If we survived this, I thought to myself, I would make every moment count.

My ears were ringing, but I gradually became aware the others were talking about the boys. Could anyone or anything come through a detonation like that unscathed, my brother was asking. Kati assured him that her comrades had allowed themselves plenty of time to take cover; she herself had participated in numerous practice raids with homemade bombs. In school they'd been trained to resist the imperialists by such improvised means, she bragged, and the risk of blowing oneself up was not as great as it appeared.

"The imperialists?" I repeated stupidly.

"She means us," said Gray. "Isn't that right, sweetheart?"

Kati nodded enthusiastically. In a sing-song, she recited a

chant in Hungarian, an imaginative little ditty about Stalin getting Uncle Sam in a headlock, or so I gathered from her loose translation. They'd been encouraged to chant it while performing calisthenics at Communist Party youth rallies, competing to see who could do the most exercises without flagging.

"Anything to keep up morale," my brother commented, taking refuge in his habitual cynicism.

Jakub shifted into a lower gear, his face impassive. He was only eighteen when he'd joined the Communist Youth, a decision born less out of conviction than of necessity. A Jewish foreigner studying music in Paris, he'd had no choice but to go underground once the Germans occupied the city and started rounding up "aliens," helped along by French gendarmes, and shipping them off to the camps in cattle cars. Sometimes I worried that I could never surmount the gap between his life and mine.

A bit farther along, Kati pointed to the mutilated body of a secret police agent dangling from a tree. He'd gotten no better than he deserved, she informed us self-righteously. On top of everything else we would witness during our time in Hungary, the sangfroid of our schoolgirl escort haunts me to this very day.

CHAPTER THREE

Hotel Duna, Budapest
October 31, 1956

József met us at the Duna the next morning and we drove him to the magazine's offices to meet our brother. "Offices" is probably too dignified a word for the tiny third-floor apartment off Republic Square, a scrubby park in a working-class district of Budapest, where he and our brother produced *The Cold Truth*. I'd been expecting a hive of literary activity, bearded poets hunched over their typewriters in the throes of inspiration, crafting odes to their courageous brothers on the barricades. Being an actress, I tend to have an overactive imagination.

The cold truth, to borrow the expression, couldn't have been further from my romantic vision. The room was cold, for sure. All the windows were blown out, shards of glass blasted across the floor, which was also littered with shell casings. Copies of the mimeographed magazine were scattered everywhere. We couldn't help treading on them when we came in the door, which we'd found ajar. Bullet holes punctured the ceiling as if someone, or several someones, had been firing into the room from the sidewalk below. A daybed was pushed against a wall, the one farthest from the broken windows, its rumpled coverlet splattered with blood.

"Good lord!" József exclaimed. "The place was intact yesterday. All of this happened after your brother and I left." A dapper, middle-aged man in tweeds, he had the fastidiousness of Noel Coward without the leavening touch of a sense of humor. Not that the scene before us called for humor.

We surveyed the room, the dingy kitchenette in the corner, its sink stacked high with cups and plates. The bookshelves laden with leather-bound tomes, most by Hungarian authors I'd never heard of, although I glimpsed the names of a few Western authors among them. Four desks occupied the center of the space, each boasting an old-fashioned typewriter, the kind with glass-topped keys. Stuck between the rollers of one of the typewriters was a sheet of paper with a dozen or so words typed in Hungarian that petered out mid-sentence, followed by a sequence of Roman numerals. I noticed a blood-smeared fingerprint on the upper right-hand corner of the page.

József noticed too. Carefully, he unrolled the sheet of paper from the cylinder far enough to allow him to read the typewritten line.

"Damned warrior ethic," he muttered. "Why couldn't he have kept his head down?"

We all stared at him in dismay. He was talking about Zoltán.

"But you just told us that the two of you left together," said Jakub.

"He must have come back."

"How can you be sure it was him?" I objected. "Anyone could have come in. The door was wide open."

"This is his desk." József sank into the chair. "I'm terribly sorry," he said, "but I lived with your brother for three

29

years. He had a bad habit of biting his nails when he was preoccupied." A scattering of fingernail parings littered the floor by his feet. I'd taken them to be splinters of glass.

Gray asked about the words on the sheet of paper in the typewriter. Had Zoltán left a message for us?

"I'm afraid not. Offhand, I'd say it was a line of poetry he was composing. Something to do with frozen tears."

Our companion now set about opening the desk drawers and removing their contents, laying them out on a corner of the desk that he'd cleared expressly for the purpose. In this way he discovered the item that brought Zoltán to life for me: a small framed black-and-white photograph of a man, a woman, and a small girl, the three of them dressed for a summer outing. Sunlight dappled their faces, which were already bright with smiles. The girl couldn't have been older than three or four. Her black hair was plaited in two tight braids and she was wearing brand-new Mary Janes and a plaid dress with a bow at the collar that matched the bows at the ends of her braids. The man was in shirtsleeves but carried a seersucker jacket draped over one shoulder. He had a high forehead and thinning hair brushed back, away from his face. Round tortoiseshell glasses gave him an owlish, intellectual look, but I was most struck by the man's light eyes. They were the same as Father's.

"That's your brother," József confirmed. "His wife's name is Anna. She's a physician. The daughter's name escapes me at the moment."

Gray studied the photo, then handed it to me. "He doesn't look much like either of us, does he?" We'd both inherited the dark coloring of our respective mothers. While my brother's complexion was swarthier than mine—his mother claimed to be part Gypsy—we bore enough of a resemblance to make it evident we were siblings. The man in the photograph looked a great deal like Father, apart from the thinning hair. Father, at sixty-four, still had a full head of hair. It was now entirely white, but I remembered when it was brown, a lighter shade than either Gray's or mine. Again, more like Zoltán's, as I noted.

"He has your smile," said Jakub, who'd been peering at the photograph over my shoulder. I examined our half brother's face, looking past the smile in an effort to discern the man underneath. He looked as if married life agreed with him, which made me glad. And he was obviously adored by the child, who was smiling up at her father, not focused straight ahead at the photographer or looking at her mother, a slender, fair-haired woman who stood rather awkwardly at the edge of the composition. She wore a white linen dress, quite simple, its timeless elegance reminding me of lawn parties at Walden Lodge in the days when my mother presided, people playing badminton or croquet while waiters in white jackets proffered glasses of rum punch and the strains of a rumba drifted across from the terrace. Zoltán's wife would have fit right in at one of those gatherings. How strange to discover I had a sister-in-law as well as a niece.

"I'd like to keep this," I said, placing the framed photograph in my handbag. If we found Zoltán, I could always give it back to him, but if we didn't, I wanted Father to know that his son had grown into manhood, that he'd been brave and talented, but above all, that he'd been happy.

"Home so soon, dearies?" Peter Ames hailed us as we exited the revolving door and entered the hotel lobby. We'd dropped József off at his apartment on the way back to the

Duna. He intended to make a few inquiries—a euphemism, we suspected, for a visit to the morgue—and would rejoin us later. We were all in low spirits, fearing the worst, but we had no intention of confiding our fears in Ames.

Gray took my arm, propelling me onward, toward the reception desk. "Keep walking," he instructed, sotto voce. "Maybe we can outpace him." He'd taken an instant dislike to the British journalist, who'd foisted himself upon us at dinner the night before; he and Gray had several acquaintances in common back in London and Ames had wasted no time in exploiting these connections.

"Outpace him? You must be kidding," said Jakub. We'd reached the desk, but Ames was closing in, moving more rapidly than you'd expect a man of his size to be capable of navigating the crowded lobby. Smaller, thinner men scurried out of his way as he surged ahead, holding aloft a highball glass as if it were a torch.

My husband was strangely fascinated by Ames. Jakub's knowledge of England derived exclusively from literature: Shakespeare, first and foremost. Milton, Pope, Spenser, Dryden, a solid grounding in Dickens, along with a smattering of the Romantic poets—his English teacher at the gymnasium he attended in Warsaw had been enamored of the classics—but Gissing's *New Grub Street* must have come his way at some point. He saw Ames as a true English type. The Fleet Street hack, willing to go to any lengths to get a scoop.

"He's a type, all right," said Gray. "The type you avoid like the plague."

The journalist did seem overly eager to assist us in locating our missing relative, jotting down the details of Zoltán's story (which he'd extracted expertly, I will admit) in his little black notebook, to pursue along with his own investigations. Gray worried we'd end up a feature article in the trashy tabloid Ames reported for, but he was a veritable fount of information regarding the revolutionary events of the previous week. Dozens of Western reporters had made their way into the country since the uprising began. Ames had ingratiated himself with every last one of them, as far as we could tell, and was only too happy to pass on whatever he heard, a conduit for all manner of rumors and wild predictions. Alas, not speaking a word of Hungarian, we had no more reliable source of news.

The desk clerk had our room keys in hand before we even asked. "Any messages?" Gray inquired. Zoltán knew where we were staying. Perhaps he'd tried to get in touch.

"I am sorry, Mr. Walden." The clerk's face bore a look of genuine regret, remorse encompassing not only his answer to my brother's question, but the decrepitude of the establishment where he was employed.

The Duna had definitely seen better days. The furniture in the lobby was shabby, the marble floor tiles cracked, the velvet drapes frayed and faded. Magnificent crystal chandeliers still hung in the dining room, their glass tinkling with every loud disturbance on the street, but they gave no light, most of the bulbs having burned out decades earlier. The whole place was sadly in need of refurbishment. Nevertheless, the staff carried on as if the hotel were still the top-notch establishment it must have been in Father's time. Indeed, the Walden name was known to them. Father's reputation as a director of high-class Hollywood costume dramas made his countrymen proud, even if the cultural arbiters of the recently overthrown regime had condemned his work as decadent capitalist rubbish.

Ames materialized beside us at the reception desk, slightly out of breath. He knocked back the remainder of his pink gin and set the empty glass down on the counter, ignoring the clerk's disapproving glare. The revolutionaries had forbidden the sale of alcohol, a gesture of mourning for the martyrs who'd died in the early days of the uprising. Other guests had the decency to confine their drinking to the privacy of their rooms; it was not at all difficult to procure liquor if one went about it discreetly. But Ames traveled with his own supply of Beefeaters and bitters and saw no reason to go without his favorite cocktail—a favorite of the Royal Navy too, Gray noted, quaffed in imperial outposts the world over.

"Did you find your brother?"

For some reason, the job of answering this question fell to me, but as I began to describe the condition of the magazine's offices, I couldn't help getting upset. What had begun more or less on a whim, the quest to find our mysterious brother in Hungary, had become serious all of a sudden. Deadly serious. Zoltán was no longer an abstraction. He had brown hair and poor eyesight. He bit his fingernails. He found time to write poetry while shooting down at unknown assailants in the street below. Most importantly, he had a wife and child who loved him. I hoped he had found his way safely back to them, but I was worried he hadn't. Why else had he failed to show up to meet us this morning as planned? If he was still alive, wouldn't he have gotten word to József and spared us the ordeal of the office?

Ames patted my shoulder in an avuncular fashion. "Chin up," he said. "I took the liberty of booking a table for lunch. There's no better restaurant in this part of the city. Go and powder your nose, dearie. I'll be waiting for you in the dining room."

Gray said he would rather starve as we headed to the elevator, but there was really no alternative to eating in the hotel. József would be reporting back with the results of his inquiries and we didn't want to miss him. Besides, where would we go?

Entering the dining room was like stepping into another era, pre-revolution and pre-Communist. Seated around us were well-dressed citizens, tucking into their goulash as if they hadn't a care in the world. How could this be? The damage was everywhere you looked. So many stores had been destroyed in the fighting that food was in short supply. Yet here we were, being served rolls with fresh butter by a servile French-speaking waiter with the delightfully inapt name of Attila who apologized for being out of caviar, but recommended the morel bisque as a first course. Or perhaps we would prefer the goose liver paté on toast points?

Jakub's voice betrayed his incredulity as he transmitted the waiter's recommendations. "Where are you getting such delicacies at a time like this?" I heard him ask.

Attila explained that Hungary's farmers had taken it upon themselves to provision the city. Wagons full of produce, dairy, pork, and poultry had started to arrive from the countryside, now that the fighting was tapering off and order was being restored. Just this morning a peasant had appeared at the service entrance to the hotel with several freshly killed geese. Hadn't we heard? The Russians were going home and a new government was preparing to rule the country democratically.

"Soon we be like America," Attila said in English, beaming at Gray and me. "Your dear father, he come back. Make beautiful movies for his country."

"Is it true, what he said?" Gray asked Ames when the waiter had left, unable to repress his curiosity despite his aversion to the man. "Are the Soviets pulling out?"

The British journalist buttered a roll and popped a

piece into his mouth. "Never trust the Russkies," he said, chewing. "Khrushchev's a sly dog. Not as evil as Stalin, mind you, but he didn't get to be party leader playing by the rules."

I was sitting with my back to the door. Jakub, who had a better view of the comings and goings in the dining room, had risen from the table in the middle of Ames's little speech. Turning in my seat, I saw him conversing with József at the maître d's stand. They spoke for several minutes. Attila had ample time to set another place before they joined us. What was József telling him? It couldn't have been good news, or they'd have announced it when they sat down, but if our brother were dead, I would have been able to tell from my husband's face.

Ames was intrigued by our Hungarian acquaintance. He opened his notebook and, pencil poised, began peppering him with questions. "Where did you learn to speak proper English? Oxbridge, I'd wager. The tweeds are a dead giveaway. Fond of Britain, are you?"

József acknowledged he had spent several years studying law at Cambridge in the 1930s. During World War II he was employed by the Foreign Office and might have stayed on in some capacity. Indeed, he sorely regretted his decision to return to Hungary in 1945, but at the time he'd felt duty-bound to serve his country in her time of need.

"We had hopes of turning our nation into a democracy. There were free elections—the first truly free elections in our history—and liberalism triumphed. The people voted for a parliamentary government with private property and a market economy, just like you have in England."

Ames nodded. "A laudable objective. But your country lacks our tradition of self-governance."

"Quite so." A pained look came into József's eyes and he

paused to massage his temples. "I'm afraid we were terribly naive."

Lázár had given us a lesson on recent Hungarian history before we left Paris, but I hadn't grasped what it meant to live through the Communist takeover until now. József had belonged to the Social Democratic Party in the immediate postwar era, and had sat in the National Assembly until the Communists seized power in 1947. Not long afterward, he was arrested, tortured, and forced to confess to a list of trumped-up charges, then sentenced to three years in Recsk, the most brutal penal camp in all of Hungary.

"Tortured!" I could hardly believe this refined man sitting across the lunch table had endured such punishment at the hands of his own government. I knew such things went on. The French army was torturing Algerians whom they suspected of being terrorists. It was in the news every day, sickening accounts of beatings, rapes, and electric shocks. Not long after our arrival in Paris, Jakub and I had attended a ceremony at the famous Mur des Fédérés in the Père Lachaise Cemetery in Paris. Former members of the Resistance who had themselves been tortured by the Gestapo stood up and spoke against the atrocities being carried out in Algeria by the French army. "We are doing there what the Germans did here," one of them said. The accusation had stuck with me.

József flexed his fingers and brought his palms to rest on the tablecloth. He'd been wearing gloves earlier, and had kept them on in the apartment because of the cold. Now I saw the backs of both hands were marked with the pinkish scar tissue that grows back over severe burns and several of his fingernails were missing.

"What they did to you—" I couldn't finish the sentence. He must have endured multiple sessions at the hands of the secret police. Yet here he sat in the Duna dining room, helping himself to another roll from the basket, asking Ames to pass the butter. That's what shocked me, as I thought about it, his ability to behave like an ordinary man after the cruelty that had been done to him. Why wasn't he enraged? I felt enraged on his behalf, and I was glad of it, glad I lived in a place where people spoke out against torture. The French had an image of themselves as a just and humane people, and I'd seen them struggling to uphold that self-image in the face of the brutality of the Algerian campaign. Here in Hungary, the struggle had barely begun.

Attila arrived with platters of chicken paprikas and dumplings and placed them before us with a flourish. The national dish, it deserved to be accompanied by a creamy Cabernet Sauvignon, he told us. They produced a fine variety in the Eger region, but since he was not permitted to serve wine, he let us know he would be bringing us coffee instead.

"Coffee with the main course?" said Ames. "Please don't tell me that you indulge in that nasty American habit. *On ne boit pas de café avec le dîner,*" he informed Attila with a dismissive flick of the wrist, exactly as a French person would have done.

"Is special coffee," the waiter assured him with a wink. "You will like." Once he had seen to it that everyone was served, he brought out a silver coffeepot and proceeded to pour each of us a cup of the special coffee, which rivaled the very best of the French Cabernets I'd sampled with Jakub. Looking around the dining room, I saw that many of the patrons were having coffee with their meals. Ames consumed a full pot, all by himself, and even József asked for a refill. By his third cup, he'd loosened up to the point where he was willing to divulge a good many things that outsiders couldn't possibly have known about the Rákosi era.

"Do tell," said Ames, licking the tip of his pencil as he prepared to take notes. "I'm all ears."

József put a finger to his lips and gestured for all of us to lean in. The Duna, he whispered, which catered to foreigners, was bugged, a listening post in the basement staffed with ÁVH agents around the clock.

The journalist's jaw dropped. "Is this true?" he demanded of Attila, who had returned to our table with dessert menus and was just then in the process of removing our empty plates.

"Is which true, sir?"

"Is the hotel bugged?"

Taken aback, the waiter denied the allegation vigorously. "No bug. Is very clean, sir."

"Bug: *ça veut dire dispositif d'écoute*," the journalist clarified, employing what I could only assume to be the French term for a listening device. His command of the language was impressive.

"*Mais oui, monsieur. Bien sûr*," Attila agreed. "Yes, sir. Is bug." Picking up the final plate, he gave a curt bow before marching smartly back to the kitchen. The rest of us looked at one another, unsure what to make of this matter-of-fact confirmation, leaving open as it did the question of whether the bugs were still being monitored.

Ames proposed continuing the conversation outside. "No point in broadcasting, if you catch my meaning."

"I'm afraid we must be on our way," said József, glancing at his watch. "We have an appointment with the chief surgeon at Saint Stephen's." After leaving us, he hadn't gone to the morgue, he'd gone home to phone various hospitals on the off chance our brother had ended up in one of them. His diligence was rewarded: someone fitting Zoltán's description had been treated at Saint Stephen's for a gunshot wound the previous night.

"Thank goodness!" I could have hugged József. Gray was beaming, and Ames reached across the table to shake his hand, but Jakub held back. He and József exchanged a look. They clearly knew something else that we didn't. Had our brother died on the operating table? I couldn't bring myself to ask, and neither could Gray, although I could see from his face the same thought had occurred to him.

"Best to be out with it," urged Ames. "Did he come through the surgery or not?"

"He came through it fine, as far as we know," said József in a tone that failed to reassure me. "But they seem to have lost him."

CHAPTER FOUR

Gray called for the check and signed for the meal, waving aside Ames's ineffectual offer to pay his portion of the bill. The three of us then went upstairs to retrieve our winter coats and hats, along with the champagne, caviar, and whatnot for József's family, which we'd left in Gray's room overnight. Ames trailed along as we ferried it down the block, but when we reached the Škoda he could see for himself there wasn't enough room for five in the Romanian playwright's car, not when one of them was a man of his girth. We stowed the gifts in the trunk and got in, eager to be gone, but the journalist held up a hand as we pulled away from the curb, motioning for József to roll down his window.

"I'll be waiting for your return, dearies. Do be careful …"

Whatever else he'd intended to say was drowned out by the clatter of a Soviet half-track, its metal treads making a fearful noise as it barreled toward us. Gray put the car in neutral, let out the clutch, shifted into second gear, and stepped on the accelerator. I was sitting next to Jakub in the back seat and I saw him brace himself for the inevitable jerk, but the car moved smoothly forward, picking up speed, and we'd soon outpaced the military machine.

"That's some trick!" said my husband, the daredevil in him thrilled by the stunt. Poor József, meanwhile, was gripping the door handle, his body tensed as if preparing to spring from the moving vehicle at any moment.

"My brother's seen a few too many gangster movies," I said. "He's imagining himself at the wheel of a getaway car. Notice the fedora? He never goes anywhere without it."

József tittered artificially without relaxing his grip on the handle. "A tough guy, are you? A ladies' man? I suppose they like that sort of thing."

"Hardly," demurred Gray. Movie-star handsome, with his shock of dark hair and the dapper little goatee he'd affected in England, it would be more accurate to say he was a gentleman's man—not that he advertised his sexual proclivities. Being blacklisted was trouble enough.

But where were all the tanks going? As we approached the green-painted iron span of Liberty Bridge, we saw a column of them crossing the Danube. The noise they made rendered conversation impossible. Gray was forced to drive up onto the sidewalk and park to get out of their way as one tank after another rumbled past us.

"They must really be leaving," Jakub shouted over the din, drawing our attention to the silent groups of bystanders on the opposite sidewalk. Hungarians would not have been watching so dispassionately the day before. Those not running for cover would very likely have been launching an ambush, as the boys we'd seen the previous day had done.

The last tank rolled across the bridge and Gray made to pull back out onto the road, but József asked him to wait. "This is a good place to talk," he said, offering around a pack of unfiltered Hungarian cigarettes. Jakub accepted one out of politeness, but Gray and I stuck to our own brands, Player's and Lucky Strikes, respectively. We all sat smoking in the closed car while József gathered his thoughts.

I found it soothing inside the Škoda, its cream-colored interior contrasting nicely with the vermillion of the body. Swank it was not; in addition to burning oil, there were dents in the hood, and the upholstery gave off a curious licorice aroma, but it nevertheless felt like home. I was content to settle back with my cigarette and look at the view across the Danube. One of Budapest's grand hotels, the Gellért, was directly across the bridge. A massive building, imposing even when viewed from the opposite bank of the river, it too had fallen into disrepair. Decaying buildings could be found in our Paris neighborhood, but these had the charm of sepia photographs, their edges blurred and softened with time. You could still make out the beauty of the original image. By contrast, Budapest's former elegance had been deliberately effaced, as if to prevent the city's residents from indulging in nostalgia for its bygone splendor. I felt sorry for them, going about in the dimmed landscape.

József stubbed out his cigarette in the car's ashtray. "I would like to tell you about your brother, before you meet him."

"Assuming we do meet him," said Gray. "He isn't making it easy for us."

"Believe me, he doesn't make things easy for anyone, least of all himself." Our companion sounded weary. "He could be so obstinate, there were times I wanted to strangle him."

Jakub nodded his head in recognition. "Those purist types can be infuriating. You're grateful to have them by your side in a battle, but in the day-to-day they can be very hard to live with."

"Very hard," agreed József. "But none of us would have survived Recsk without Zoltán, I am convinced of it. None of us. He was a genuine hero."

We listened as he described his ordeal. Recsk was located in a mountainous region northeast of Budapest. To get there you took a train—not a passenger train, he explained, but a locked freight car you shared with fifty other men.

A freight car. The idea that the Hungarian government would have chosen this means of transporting prisoners, after the use to which freight cars had been put by the Nazis, appalled me, and I could see from the expressions on Gray's and Jakub's faces that it appalled them as well.

"What year was this?" asked my brother.

"1951." József resumed his story. He and Zoltán had ended up in the same car. They were not the only ones with an education. Engineers, doctors, teachers, and civil servants were also among the ranks of prisoners, few of them suited for the relentless, backbreaking work they were assigned.

At Recsk they toiled in the summer sun and in the autumn rain, cutting down trees on the mountain slope to clear the ground for a quarry. When winter came and the mountainside was bare, they pried stones out of the frozen earth and hauled them down to the bottom on stretchers, where other prisoners broke them up with sledge hammers. The next season they were put to work building a road, to take the rocks from the quarry to the railroad station. All during this time, whether sawing wood or excavating tree stumps, while sliding in the mud on their way down the mountain with their load of stones, waiting outside the barracks for the guards to finish the evening count, or huddled in their wooden bunks at night, they talked about poetry. Zoltán, who had an excellent memory, could recite stanza after stanza of his favorite poems by heart. The authors of those poems were his true companions, and he brought them into the bleak world of Recsk to give solace to his fellow laborers, the educated and the uneducated alike.

"The men never tired of hearing him recite Dante. I believe he had memorized the better part of the *Divine Comedy*," said József.

"Ah, Dante." Gray sighed, and from some recess of his own memory he drew words I immediately recognized as the opening of the *Inferno*.

"Midway upon the journey of our life
"I found myself within a forest dark.
"For the straightforward pathway had been lost."

József did a double take. "Remarkable. You're quite like him, you know."

"I'm certainly no hero," my brother insisted. "Just ask Cara."

"Well, you are pretty hard to live with," I said, earning a laugh. But I saw Gray's refusal to name names before McCarthy's committee as quite heroic, and as a playwright, he didn't take the easy way out. His portrait of Dory in "Out of Place" was harsh as only the truth can be: terrible, beautiful, lacerating in its honesty. The play wounded me, but I was glad of it. Being wounded was better than being deadened to the pain of our friend's death. I would never forget Dory. I never wanted to.

People say good art is redemptive. I used to think they meant it was uplifting, conveying hope the way a sunrise conveys the promise of a bright new day. But bleak vistas can be redemptive too, even when there is no hope. *Abandon hope, all who enter here.* The dreadful inscription that Dante placed on the gates of Hell. Zoltán had brought the poet's unflinching vision into the darkness of Recsk to remind his fellow prisoners of the terrible beautiful pain of being alive, and that may very well have been what saved them.

"Even a nightmare can be endured, if you are given the words to describe it," I suggested. Not being gifted with language like either of my brothers, the one I knew, and the one I was beginning to know, I struggled to express my thoughts. "Is that what you're saying?"

"Yes," said József. "You put it beautifully." He looked from Gray to me. "I must say, the three of you are quite some family."

The praise embarrassed me and I sought to shift attention back to our brother. "I still don't understand what Zoltán did to get himself sent to Recsk. He was just a poet."

Jakub bestowed a kiss on my forehead. "Poetry stirs the soul, *najdroższa*. Plato wanted to banish all the poets from his Republic."

"So does Senator McCarthy," said Gray. "And he's making a damn good job of it, if you ask me."

"But Plato was right, and your Senator McCarthy too: words are dangerous," József pointed out. "Poets like your brother started the revolution. They published manifestos demanding freedom in the months leading up to the event and organized the protest marches on the first day. Even more importantly, they kept hope alive during the worst years of the Rákosi era. They wrote the truth, not the absurd lies the government newspapers were putting about, and somehow they found a way to get their words read. Zoltán was already writing poems in the late forties. I knew them long before I knew him."

Gray started the engine and eased the Škoda off the curb. "Let's see if we can find this dangerous poet-brother of ours, shall we?"

Saint Stephen's was a long, low red brick building in the neoclassical style, part of a complex of medical clinics along Üllői út. Stately Greek columns flanked the entrance, which was crowned by a statue of Saint Stephen (we presumed) tending to the poor, sick, and elderly.

Inside the hospital, the scene was sheer chaos, wounded people everywhere you looked. Some lay on gurneys parked bumper-to-bumper in the corridors, awaiting surgery. Other more recent arrivals lay on stretchers on the floor. Nurses and orderlies in bloodstained smocks moved between them, tending to the most grievously injured.

"He could be here," I said, scanning the faces of the wounded in a vain effort to recognize our brother's features.

József made a dismissive noise in his throat. "He could be anywhere. All of Budapest is like this." He'd grown hard, remote, since we'd entered the hospital, as if a glass shield had come between him and the surrounding world. This was the reality of the Hungarian revolution, the tragic counterpoint to the bravado we'd witnessed the day before in the streets. Just there in front of us, a teenaged boy lay bleeding on a gurney, the right side of his face and neck pocked by shrapnel. One eye was nearly swollen shut, but he was watching us all the same and I felt pierced by his anguished gaze. Had József's son looked like that, when his friends brought him home? Of course, I couldn't ask, and I certainly couldn't blame him if shutting down was the way he coped, after everything he'd undergone.

But shutting down was not my way. I sought my husband's hand to anchor me as we stumbled along, József guiding us ever deeper into Saint Stephen's depths.

"*Najdroższa*, I'm here." Jakub gripped my hand tightly. Maybe I was as much an anchor for him as he was for me. Poor Gray had fallen behind us and we waited for him to

47

catch up. We were witnessing the end of the world and I was absorbing all of it. The screams of the wounded. The agony of parents struggling without success to ease their children's pain. The hopelessness on the faces of hospital workers who could not hold back death.

Finally, we reached the office of the chief surgeon, the doctor who had operated on Zoltán. An erudite man with medical degrees from Vienna displayed on the wall behind his desk and a beard like Sigmund Freud's, Dr. Keller insisted on brewing us tea, heating the water on a small primus stove that sat next to a metal tray of surgical instruments. As he bustled about, filling the kettle, spooning loose tea into a china pot, setting cups and saucers and a sugar bowl on the work table where he bade us sit, he apologized for the state of the hospital, concerned lest "the Western visitors" think that medical care in Hungary was primitive. They were out of room and out of medical supplies, he explained with József translating. No antibiotics, no anesthetics, no morphine. Imagine operating on a fully conscious patient and not being able to give him anything for the pain. Or trying to prevent infections from spreading: a losing battle, keeping the equipment sterile amid periodic power losses. And yet, despite these circumstances, he wanted us to know, patients like our brother received the best care possible. Within an hour of having a bullet removed from his upper arm, he'd left the hospital on his own steam.

"I don't suppose he told anyone where he was going," said Gray.

"Knowing Zoltán, I'd imagine he went right back out to get himself shot at," József muttered, but he dutifully relayed the question, translating the surgeon's response as we drank our tea.

Dr. Keller assumed our brother had gone home to his wife.

She was a colleague of his, Szabó Anna, a pediatrician who ran a children's home in one of Budapest's outlying districts. The family lived on the premises and our brother was actually better off there than in the hospital. Üllői út was the Soviets' main route into the city, and Saint Stephen's might well be targeted when they came back.

"He wants to know when you plan on leaving," said József. "He's worried that you'll be trapped in Hungary when the Soviets come back."

"We'll be careful not to let that happen," my husband told him, but this was not the answer the doctor wanted to hear. József was treated to a diatribe on the subject of Soviet barbarity, the majority of which he did not bother to translate, although what we heard was bad enough. We learned Dr. Keller had lived through the siege in World War II. In the winter of '44, he and the few doctors who had survived the battle for Budapest were reduced to operating out of ancient caves carved into the hill beneath Buda Castle.

"He wants you to know that the Russians showed no mercy when they liberated the city," said József. "They raped the nurses, looted the hospital, shot people in their beds. His son, Bela was taken to a work-camp, *munkatábor*—"

"*Malenkii robot*," the surgeon asserted, vigorously nodding his head. "*Beszéljen nekik erről!*"

"*Igen, igen. Megmondom nekik.*"

I didn't know what they were talking about, but Dr. Keller's entire demeanor had changed. Gone was the air of authority, the calming assurance of an experienced physician that served to put patients at ease. Nobody who saw the shattered man now sitting across the table from us would have dared to put their life in his hands.

"They took his son, Bela, for forced labor. He was gone for three years," said József, "and when he came back, he was ruined. *Tönkretették*."

"*Igen, tönkretették*," repeated the surgeon, tears in his eyes. "*Elment az esze.*"

József translated: "He has lost his mind."

"Please tell him we're so very sorry." I was aware of how inadequate that sounded, but what else could any of us say? Here was a man who had spent his career repairing damaged bodies, sewing up wounds, a man devoted to healing who could not heal the one person who mattered most to him.

Jakub's thoughts were moving in the same direction as mine. "We ought to let him get back to work," he said, rising from the table in preparation to thanking the physician and making our goodbyes. Dr. Keller escorted us out through a back hallway. Stopping in front of a set of double doors that gave onto the clinic's side entrance, he put a hand on Gray's shoulder and spoke directly to my brother. "*Bármennyire örülök, hogy láthattam, most mégis az volna a legjobb, ha elmenne*" were his parting words. József rendered them into English: as nice as it's been to meet you, what I'd really like you to do now is to go away.

A battered ambulance van was pulling up as we exited the building. We hurried past, anxious to be off before it disgorged its wounded passengers. We had seen enough.

Üllői út took us out of the city and through the heart of an industrial area that had endured a good deal of fighting. At times we were forced to back up the way we'd come, or to detour for several blocks as we'd done the previous day. Trolley tracks had been dug up, the metal used to reinforce the structures, the trams themselves turned on their sides and dragged over to form part of the blockade. Workers had seized control of a factory here in the early days of the uprising and they were apparently still inside, József told us, vowing to halt production until Hungary was free. We saw defiant slogans painted on the walls, but all seemed quiet that afternoon.

Pesterzsébet, the adjacent district where the children's home was located, was less damaged and far busier. The revolutionaries were firmly in control of this suburb and it showed. People chatted on the sidewalks—the first natural-seeming behavior we'd observed since entering the country—and we were able to proceed along the main street without encountering a single sign of warfare. We passed the parish church, an imposing edifice with a tall steeple that towered above the surrounding one-story structures. The children's home turned out to be one of these, a stuccoed building with a red tile roof set back a slight distance from the road. As Gray maneuvered the car into a parking spot out front, I watched a group of little girls playing in the walled-off courtyard attached to the property. Was one of them Zoltán's daughter?

The afternoon had turned overcast and a light wind was blowing, scattering the leaves of a stately sycamore that occupied the center of the cleared space. Gleefully the girls lunged for the falling leaves, she who caught one before it touched the ground earning the approval of an older girl on crutches who performed the role of playground monitor. After everything we'd witnessed in the past twenty-four hours, it felt unreal to me, seeing children play, their laughter ringing in the chilly air. How quickly I'd grown accustomed to the turmoil.

József was having second thoughts about showing up

unexpected at Zoltán's front door. Although he knew where our brother lived, he'd never been invited inside the house and had only met Anna on one occasion. They were more like comrades-in-arms than friends, he said. Heroes didn't have friends.

"Your brother might regard my turning up here with the three of you in tow as suspicious. He might even see it as threatening. In his place, I certainly would."

"You can't know that for sure," said Gray. "You're just going on a hunch."

"One learns to trust one's hunches, living under a dictatorship," József replied, the shield firmly in place once more.

His words sent a chill through me. Ordinarily I was a trusting soul, and little in my experience had inclined me otherwise, but József's stories, his very demeanor, were making me paranoid. I could not imagine living in a state of constant watchfulness, but he'd been doing it for so long it had obviously become second nature.

My husband, as usual, was several steps ahead of me. "In that case, I wonder if we should be trusting you," he said with deceptive mildness.

József looked hard at Jakub and something passed between them. A flicker of appreciation on the Hungarian's part, I think, as in a high-stakes chess game where one player is forced to recognize that he'd underestimated his opponent's skill, met by an acknowledgment on the part of my husband that he too would be on his guard from that point on.

"Be that as it may," said Gray, returning to the matter at hand, "we're here now and you can't ask us to turn back, after coming all this way."

We decided I would go to the door with József. If Zoltán

appeared, Gray and Jakub would join us, but we didn't want to alarm the household by having all of us there at the outset. Nervously I pushed open the front gate and walked up the path. I so wanted it to be Zoltán himself who came to the door. I wanted him to be okay—that was the main thing—but hearing of how he had surmounted his ordeal in Recsk, I couldn't wait to meet this extraordinary person.

"*Ó csókolom!*" The girl on crutches was hobbling toward us, a bright smile on her face. József and I had reached the door and I saw him hesitating over whether he should knock or whether he should simply ask the girl if Zoltán was home, but the decision was taken out of his hands. The door was opened by a severe woman wearing a dark brown dress, a cameo brooch her only adornment. She was no taller than me, and of a slight build, her silver hair pinned up in a bun, but she gave the impression of such strength that I felt instantly intimidated.

József adopted a conciliatory tone. "*Jó napot—*" he began, but the woman cut him off.

"*Nem,*" she murmured to herself. "*Ez lehetetlen!*" Regarding the two of us with unalloyed hostility, she shook her head and seemed ready to retreat into the house and slam the door in our faces, but by then the girl on crutches had reached us.

"*Ugye tetszik tudni ki ezek?*" she said to the woman. She was still smiling as she spoke, looking from one to the other of us as if she expected to be introduced, but the woman had no intention of doing that. She shouted at the girl and shooed her away. József made a valiant attempt to engage the woman in conversation before she could shoo us away too, but she refused to be drawn out, answering his queries in a perfunctory way with her arms crossed over her chest, willing the exchange to end. She kept her voice low and

I caught her glancing at the houses across the street, as if to reassure herself that no neighbors were witnessing the exchange on her doorstep.

"That has to be the most terrifying housekeeper I've ever met," I commented to József, once we were back in the car. Mrs. Danvers, the housekeeper played by Judith Anderson in *Rebecca*, came to mind. A guard dog couldn't have been any more effective in keeping unwelcome visitors at bay.

"That wasn't the housekeeper," he said. "That was Anna, your brother's wife."

"She can't be!" I consulted the framed photograph in my purse. Yes, the woman at the door appeared to be the same height as the woman in the picture, but she looked so much older. Seeing the contrast, I appreciated for the first time the trauma the Communist dictatorship had inflicted on Hungary's people, not only on those like József who'd suffered directly at the hands of the regime, but on everyone who lived through the era. The years she'd spent alone while Zoltán was in prison had taken a heavy toll.

József was giving a synopsis of our encounter to Jakub and Gray. "She refused to answer any questions about your brother. I have no idea when she last saw him, or whether they're still married, for that matter, but I'll tell you this: the poor creature is scared to death." He felt badly for having added to her worries, particularly as it was all to no avail. We were no closer to finding Zoltán.

Privately, I disagreed. I couldn't explain why, but I had the impression the girl knew exactly who I was and why I'd come. She'd sought my eyes as she turned to go back to her charges. *Please,* I sensed her silent plea. *Find him.*

CHAPTER FIVE

The Gypsy band in the Duna bar struck up a tango, of all things, and the next instant Jakub and I were dancing cheek to cheek, his hand exerting the lightest pressure in the middle of my back, enough to signal when it was time to pivot before resuming our sinuous walk around the floor. A slight bend of the knee, a sideways swivel, and Jakub turned me around in a languorous circle, my right foot trailing behind until I lifted it, at his prompting, into a perfectly executed leg wrap.

"Brava, *najdroższa.*"

I leaned into him and nibbled his earlobe. Never once during the obligatory ballroom dancing lessons at the Wentworth Academy for Young Ladies had I grasped the essential feature of the tango, the melting movement where two become one, but improvising figures to the driving rhythm of the guitar, violin, and accordion in the arms of my beloved was already second nature. The minor chords matched my mood, too—far better than the jaunty folk melodies with which the set had begun.

"You probably need to be Magyar to appreciate them," Gray had said, already in his cups. To celebrate the dissolution of the old Hungarian Communist Party and the formation of a new government not beholden to the Soviet Union, the hotel had opened its ample cellars. To hell with revolutionary pronouncements! Champagne flowed freely, along with a variety of regional wines and a very fine pálinka that even Jakub was forced to admit gave his cherished slivovitz a run for its money. But none of us was in festive spirits that evening; we could not share the optimism of the people around us.

On the return trip, József relayed the substance of Dr. Keller's diatribe as Gray drove us back into the ruined city. The surgeon had ties to the provisional government that now controlled Hungary. He'd treated the new minister of the press, Géza Losonczy, after his release from prison and continued to monitor his health. The poor man had emerged from his time in captivity in dire shape and would never recover fully.

"He advised Losonczy against accepting the post," said József, "but Losonczy told him it didn't matter."

Jakub, as usual, was quick on the uptake. "He figured he'd die either way." He grew thoughtful. "Dr. Keller heard something from Losonczy, didn't he? Some news that the government knows and is not telling the people."

"There are reports of Soviet forces amassing on the borders."

"But we saw the tanks leaving!" I protested.

József shook his head. "All for show. Poland and Czechoslovakia are watching what happens here. Do you think Khrushchev is going to stand by and allow the satellites to slip away, one by one? The Russians are biding their time, and when the moment is right, they'll be back to put the rebellion down. Decisively."

"America won't let that happen," insisted Gray. I was sitting directly behind him and was unable to see his profile, but from the tense set of his shoulders, I could tell he was growing angry. "I mean, Christ. The Republicans have been obsessing about Communism for years, for decades, and here's a country trying to get free of it. We'll intervene. We've got to. Eisenhower's a general. He'll know how to stop those bastards."

"Eisenhower's attention is elsewhere at the moment, I'm afraid," said our companion.

"Are you talking about the Israeli attack?" Gray asked. "That was bound to happen sooner or later, after Nasser nationalized the Suez Canal. But I read in the papers in Vienna yesterday that the French and British sent ultimatums to both sides, demanding a ceasefire."

"The French and the British are bombing Egypt as we speak."

My brother swerved to avoid a chunk of masonry, a cornice from one of the blasted buildings that lined the wide avenue. "You can't be serious," he said when he'd straightened us out.

"I wish I weren't."

Now it was Jakub's turn to be alarmed. "What about the Soviets? They're Nassar's ally."

"There's been mention of nuclear weapons." József's voice was grim.

I gasped. "The bomb!" In a heartbeat, we'd gone from talk of the revolution in Hungary to the skirmish in Egypt to the threat of thermonuclear war.

"The president isn't about to risk a nuclear war over the Suez Canal," my brother hastened to assure me. "Certainly not a week before the election."

I wanted to believe him, but it felt as if we were on the brink of disaster. The world could end in a flash. We all knew it, and yet most people acted as if the danger wasn't real. I'll admit I could put it out of my mind for days at a time, but the fear was always there, hovering darkly around the edges of my awareness. Bertrand Russell predicted universal death if we could not forget our quarrels; Gray and I heard him say it on the BBC. All it would take was a serious confrontation between the United States and the Soviet Union, he'd warned, and now here we were, facing two serious confrontations in the space of a single week.

"The British and French couldn't have chosen a worse time to launch an invasion," said my husband. "You're truly lost, aren't you?"

In response, József slapped his palm against the dashboard. "Listen to me. We've got to get your brother out of here. He won't stand a chance, once the Soviets return. They'll go after people like him straightaway."

"But we haven't a clue where he is," said Gray. "His own wife doesn't even know."

"Or if she does know, she isn't telling," I added.

"One of the other poets might be harboring him. I'll phone around this evening." József paused to think. "Your father must be an American citizen by now."

My brother confirmed this. "A naturalized citizen, yes. Has been for years."

"Is that going to get Zoltán in trouble?" I worried, wondering what was behind the question.

"No," said József, brightening and taking charge. "That's what's going to get him out of trouble." He was more animated than we'd ever seen him, with a hint of a drill sergeant about him. "Pay attention, now. Here's what you're going to do. Tomorrow morning you will go to the American embassy and apply for a visa. As the son of an American citizen, Zoltán is entitled to one and it's his best chance of getting out of the country after you leave. If he shows up at the border with an American visa, they'll have to let him through."

"How long before the Soviets come back?" Jakub asked.

"Days or weeks?"

"Days, according to Dr. Keller."

We arranged to meet at the Duna at eleven the next morning. József had circled the location of the embassy on our map. It was only a short walk from the hotel and he'd advised us to go on foot, owing to the severity of the damage along the way. Indeed, it took time getting back after we dropped him off, although his apartment was less than a mile away. Structural damage inflicted during the days of heavy shelling was causing buildings to collapse, and we saw residents with handcarts picking through the rubble, salvaging what they could from their former homes.

"They're awfully stoic, aren't they?" observed Jakub, but to me they looked stunned, going mechanically about their task as if at a loss for something to do. Watching them collect their possessions, I remembered the gifts in the trunk and was ashamed. Champagne, chocolates, caviar: what in the world were we thinking? We should have brought a carload of medical supplies instead. Useful items like flour, dried beans, and blankets.

Gray had maneuvered the Škoda into a parking spot in front of the Duna and made straight for the bar. He was eager to chat up some of the foreign correspondents and hear what their governments were saying about the Suez Crisis. We'd found Ames presiding over a table of inebriated journalists of various nationalities. Blearily, they'd made room for us, and my brother had wasted no time in catching up on the news—along with the drinking, alas. Well before Jakub and I stepped out on the dance floor, he'd reached the point of no return. I seriously doubted he was learning anything of value, but there, as it turned out, I was mistaken.

The tango number was succeeded by a bossa nova that somehow devolved into a conga line, from which Jakub and I had difficulty extricating ourselves. Snaking past the journalists' table, I'd noticed my brother engaged in a tête-à-tête with a man I'd never seen before, a tall fellow with Brylcreemed hair and the physique of a body builder. Gray was attracted to muscular guys and this one was exactly his type, Brylcreem aside. They were still talking intimately when I sat back down. Jakub had gone off to get us two glasses of water. With all the chatter from the many conversations being conducted in half a dozen languages around the table, it took me a minute to realize the two of them were conversing in Hungarian.

"What in the world?" I blurted out.

Gray took note of my presence for the first time. "Cara," he said. At least I recognized my name. The rest of the sentence rushed by, incomprehensible to me but not, apparently, to his good-looking pal, who interrupted to add some gloss of his own, eliciting an even longer response from Gray. All in fluent Hungarian.

I felt as if I were watching a dubbed film. Two summers earlier I'd had a part in a B movie shot in Sicily by an Italian director and featuring an international cast. It had been strange at the London premiere, seeing my lips form English phrases as the dialogue came out of my mouth in Italian. Only Gray's lips were moving in sync with his dialogue.

"Would you mind saying that again, in English?" Honestly, I half expected the words to fall out of my own mouth in a foreign tongue (was it something to do with the pálinka?) but, no, I was most assuredly speaking English.

Gray's companion was instantly apologetic. "Please excuse me, mademoiselle," he said in a heavy accent. "I naturally assumed that since your brother speaks such excellent Hungarian, you would too."

"My brother speaks excellent Hungarian?" I pointed to Gray. "Do you mean *this* brother?"

"Why, yes." A look of bafflement crossed his face, no doubt matching the look on my face. "Did I misunderstand you?" he asked Gray. "Is this lovely girl not your sister?"

Jakub had returned with the water as this confused exchange was taking place. His face too bore a look of bafflement as he set the glasses down amid the clutter of empty bottles and overfull ashtrays and took a seat next to me.

Olé! cried Gray with a flourish of his hand, knocking over a wineglass in his exuberance. This outburst did nothing to clear up the confusion, but while I was staunching the tide of spilled wine with a napkin, Jakub deftly stepped in and explained I was actually Gray's half sister. My clever husband also figured out how Gray had come by his knowledge of Hungarian.

"It was your cradle language, wasn't it?" he guessed, the language spoken by our father and Gray's mother between themselves and the first language my brother had acquired, even if he'd had no occasion to use it beyond boyhood. In fact, Father once told me that Gray (whose given name was Géza) had insisted on being called Jimmy when he started first grade, the better to blend in with the American kids. He probably hadn't uttered so much as a word in Hungarian in the decades since, but the language was lodged somewhere in that brain of his.

"So why have I never heard you speak Hungarian until now?" I felt betrayed, as if he'd been holding out on me. Granted, we were born fifteen years apart and he was off at Yale by the time I was three. There was no reason why I should have been privy to the domestic details of his earliest years, but this particular detail felt like something I ought to have known.

My brother shrugged. "Evidently I needed to be good and drunk."

"I've seen you drunk plenty of times," I countered.

"Drunk, yes. But never in the company of a handsome Hungarian."

Definitely the pálinka, I decided, but Gray wasn't completely blotto. Belatedly remembering his manners, he introduced us to his tablemate, Ferenc Márkus, otherwise known as "Frankie," a local stringer for one of the Western wire services. The two of them had been speaking Hungarian to prevent *others*—here Gray indicated Ames, his neighbor, with a jerk of his head—from overhearing.

"No worries there," Jakub murmured. Sprawled across the table like some bloated sea creature washed ashore, the British journalist was in no condition to absorb any information he might overhear, but as Frankie told us what he'd been telling Gray, I appreciated their circumspection.

"Dr. Szabó is a specialist in children's psychiatric disorders," said Frankie. "Strictly speaking, the institution she runs is not an orphanage. The girls you saw have parents, but they've been interned." He paused, to give us time to let this information sink in.

"That can't be easy," I said, "having your parents taken from you."

Frankie agreed. "The girls have problems. Emotional problems. Bedwetting, nightmares, difficulty paying attention in school." Some of them were too much for their relatives to handle, he went on to explain, but such was the stigma of being associated in any way with an accused enemy of the people that family members often refused to take in even the well-adjusted children—as if the trauma of losing their parents wasn't bad enough.

I knew only too well what it meant to lose a parent at

a young age, how in a child's mind everything took on significance. The characters in fairytales were always punished for their mistakes and there had been times when I blamed myself for Vivien's death. Hansel and Gretel's greed had gotten them locked up by the witch. In "Sleeping Beauty," the princess was cursed by an evil fairy who someone had neglected to invite to the infant's christening. What had I done to deserve my punishment? I spent an awful lot of time as a child trying to figure this out. Bad things happened for a reason. Everybody knew that. If I could just stop doing whatever it was I was being punished for, then I could undo the spell.

That sad little girl still lives inside me, and each time I sing a melancholy song, or take on a tragic role, I draw on her sorrow. I've learned I can go into that lonely place and come out whole again, but I had a loving father and an older brother who'd always looked out for me. And needless to say, the Wentworth Academy was a far cry from a public institution like the children's home. Even so, the girls had not seemed disturbed. In the short time I'd observed them playing in the courtyard, I'd seen no sign of distress. They seemed like perfectly normal children, which was saying a great deal as these were hardly normal times. Zoltán's wife had come across as a forbidding figure when she'd confronted us earlier, but I now saw her fierceness as entirely warranted, if not admirable: the behavior of a mother bear defending her cubs. It was no small thing she'd managed to do, creating an oasis of calm amid the crisis, a safe haven where damaged children could still play as battles raged nearby.

Jakub had been listening closely as Frankie described the home. I could tell he was trying to figure something out, some aspect of the situation that didn't quite fit. "Dr. Szabó is employed by the state?" he asked.

"Naturally." Frankie was amused by the question. "There is no private enterprise here."

"And she has been running this home for how long?"

"Oh, five or six years, I should think."

"How could the wife of an *accused enemy of the people* have been allowed to remain in charge of a facility like that? Wouldn't she have fallen under suspicion when her husband was arrested?"

"Certainly, she was under suspicion." Frankie's lips turned up in the semblance of a smile, but there was no mirth behind it. Like József in the hospital, his feelings seemed to have disappeared from view, leaving behind a cardboard rendition of himself whose true opinions were impossible to discern. He seemed reluctant to elaborate any further in English, but Gray was able to get a bit more out of him by switching back to Hungarian.

"Frankie's sure the ÁVH kept an open file on both of them," he told us later. "But Dr. Szabó might have been of more use to them right where she was. She might have led them unwittingly to other so-called enemies, if you catch my drift. They probably had an informant in the neighborhood who kept an eye on all the comings and goings at the home."

We were back in his room and it was well past midnight. Between the dancing, the late hour, and our fitful sleep the night before, Jakub and I were dead on our feet. We sat slumped together on one of the room's narrow beds, struggling to keep our eyes open as Gray bounded about in his stocking feet, too keyed up to stay in one place. Alcohol made most people sleepy, but drinking, initially at least, had the opposite effect on my brother.

I stifled a yawn. "That explains Dr. Szabó's desire to get rid of us so quickly." The more I learned about her, the more she grew in my estimation. She would have put up with the surveillance to preserve her little refuge. She seemed prepared to go to any lengths to protect her young charges, which raised a new question in my mind: "What if Zoltán were there the whole time and she didn't want us to know?"

"That makes no sense." Gray plopped himself down on the opposite bed. "Why would she have been hiding him from us? We're no threat to anyone."

"Aren't we, though?" I pursued. "József said they'll go for the ringleaders first. She doesn't want to lose him again, and can you blame her? If speaking English is enough to draw suspicion down on somebody, having your American relatives show up at your front door is bound to get you arrested."

Jakub put his hands on my shoulders and pulled me in for a kiss. "Of course! If there's an informer in the neighborhood, she'd have needed to be extra careful. Not only would it have been dangerous to be seen talking with us, but she wouldn't have wanted anyone to know that Zoltán was injured."

"Because that would be a dead giveaway he'd been involved in the fighting," I said, completing the thought.

"Exactly!"

"Do I get another kiss?"

"Correct me if I'm wrong," said my husband, kissing the tip of his finger and running it down the bridge of my nose, "but it sounds to me as if you have something more in mind."

I caught his finger and brought it into my mouth, feeling myself grow moist as I sucked it. Aware, too, from the change in his breathing, that Jakub was growing aroused.

"Go play in your own room, children," said Gray with an indulgent smile. "I'm going to try and get some sleep."

Jakub pulled himself to his feet in preparation to leading

me off to bed, but I ignored the hand he was offering. Something was nagging at me, some crucial detail I'd overlooked. The girl on crutches: why didn't Dr. Szabó want her talking to us? What did she know? She wasn't much older than the other girls in the courtyard and I could see no reason why she'd have been privy to information Zoltán and his wife hadn't shared with the others. Unless she was their daughter? Unlikely. The girl in the picture was standing on two good legs. Had she contracted polio since the photo was taken? I still had a clear image in my mind of the girl on crutches to compare to the photograph, but my handbag was in the adjoining room.

I stood up and moved toward the connecting door between Gray's room and ours. One hand on the knob, I turned, expecting Jakub to be right behind me, but he was standing facing Gray, who was now stretched out on the bed, eyes closed, drifting off into unconsciousness. That's how it happened with him when he'd had too much to drink. One minute he'd be voluble, wired. The next thing you knew, he'd be flat out and there'd be no rousing him.

"What about this Frankie?" my husband said, a frown marring his handsome face. I badly wanted to be alone with him in our room, but he was still troubled by the Hungarian stringer. "How did he get to be such an expert on ÁVH files and surveillance tactics?"

My brother covered a yawn as he struggled to remember what the Hungarian reporter might have confided about his own background. "He used to work for the Communist newspaper, I believe. The state paper. Something-or-other *Nep*, it was called."

"He wrote propaganda, you mean," said Jakub.

"Well, yes. He didn't call it that, but he didn't brag about it either. He fed stories to the United Press, too, on the side. I don't imagine his bosses at *Nep* would have been too happy about that. He told me he could have been tried for treason, if they'd found out. Incidentally, the paper's been shut down by the new regime. He's hoping to get hired full-time by United Press. I think he initially took me for one of their reporters and wanted me to put in a good word for him."

Jakub was still frowning. "I wonder who fed him the stories that he fed to UPI?"

"What are you saying?" I asked, my anxious tone causing Jakub to pause before he answered.

"I'm sorry to scare you, *najdroższa,* but a little fear is probably a good thing, under the circumstances." Here he fixed Gray with a stare, and I saw my brother wilt. "Either your friend Frankie was very stupid, or he had more than one employer."

"Hmmm," said Gray. "You think the government was using him to funnel disinformation? I'm not sure I buy that."

My husband lost his temper. "Nobody with half a brain, least of all a reporter for the state-run newspaper, would have risked moonlighting for a Western news organization during the Rákosi years. Or, to put it another way, if he had been slipping them stories without sanction, I very much doubt he'd still be around to brag about it."

"So what's he doing, hanging around with the likes of us in the Duna bar?"

I was surprised to see Gray standing up to Jakub. I myself was intimidated, it was so rare to see him angry, and I think he was regretting the outburst, because when he spoke again, his tone was calmer.

"Ingratiating himself with Westerners must be the way he's used to operating, playing both sides. Now he's in a position to sell his knowledge of the regime to our side, maybe earn himself a ticket out of Hungary."

"Or he's hoping to gain information that he can sell back to his side," muttered my brother, a guilty look on his face as he mentally reviewed what he could remember of the conversation he'd carried on with the ÁVH informer.

For my part, I was thinking that this high-minded little rescue mission behind the Iron Curtain was turning out to be far more complicated than any of us could have anticipated.

CHAPTER SIX

November 1, 1956

We stepped out of the hotel the next morning into a different Budapest, a sunlit city no longer in the throes of a revolution. All along the riverfront we saw people cleaning up, sweeping the pavements of broken glass, piling rubble at the curb, moving debris off the tracks to allow the trams to run again. Downed wires still dangled from the overhead power lines, but someone had wrapped white paper around the live ends. Shops were reopening— amazingly, it seemed as if nothing had been looted in the week of fighting—and the cafés were full of patrons.

"Would you take a look at that!" exclaimed Gray, indicating a fancy establishment whose fin-de-siècle allure was somewhat marred by the heavy shelling that had pitted the building's marble facade. Yet inside, impeccably groomed waiters wearing starched aprons were serving coffee and pastry in a room furnished with velvet upholstery, gold leaf glittering from the fixtures and reflected in the many mirrors that hung from the walls.

I'd stopped to watch the scene, dazzled by this glimpse of an earlier, more civilized time. This must have been the way Budapest looked when Father lived there. No wonder he got nostalgic when he and his Hungarian friends in the film industry got together.

"Can't you just imagine Father in this froufrou café?" I asked my brother.

"In Warsaw we had such cafés," said Jakub. A casual comment, but behind it, I knew, lay his entire history. Before the war, Jakub's parents were well-to-do. He and his sister had been brought up by a French governess and the family traveled quite a bit, summering on the Riviera and skiing in the Swiss Alps. These excursions had instilled a wanderlust in my husband, or so I'd assumed; his jazz trio never stayed in one place for very long and I'd reconciled myself to adopting their itinerant lifestyle. Now an alternative explanation for his restlessness suggested itself. Jakub's Warsaw was gone, destroyed, and I could only think he'd found it less painful to move about, retrieving the odd memory by visiting places he'd known in happier days, rather than brooding over his vanished past.

"Were you taken there as a boy?" Bit by bit, I was assembling a picture of his childhood.

"As a boy, yes, wearing short pants. My sister Bracha used to make fun of my knobby knees and once, to get even, while sitting in a pastry shop very much like this one, I dipped the end of her braid in whipped cream."

"She must have really tormented you to have deserved that," said Gray.

"Oh, yes. She knew all my weak points."

Bracha had been studying medicine when the Germans invaded Poland. She continued her studies clandestinely in the ghetto, in an underground school set up for Jewish students barred from Warsaw University. Jakub had met one of her professors after the war, a non-Jew who'd risked a lot to keep the school going. "This country will never recover," he'd told my husband. "People like your sister. We've lost our life's blood."

We'd been alone when Jakub recounted this story, and I remembered holding him in my arms for a very long time, grieving in silence for my beloved's unbearable loss. Here on the street, the only comfort I could provide was to take his hand, aware as always of the sheltered life I'd led in comparison to his, and to everyone around us.

Budapest too was taking stock of its losses. It was All Saint's Day, an occasion for solemn remembrance, and the plaza in front of the Parliament building was filled with candles. Groups of mourners clustered here and there, women in their kerchiefs, the men's collars turned up against the damp chill coming off the river. Here, where Soviet tanks had fired on the demonstrators on the second day of the uprising, killing dozens and wounding several hundred more, the mood was somber. Black flags hung from the windows of the buildings overlooking the plaza. For years, Hungarians had been prevented from practicing their religion, but of course they hadn't stopped believing in God. Now the Hungarian cardinal, József Mindszenty, imprisoned by the regime in 1949, was finally free and for the faithful, a demonstration of devotion was long overdue.

Cutting through Parliament Square to reach the embassy, we passed a marble obelisk adorned with a hammer and sickle, a bronze relief at its base commemorating the liberation of Hungary by the Red Army. The monument had been defaced with the slogan *Ruszkik haza!* Russians go home. We'd seen the slogan painted defiantly on the side of a burned-out tank in Republic Square the day before, but the message appeared almost wistful to me, and well on its way to becoming a relic. As if to underscore the need for haste in getting ourselves out of Hungary, a plane flew overhead at that very moment, the roar of its engines loud enough to make everyone in the square glance upward.

"Christ! That was a MiG," said Gray, once the noise had diminished.

Jakub was disconcerted by this information. "Are you sure?"

"Positive. It was too high to see the markings, but it's the same model they used against our B-29s in Korea."

We weren't the only ones rattled by the Soviet fighter jet buzzing the city. Most of the people around us seemed to be on edge. Our initial impression that Budapest was returning to normal had been dispelled within the space of a fifteen-minute walk. The situation was even more tense at the embassy, where a handful of overworked clerks stationed behind a counter at the far end of the busy lobby strove to maintain order: American citizens in one line, Hungarian dependents in another. Anyone not affiliated with an American through blood or marriage was asked to come back another day, which was as good as telling them not to bother coming back at all, and many did not go willingly. A harried white-haired man seemed to have been assigned the job of reasoning with the most recalcitrant of the petitioners.

We reached the front of the line for American citizens and were directed to a collegiate-looking fellow with a crewcut whose name tag identified him as Bud Stilton. The young clerk didn't bother to ask our business; he just assumed we wanted to get out of the country like everyone else.

"You're in luck. We're putting together a convoy bright and early tomorrow morning to evacuate the wives and children of embassy employees. I'll put you on the list. Where are you staying?" he asked, after checking our documents. "You'll need to be here at seven."

Gray gave him the name and address of the Duna and told him we had our own car.

72

"That's excellent. Would you be willing to take an extra passenger? We're short on vehicles."

"We might have a fourth passenger," my brother said. "If we can find him."

"How's that?"

"We were supposed to meet a relative of ours, but he's gone missing."

A worried expression crossed Bud Stilton's face. "A relative, you say?" He pulled a piece of lined paper from the drawer beneath the counter, took out a pen, and prepared to take notes. "How did you get separated?"

"We didn't get separated," Gray explained. "He lives here and we were hoping to get him a visa—"

"You mean he's not an American?" interrupted the clerk, noticeably less worried. He screwed the cap back on his pen and laid it down on the counter.

"No, he's Hungarian. But his father—our father, I should say; he's our half brother—is an American citizen. We were hoping to procure him a visa."

Bud Stilton had no interest in figuring out our relationship to Zoltán, but he did take pity on us. "I'm not able to issue visas, unfortunately, but I won't make you wait in line again. Park yourselves over there," he said, indicating a roped-off section of the lobby. "I'll send my colleague over as soon as he's free. And remember: be here tomorrow at 7 a.m. sharp."

We found a bench along the wall in the roped-off area, next to a flag stand displaying the stars and stripes, and settled down to wait. Behind us hung a framed photo of President Eisenhower, the standard Ike portrait you'd see in any courthouse or government building back home. I found it reassuring, these indications that we were on United States territory. After two days of needing constantly to be on my guard, I felt I could relax a bit, exhale. For the first time in my life, I appreciated what it meant to live in a democracy.

Gray extracted a pack of Player's from his flap pocket. "Cigarette?" he offered. He shook one out and passed the pack to Jakub, who took two, gave one to me, and lit it with a flick of his Zippo. I loved his old-world manners.

"Ah, Player's." The white-haired man approached our group. "I haven't had one of those in donkey's years. Would you mind?" he asked, his accent that odd blend of British and American inflections you heard in people who'd grown up in one of those countries and ended up living in the other. I'd noticed it happening to Gray, a lengthening of his vowels and a descending note at the end of a sentence, even when asking a question.

Jakub handed over his own as-yet-unlit cigarette and offered the man a light. By the time he'd lit one for himself and returned the pack to Gray, our companion was puffing away, sunk in a nicotine fugue. I realized there was no ashtray nearby and went in search of one. When I returned, dragging a metal stand ashtray back to the bench where we'd been sitting, he and my brother were carrying on a lively conversation about cricket. Someone named Laker had taken forty-six wickets that summer in a five-Test series against Australia, and Gray'd been in the stands at Lord's for the second match, which England apparently lost.

"He wasn't on top of his game that day," my brother was saying. "I wish I'd seen him at Old Trafford. Nineteen for ninety!"

Jakub gave me a quizzical look, but I hadn't the faintest idea what they were talking about. I'd never managed to figure out the point of the game when we were in England, but Gray was keen on the sport. He'd made friends with some theater people who followed it avidly, traveling with them to matches on weekends.

"It must have been quite something," the white-haired man agreed. "I was fortunate enough to have attended the third Test at Leeds in 1930."

"Is that the match where Bradman scored a century before lunch?"

"He did indeed. And he added a second by teatime."

Gray expressed his appreciation for the cricketer's skill. Then he noticed me, and the ashtray. "Ah, so that's where you went. Cara, this is Mr. Miner. My sister, Cara."

Miner transferred his cigarette from his right hand to his left and offered me his right hand to shake. "Nicholas, I insist." His grip was loose, his attention elsewhere. I followed his gaze. A family in the line for Hungarian dependents—two parents, two small children, and an elderly woman struggling to keep hold of a squirming infant—were being directed his way. Stubbing out the remainder of his cigarette, he excused himself with an apologetic shrug and went over to deal with them. As the only Hungarian-speaking official on the premises, Gray explained, he was in great demand as a translator.

"One Hungarian speaker for an operation of this scale?"

"I'm sure there are lower-level Hungarian employees," Jakub assured me. "Janitors and secretaries. But Hungarian isn't an easy language to learn. It's pretty much in a group all by itself."

"Let's find someplace a bit more private, shall we?" said Nicholas upon his return. He led us through a doorway marked "Authorized Personnel Only" to a back hallway, up a flight of stairs, down a corridor and into a formal reception room whose furnishings reminded me of the front parlor in the dormitory of my Connecticut boarding school, the only place where we girls were permitted to entertain male visitors. The same brass-studded leather sofas and upright armchairs, the tasteful oriental rugs, the standing lamps with their fringed shades that used to make me think of dowager aunts hovering close by, alert to the slightest impropriety. Potted ferns stood on either side of the room's tall windows, whose floral drapes were drawn, giving the room a stealthy, nighttime feel although it was midmorning.

Nicholas ushered us over to one of the sofas and seated himself in an armchair directly across from us. Leaning forward, he rested his elbows on his knees and gave the three of us his full attention. "So, tell me about this missing Hungarian relative of yours. I understand you're trying to procure him a visa?"

"Zoltán. He's our half brother, our father's son from his first marriage," said Gray. "You may have heard of our father, Robbie Walden."

"Naturally I've heard of Robbie Walden! Your father is still viewed by many in Hungary as a national treasure, even if he did change his name like all the others."

"Which others?" Jakub asked. "Who else changed their name?"

Nicholas went on to explain how the Austro-Hungarian Empire had fallen apart after its defeat in World War I. Hungary was dismembered, losing two-thirds of its territory, and the country was plunged into political disarray. Various factions vied to fill the void. A liberal aristocrat attempted to establish a Western-style democracy, which failed in a matter of months. Then came an equally short-lived Soviet Republic modeled on the newly established revolutionary regime in Russia whose leader, Béla Kun, had been a protégé of Lenin's.

Gray's interest was piqued. "Kun knew Lenin personally? I never heard that before."

"Oh, yes. Lenin trained him and sent him back to his own country to instigate a revolution," said Nicholas. "He promised to send the Red Army, to help Hungary reclaim the territories it had lost by the terms of the armistice. Unfortunately, Lenin was too busy putting down the counterrevolution in Russia to keep his promise. Kun was overthrown and his supporters were purged when Admiral Horthy took power."

I shivered involuntarily as the meaning of the word "purged" sunk in. "All of Kun's supporters were killed, do you mean?"

"Not only Kun's actual supporters, but anyone suspected of sympathizing with the Reds." Nicholas shook his head. "Horthy's forces were quite brutal. In addition to being a Bolshevik, Kun was a Jew. There were pogroms, I'm sorry to say. A bloodbath is what it was. No other word to describe it. Worse than now. Your father was lucky to have left Hungary when he did. The rest of the revolutionaries were slaughtered."

"Father?" Gray shook his head. "He was no Bolshevik, I can assure you. He left Hungary because he was having an affair and his mistress was pregnant."

A narrowing of his blue eyes indicated Nicholas's disapproval, but he said nothing. The silence grew awkward and I found myself wanting to speak up in Father's defense.

"I think he regretted leaving Zoltán behind," I said. "Maybe not at the time, but afterward, although by then it was obviously too late."

Both Gray and Jakub knew what lay behind this remark of mine. I sensed their concern, and didn't dare turn my head to look at either of them for fear I'd end up crying in front of Nicholas. At seventeen, I'd had a baby out of wedlock. The baby's father was a famous actor whose career would have been ruined if word got out that he'd seduced a minor. My own parents had gotten married under the very same circumstances, but the father of my son had no intention of marrying me. He was, in every respect, a cad. The studio employed a fixer whose chief responsibility was to keep his name out of the papers, and more than one paternity suit was lodged against him. I was told all of this, but it made no difference in my feelings. Like most girls my age, I'd been in love with Taylor Reed forever. There wasn't one of his pictures I hadn't seen, and I'd memorized the best lines in many of them. My school friends and I took turns acting out the ending to *Remember Me, Darling*, the tearful scene where the girl he'd left behind to marry an heiress lies dying in his arms and he confesses—too late—that he still loves her.

The real scene between Taylor and me played out quite differently. "I'll pay for you to get rid of it," he said when I told him that I was expecting. There were ways of getting an abortion in those days if you had money, private clinics where women went, some of them in Switzerland. Father had offered to send me to one of these places, but I wanted Taylor's baby. Both he and Gray would have supported me, no matter what decision I made, but they both believed the baby would be better off growing up in a stable home with two parents, a married couple, and in the end I allowed myself to be persuaded. I often thought of my son, especially at this time of year. He'd been born in October and would have just turned five.

"A good many of us have regrets about choices we made in our youth," said Nicholas kindly. "I'm sure your father will be glad to be reunited with his son. Tell me his name and I'll see if I can't expedite a visa. You're leaving with the convoy tomorrow, is that right?"

"Tomorrow morning, yes," said Gray. "And the name is Szabó. Zoltán Szabó."

"Zoltán Szabó? Could it be?" The blue eyes widened in disbelief. "How old did you say your brother was?"

"He would have been born in 1915."

"1915." Our companion did a rapid calculation in his head. "He would be the right age. But this is unbelievable. He's still alive, that devil!"

"Do you mean to tell us that you know him?" I asked.

Nicholas laughed with delight. "I believe so. Zoltán Szabó. Yes, it must be him. It was years ago, mind you, during wartime. We were in Marseille, and he was using a *nom de guerre*, but I'd known him originally under his own name."

"Marseille?" Jakub was suddenly alert. "What were you doing there during the war, if you don't mind my asking?"

"I was working with a relief agency, helping refugees get out of France."

"'Helping them' as in smuggling them out of the country, do you mean?"

Nicholas gave him an appraising look, as if noticing him properly for the first time. He rattled off a question in French, to which my husband replied curtly, and quite pointedly in English. "No," he said. "I was in Paris."

"But you're not French, are you? I detect a slight Slavic intonation."

"I'm Polish."

"Ah, yes. I hear it now. You form your vowels in the front of your mouth, whereas with English or German—and the romance languages, for that matter—the sounds come from further back in the throat."

Now it was Jakub's turn to probe. "How many languages do you speak, Mr. Miner?"

"Fluently? Only English and French, I'm afraid."

"And not fluently?"

Nicholas mumbled something about speaking versus understanding, the gist of it being (if I understood him properly) that he'd read modern languages at university and had a working knowledge of Spanish, Italian, German, and Hungarian.

My brother let out a whistle of appreciation. "That's quite some résumé!"

"Not Russian?" said Jakub in a low voice. Something about the man was clearly rubbing him the wrong way, offsetting his habitual politeness. I could feel the tension in his body although we were not touching.

Nicholas acted as if he hadn't heard the question. "Zoltán Szabó," he repeated, addressing himself wholly to Gray and me. "Your brother was absolutely indispensable to our work, I'll have you know."

I was having a hard time putting together all the facets of Zoltán we'd been shown. Poet, prisoner, and now, evidently, an underground operative who traveled under an assumed name, no less. I definitely wanted to be on hand when he and Father met.

"What did he do?" I asked.

"He was a guide. We recruited him to ferry people over the Pyrenees. He knew the escape routes. He'd fought in Spain, you see, with the International Brigades."

"Did he!" exclaimed Gray. "I can't wait until Father hears that."

During his college days, my brother had demonstrated against fascism in Spain, at one point toying with the idea of joining the International Brigades himself. This activity had put him at odds with Father at the time, and was what got him blacklisted in 1951. Premature anti-fascism (as it was called) branded you as pink, regardless of whether you had been a card-carrying Communist or merely a fellow traveler like Gray.

Next to me on the sofa, Jakub was fidgeting with a button on his cuff. "How did you come to recruit Zoltán, Mr. Miner?" he asked offhandedly. "Were you in Spain too?"

Our companion stood up, a signal that the three of us were to follow him back downstairs. "I'm afraid I'm wanted at my post, but I will personally see to it that Zoltán Szabó is issued a visa this very morning. I had a great deal of respect for your brother. He was a bit of a dreamer, but he proved himself on more than one occasion to be absolutely fearless."

"Fearless or reckless?" I wondered aloud, falling into step beside him as we walked down the corridor.

Nicholas gave a slight chuckle. "I'll admit, it was sometimes hard to tell the difference. I will say this: your brother went by Icarus and the name suited him to a T."

"He flew into the sun, didn't he?" Knowing that Zoltán had chosen this name for himself filled me with foreboding. Why, out of all the possible figures of classical antiquity, had he chosen this myth? It made him sound like even more of a risk taker than my husband.

"Oh, I wouldn't be too concerned, if I were you," said Nicholas, still amused. "Icarus knew how to disappear."

CHAPTER SEVEN

"What is it?" I asked Jakub the instant we were outside. "Why don't you trust him?" Once again, I was out of my depth, but it's amazing how quickly you can get used to living in a state of perpetual confusion. Hungary was so unlike the world I knew. Nothing I'd learned as an actress seemed remotely relevant to the drama playing out here. In the theater, reading between the lines meant going deeper into a character to find her motivations. Inventing a history that felt plausible and then inhabiting it on stage: challenging enough to do well, night after night, but the stakes were hardly life and death. Sooner or later the run would end, you'd discard the role, and step back into your ordinary self.

Reading between the lines was no exercise in make-believe in Communist Hungary. It was a daily necessity and it didn't look as if the run of this particular drama would be ending anytime soon, optimistic pronouncements from the provisional government notwithstanding. Neophytes such as Gray and myself were left with no choice but to take our cues from a seasoned player like Jakub.

"A man of his sort," he replied after giving the matter some thought. "Well, let's just say it's hard to know which side he's on."

"I'd have thought he was on our side," said Gray.

"The American side, you mean?"

"Well, yes. Seeing as how he works at the embassy, I assumed ..."

Jakub's reply was terse. "Don't assume anything."

I found myself looking anxiously around us, although there didn't appear to be anyone within earshot. We'd had to wait for Zoltán's visa to be processed and in the length of the time we'd been inside the embassy, the weather had turned blustery, with a hint of snow in the air. The candlelighting vigil in Parliament Square had dwindled to a handful of mourners. On the opposite bank of the Danube, perched on the crest of a hill, loomed Buda Castle, shrouded in fog.

Gray paused in his march across the plaza to light a cigarette, cupping his hand around the flame to keep it from blowing out, and we all stood shivering on the sidewalk until he'd got it lit. I watched him inhale, pulling the smoke deeply into his lungs as he weighed the evidence for himself.

"The language business is worrying you," he said to Jakub, smoke mingling with his frosty breath as he exhaled.

"Not only that. Did you notice the way he sidestepped my question when I asked how he and Zoltán met?"

"He sidestepped a number of questions, as I recall."

"True, but I found his evasiveness when I tried to pin him down on Spain most telling. He didn't deny being there, but he certainly didn't want to talk about it."

My brother drew pensively on his cigarette. "You think he was with Comintern?"

"Hold it," I interrupted. "What are you two talking about?"

Gray took a final puff and tossed his cigarette into the gutter. "You remember the last time we talked about the spread of Communism after the Russian revolution, Cara? Communist parties sprung up all over the place, but these were homegrown affairs. Autonomous. Each had its own concerns, and its own way of working for change, depending on conditions in the country where it was born."

Too late, I realized I'd let myself in for one of his lectures on politics. Granted, he'd taught me a great deal over the years, but I wasn't sure that a windy street corner in the heart of strife-ridden Budapest was the place to resume my political education. Unfortunately, I wasn't given a choice.

"Comintern was set up by the Soviet Union to bring the local outfits into line. Its agents infiltrated Communist parties around the world in order to control them. During the Spanish Civil War, they recruited volunteers from all over Europe and America to defend the Spanish Republic."

"They also set up a number of bogus relief agencies as fronts to funnel arms to the Republican side," Jakub noted. "I suspect Miner worked for one of them."

"Is that such a bad thing?" I didn't know a lot about the Spanish Civil War, but I remembered from an earlier lecture of Gray's that the Soviet Union had been the only nation willing to aid the doomed Republic. You had to stand up for what you believed in, he'd said. The rest of the world stood by and watched while Hitler and Mussolini bombed the country to bits, all in support of their fellow dictator, Generalissimo Franco, who still ruled Spain with an iron fist. But now Gray was telling me Miner's activity was a very bad thing, reminding me the Communists were only one party in the coalition that made up the Popular Front, as the government of the Spanish Republic was called.

"They wanted to run the show so badly that they sabotaged their own side! My God, the stories Orwell told in *Homage to Catalonia* were enough to turn your stomach. And the show trials! Well, they had them here, too, didn't they? But the writing was already on the wall with Bukharin." He seemed prepared to discourse at greater length on the

Russians' treachery, but Jakub guided the conversation back to his suspicions regarding Nicholas.

"If Miner was in Spain during the civil war, we have to assume he was a Soviet agent."

"Was or is?" I wanted to know.

"It's not something you pick up and discard like a hobby, *najdroższa*."

József was pacing the sidewalk in front of the Duna. "How did it go at the embassy? Were you successful?"

"We got the visa," said Gray, pulling the document out of its envelope to show him. "What about you? Any news of Zoltán?"

"I'm afraid not. I thought we might go to the magazine's offices and see if he hasn't been back there since yesterday. It's possible he's left you a message."

Jakub had wanted to wait until we were en route before giving his account of our visit to the embassy. As it turned out, József was so busy giving directions it wasn't until we were parked that my husband had the opportunity to share his suspicions that Nicholas was a Soviet agent of long standing.

Our companion was skeptical. "The man is no amateur," he commented. "Assuming you're correct, he'd have to have spent years burrowing his way into a position of responsibility at the embassy. All of that work would come to nothing if he were exposed, and the Americans would hardly take kindly to the discovery of a spy in their midst. I sincerely doubt he'd have unmasked himself to the three of you. It would've been like slitting his own throat!"

"He did it inadvertently," said Jakub. "Miner's skilled

at languages. He picked up on my accent, pegged me as a Slavic speaker."

"It takes one to know one, eh? Sorry, I'm still not convinced. He might just as easily speak Serbo-Croatian or Czech."

"I'm willing to bet he speaks Russian."

"What if he does? A knowledge of Russian isn't damning in and of itself. For all we know, he's spying for the Americans and using his post at the embassy as a cover. That's how it's done these days, apparently."

My husband refused to back down. "In that case, he must be a double agent. Would you like to know what he did during the war? He was in France, heading up some kind of refugee agency, and before that he seems to have been in Spain, although I couldn't get him to admit it outright."

This got József's attention. "You weren't foolish enough to press the man over his political affiliations?"

Jakub looked down at his lap. "I didn't hide my suspicions."

"There's such a thing as being too clever for your own good," József rebuked him. "If he is what you say he is, you've as good as told him you're onto him. What do you expect him to do now, wait for you to report him to the ambassador?"

"You're not suggesting that he'll be coming after us, are you?" Gray's question came out louder than he'd intended, betraying his alarm.

József didn't even bother to reply. Reaching into a pocket of his overcoat, he extracted a pack of cigarettes and tipped one out. Gray had to light it for him, his hands were shaking so badly. The man wasn't cut out for subterfuge; he was meant to be working a desk job in some government bureaucracy. We watched him smoke, each of us lost in our own thoughts.

I was feeling shaky too, and not only because of the threat posed by Nicholas. Jakub sat at the wheel, staring out through the windshield in utter despair. I didn't know how to reach him in this black mood. Was he blaming himself for his lapse, for failing to protect me in the same way he believed he'd failed to save his family? Useless to point out that Gray and I had made more than our share of mistakes over the course of the past two days. There was ample guilt to go around; none of us was blameless. Wasn't it József who'd sent us on the errand to get Zoltán a visa? If we hadn't gone to the embassy, we'd never have met Nicholas. We'd have been on our way back to Paris by now, abandoning Hungary to its tragedy. Jakub shouldn't have to bear the entire burden of keeping me safe.

"What's stopping us from leaving this afternoon?" The solution offered itself up to me and it was so simple I found myself giggling. By the time Nicholas realized we weren't joining the convoy, we'd be long gone.

My brother was giddy with relief. "Cara, you're brilliant! Isn't my sister brilliant?" he asked the others.

"Absolutely," agreed Jakub, planting a kiss on my lips. Even József liked the idea. He thought we should leave immediately, without going back to the Duna to retrieve our belongings, in case someone was watching the hotel.

"We'll just check the office one last time, and then I'll see you off," he said.

The streets leading into Republic Square were closed off and we'd had to park blocks away from the apartment. As we made our way there on foot, we found ourselves in a crowd of onlookers, all watching as the entire square was being dug up. Workers using excavating equipment were being aided by dozens and dozens of ordinary people wielding pickaxes and shovels. They'd break through the frozen ground using the heavy machinery and scoop out as much earth as they could, then people would get inside the hole and continue the work by hand. Several holes were being dug out at once and as we drew nearer, we saw the people in one hole signaling that the work in all the others should stop. A hush descended upon the crowd as all the equipment was turned off. People rushed over to the suspicious hole and put their ears to the ground, encouraging others to do the same. I counted some thirty people listening before the strange ritual ended and the machines started up again as people returned to digging in their own holes.

"What in the world is going on?" Gray exclaimed. "Have they all gone bonkers?"

"They're looking for a secret underground ÁVH prison."

A young couple wheeling a baby carriage had come up behind us. Ilona and Villi were both schoolteachers and clearly relished the opportunity to practice their English on native speakers. After we'd introduced ourselves, I asked Ilona how she could tell we weren't Hungarians.

"Your coat is very beautiful." She cast an appreciative eye over the navy wool velour swagger coat with a beaver collar I'd bought myself in London the previous winter. Ilona herself was wearing a threadbare man's overcoat far too large for her slender frame—her husband's overcoat, I guessed, seeing as how Villi wore only a trench coat. With the collar turned up and the brim of his hat pulled low, a cigarette dangling rakishly from his lips, he looked like Humphrey Bogart in Casablanca, minus the uncompromising set of actor's jaw.

The outward resemblance to Bogey was quite deliberate, we learned. Our new acquaintances belonged to a clandestine film society that screened banned Western movies. They'd named their small daughter Erzsébet after Elizabeth Taylor,

Ilona confided; *National Velvet* was her favorite picture.

I peeked in at the baby, bundled up in a snowsuit beneath a pink crocheted blanket. "Hello, Erzsébet," I whispered. She turned her head and regarded me with serious interest, her small round face a study in concentration.

"Her first American," said Villi, smiling fondly at his wife. The love in his soft brown eyes, the hopefulness in his voice as he imagined a future in which his daughter would grow up to meet more Americans, made me ashamed. Villi and Ilona assumed we'd come to share their country's jubilation at having thrown off the Soviet yoke, and here we were, me in my expensive coat, gawking like tourists at the frenzied activity on the square while making plans to get out of Hungary as soon as possible. I wanted to urge the couple to leave too; America would do nothing to save them and little Erzsébet, I wanted to tell them. Speaking English was a liability. Watching banned films could get them in trouble. Naturally, I said none of these things.

Gray was quizzing Villi about the hole-digging operation in the square. "Is it true, that the regime hid their prisons underground?"

Villi made a dismissive gesture in the direction of the people in the square. "They think so," he said.

"What do you think?"

"I think Hungarians are delirious with freedom."

"Delirious with freedom," my brother repeated, savoring the words. He collected phrases the way others collected souvenirs on their travels. "Rather like a person in the grip of a fever?"

"With fever comes a great thirst," replied Villi darkly. He proceeded to describe the events he'd witnessed earlier in the week, the horrifying prelude to the digging in the square. A short distance from where we were standing was Communist Party headquarters, he told us. Dozens of ÁVH officers had barricaded themselves inside. They'd taken prisoners and had threatened to shoot the hostages, the standoff persisting for several days. Finally, a delegation was allowed inside to negotiate. Some of them brought arms, apparently, and shooting was heard from within. Tanks arrived—nobody was sure who sent them—and began bombarding the building, forcing the officers to surrender. As soon as they did, crowds stormed the place and dragged the ÁVH men out. The mob lynched them; he'd seen it with his own eyes. People tearing at the bodies, kicking, spitting on the desecrated corpses—

He stopped. Ilona was glowering at him. "*Miért mondod el nekik mindezt?*" she hissed.

"I'm sorry," he apologized. "My wife says I shouldn't be telling you about this. You will think we Hungarians are barbarians."

"I've seen it elsewhere," said Jakub. A haunted look had come into his eyes. "In France, they killed collaborators after the war."

"Oh, my darling." I pulled my coat's beaver collar more closely around my neck. Here was something else I hadn't known, that he'd witnessed scenes of vengeance like the ones Villi was describing. Every day we spent in Hungary brought new revelations, complicating my understanding of my husband. How, after seeing the absolute worst in people, and after losing his family, had he himself not succumbed to anger or despair? I listened to him tell the others about the violence unleashed against anyone accused of consorting with the enemy. Summary executions, shaving the heads of women who'd slept with German soldiers. I hadn't known any of it, and there we were, living among people in Paris who had surely witnessed all of these things, if they hadn't participated in them.

"The term they used was *épuration,*" he said. "Purification. Nobody knows for sure how many Frenchmen died at the hands of other Frenchmen following the liberation, but I've heard it numbered in the thousands."

"Thousands!" We were all shocked, even József and the Hungarian couple. Knowing of the brutality and oppression under Rákosi these past seven years, "purification" might be tempting here too.

"When did it stop?" asked my brother.

"De Gaulle put an end to it eventually."

"I wish someone would put an end to this," said Villi, returning his attention to the diggers.

Nothing had changed in the apartment since our visit the previous day. Nobody had removed the bloodstained coverlet or swept the floor. The windows remained shattered, no effort made to cover the gaping panes with cardboard. Zoltán's typewriter sat on the middle of his desk, the unfinished poem still trapped between the rollers.

"What does this say exactly?" My brother had gone over to peer at the page.

József parsed the words. "The literal translation of the lines would be 'and the frost bound the tears between those orbs, and held them there.'"

"Orbs? Don't you mean eyeballs? He's talking about tears."

"It is rather archaic, but your brother used the word *gömb.* Perhaps he needed it for the rhyme? *Szemgolyó* is the contemporary term for eyeball."

"Curious," said Gray, glancing over the typewritten lines. "Was he in the habit of numbering his poems?"

József shook his head. "I've never known him to use Roman numerals." Gingerly, he unrolled the sheet of paper from the cylinder and pulled it out, taking care not to touch the bloody fingerprint on the upper edge. "Thirty-two, followed by the Arabic numbers forty-five and forty-six, separated by a hyphen … It sounds like a chapter in a book, doesn't it, followed by the page numbers perhaps?"

"He left us a clue!" I crowed, grabbing Jakub's hand in excitement. "It's the same thing you did in the war, passing messages in books."

One day, while strolling along the Seine, the two of us had stopped to browse at the stall of one of the booksellers—the *bouquinistes,* as they were called. Idly, my husband had picked up a novella by Prosper Merimée.

"*Vous ne disposez pas de son autre, avez-vous?*" he said to the bookseller.

"*Lequel, monsieur?*" the man responded with a distracted air.

"Columba."

This got his attention. The bookseller scrutinized Jakub. Then his face broke into a smile. "*Mon Dieu, combien d'années a-t-il été? Je ne vous reconnaît pas sans la soutane!*"

I'd known that my husband had gone about disguised as a seminary student during his time in the Resistance, but I hadn't realized that he'd frequented the *bouquinistes* in religious garb, or that the works of a less-than-first-rate nineteenth-century author and playwright were the preferred vehicle for clandestine communications within his cell. He and this fellow had evidently been in cahoots, and the *bouquiniste* was so overjoyed to see Jakub again, once he recognized him without his cassock, that he closed the stall and took us off to a café, where he ordered a bottle of pink champagne.

Now Jakub and I watched as Gray crunched his way across the broken glass on the floor to the bookshelves, where he began reading the spines of the leather-bound volumes. I was expecting him to ask for help—there were an awful lot of books to go through—but József seemed to know exactly what our brother was looking for and directed him to the proper spot.

"Second shelf. You'll find all three volumes of the Babits translation, side by side."

Gray selected the first of the identically bound books and brought it over to the desk. "Canto thirty-two of the *Inferno*, lines forty-five through forty-six," he prompted as József leafed through the pages.

"Dante," murmured my husband. "I should have guessed."

"Well, well, well. Your brother did leave us a message after all," said József. Tucked inside the book was a small sheaf of pages that looked as if they had been torn from a stenographer's pad, each page bearing a series of handwritten entries in black ink.

"What have you got there?" asked Gray, craning his neck to see over his shoulder.

"Surveillance reports." József frowned as he skimmed through them. "They're from before your brother was arrested." He showed us where each was dated—they were all from a two-week period in the summer of 1951—and proceeded to summarize their contents.

Zoltán (Z) was observed meeting with another party (P) in Vörösmarty tér. The two adjourned to a coffeehouse, where they encountered a third party (T), who had arrived a good deal earlier to secure a table in the back. Five days later, they met again at the Oktogon and entered the metro, surfacing farther down Andrássy út. P parted company from the others at this point, and the watcher followed T and our brother as far as Saint Stephens Basilica, where they shook hands and separated. The very next evening, the three of them were together again in Zoltán's house, where they were overheard discussing the fate of a fourth man, Kálmán. T suspected he'd been apprehended by the secret police and warned the others that it would be unwise to meet again. While the notes on the previous encounters were brief, the account of this conversation was fairly detailed, filling up both sides of several pieces of notebook paper.

"It looks to me like the children's home was bugged," said Gray.

"No bug, is very clean," I quipped. But I honestly didn't think there was a bug. It seemed more plausible that one of the parties, P or T, was an informer.

József agreed with my assessment, pointing out that the notes on the conversation were incomplete. "This isn't a verbatim transcript of everything they discussed, it reads more like personal recollections after the fact."

"In other words," said Jakub, his thoughts moving in tandem with my own, "Zoltán was betrayed by someone he trusted, someone he'd invited into his own living room."

Disquieting as this was, I was glad to have my speculations confirmed. Maybe I was starting to think like a spy—not that I expected to have much use for such skills, once Jakub and I resumed our married life in Paris—but at least I'd learned something from this ill-advised escapade. I might not be able to match my husband's depth as far as his wartime escapades were concerned, but I was beginning to understand the shadowy world he'd frequented. One thing was still bothering me, though. The notebook pages were clearly part of some secret file the ÁVH was keeping on Zoltán. But that was five years ago. How did he get hold of them? I put this question to József.

"All sorts of nasty secrets have come to light in recent days," he told us. "Your brother may have 'liberated' his file from Communist Party headquarters after the revolutionaries sacked it."

"But why did he leave it here for us to find?" asked my brother, picking up the topmost page and scrutinizing the Hungarian words as if by looking hard enough, their secret would be revealed.

Jakub proposed an answer: "Better the evidence should fall into our hands than someone else's, although, for the life of me, I don't know what he expects us to do with it."

"Publish it," said József. "People in the West should know what went on here. That's what he wants from you." He shook his head. "It's all your brother has ever wanted, for as long as I've known him. The truth."

The cold truth, I thought to myself, tears welling up in my eyes. Everything we'd heard about Zoltán was accurate: his courage, his integrity, the warrior ethic that made him act always for the greater good, for posterity, regardless of his own safety. How he'd managed to survive this long was a miracle; a man with his principles would have fared no better in McCarthy's America than in Rákosi's Hungary. And yet his belief in the power of words was so inspiring. Of course we would do what he wanted.

"*Najdroższa*, you're crying." Jakub was all tender concern, pulling me close and brushing away my tears with the back of his hand.

"I wish we could have met him," I sniffed. "And Father too. He ought to know the kind of person his son is."

"There is one thing we can do," said Gray. I watched him

remove the envelope containing the visa from an inside pocket of his sports jacket. "We'll leave this for him right here, in case he returns. I know just the place."

First, he folded the notebook pages in half and placed them in his jacket pocket. Then, turning to the section of the *Inferno* where he'd found the surveillance reports, he slipped the visa between the pages and returned the book to its place on the shelf.

CHAPTER EIGHT

Church bells were ringing as we made our way back to the Škoda. I was expecting the sound to be drowned out by the noise of the excavating equipment the nearer we got to the digging operation, but there was dead silence when we reached the square. Not a soul was moving. The steam shovel operators had emerged from their machines and the diggers had all climbed out of their holes to stand in silence beside their shovels and pickaxes, heads bowed.

"What's going on?" said Gray. "Don't tell me they found the underground prison."

József looked at his watch. "They're observing a moment of silence for the martyrs."

It was like Armistice Day. The English marked the end of World War I with a two-minute silence on November 11. The first year that Gray and I were in London, I'd found it unsettling to be out in the streets when everything stopped. The scene before us was eerie in the same way, but the commemoration here was premature. Hungary's ordeal had not ended; we were just at intermission.

Out of respect, we waited until the digging resumed before proceeding to the car. With the rattles and clunks of the heavy machinery accompanying us once more, we reached the Škoda only to discover that one of the rear tires was flat.

Jakub squatted beside the wheel and surveyed the

damage. "We seem to have punctured it on something." He had to shout to be heard over the racket.

"Or someone punctured it for us," József yelled back, disinclined, as ever, to believe in accidents. I didn't think we needed to go beyond the debris in the streets to explain the flat, but I wasn't about to bet my life on it. Not after reading the surveillance reports on Zoltán. Anything was possible in this country.

Gray opened the trunk to check the spare. He had to move the gifts and the extra cans of oil to the back seat in order to get at it, and then he'd spent a few minutes prodding the tire, to assess its condition. The spare was soft, he informed us, most likely due to a slow leak, although given the Romanian playwright's lackadaisical approach to car maintenance, there was no telling what had caused it or how long it had been that way. He thought we'd be okay driving on an underinflated tire for a short distance, but Austria was out of the question.

"Can it be repaired?" my husband asked.

"Plugging the hole in the front tire might be easier," said Gray. "But that'll take time, assuming we can even find a garage that's open."

Fortunately, the trunk contained both a wrench and a jack. While Gray and Jakub changed the tire, József and I looked on or, to be more accurate, I looked on while József anxiously scanned the street, hoping to spot any adversaries before they had time to assault us. He was fairly confident we would find a service station along our route. He'd noticed one earlier on an undamaged section of Rákóczi út, one of Budapest's major arteries.

"Rákosi, like the dictator?" I said.

"Certainly not!" This Rákóczi was a national hero, I was informed, an aristocrat who led an unsuccessful uprising against the Habsburgs. Of all the unsuccessful Hungarian uprisings, Rákóczi's was second only to 1848. Franz Liszt composed a rhapsody about it.

Jakub, who was engaged just then in tightening the lug nuts on the wheel, paused in his labors. "The Rákóczi March." He proceeded to hum the opening bars, which I recognized from music appreciation class at the Wentworth Academy. The piece had been arranged for violin, he informed us, and he had performed it as one of his audition pieces for music school.

"Someday," said József, "when we meet again under happier circumstances, I would like to hear you play it."

"It will be my pleasure," my husband told him, returning to his project.

The drive back took us through the university district, the site where the fighting had begun on October 23. József pointed out the radio station where his son, Péti, had been injured. He'd been part of a student delegation that had attempted to storm the building in order to broadcast their demands on the air. They had no weapons at first, making them easy targets for the ÁVH men who'd barricaded themselves inside and were shooting at the students, but army units sent in by the government to rescue them wound up defecting to the demonstrators' side, turning over their guns and ammunition. They were soon joined by workers from the munitions factory, who brought more arms. By morning the revolutionaries had captured the building.

"He sounds very brave," commented Gray.

József shook his head. "Young people have no understanding of the dangers they run." Péti had been shot in the leg, and while the bullet missed hitting an artery, the damage was fairly severe. The boy would always walk with a limp, but there were larger consequences to the disability, he told us. Once order was restored, József envisioned the authorities going house-to-house, arresting all they suspected of having participated in the uprising. Anyone with an injury like Péti's would be implicated. I felt selfish for having taken so much of József's time and attention. He had enough on his plate without adding our fruitless pursuit of Zoltán to his problems. But maybe there was something we could do to help.

"Why don't we take your son with us?" I looked to Jakub and Gray, who both nodded their affirmation. It seemed the least we could do, after everything József had done for us. He and his wife could join us in Vienna—we could look after Péti until they arrived—and I was sure that Lázár would do everything he could to help them get settled in Paris. It was what he'd wanted all along, to bring his family to safety.

"That's very generous of you, but Péti's in no shape to travel," said József.

He looked so discouraged, and it was evident he was still struggling to reconcile himself to the future that lay in store. I wanted to argue with him, but already he was getting that closed-off expression on his face, retreating behind his wall.

"Turn left at the next intersection," he directed.

My brother did as instructed and, sure enough, there was the garage. The place resembled a 1930s filling station, with clock face pumps, the kind that showed the gallons but required you to calculate the price in your head. There were three pumps but only one of them seemed to be dispensing gas, and the attendant looked frantic. We joined the queue to fill up while József went inside to inquire about having the tire repaired, returning almost immediately with discouraging news. We were not the only ones in Budapest with a punctured tire. The wait to have it repaired would be even longer than the wait for gas.

"Why don't we just buy a new one and be done with it?" Gray reached for his wallet and pulled out his stash of forints. We'd purchased a large quantity of the Hungarian currency in Paris before setting off but had spent very little.

"I already asked about that," said József. "They ran out days ago."

We debated our options as we sat in line. We could pump up the soft tire—the service station had air—but we couldn't trust it to get us to the border. Alternatively, we could leave the tire with the garage overnight and they'd have it ready the next morning. None of us liked the idea of spending another night at the Duna, but József argued that we'd be safest returning to a place where we were known, provided we remained vigilant.

"We have to assume that you're being watched. They'll be looking for an opportunity to get you off alone somewhere. Pack up your belongings the minute you get back, all of them, and keep them nearby. You don't want to return to your rooms for any reason tonight."

This struck Jakub as excessive. "Are you recommending that we sleep in the lobby?"

"I wouldn't recommend sleeping at all, unless you take it in turns," said József. "And the last place you want to be is your hotel room. Privacy is a luxury you can't afford. Listen to me: you must keep to the public areas of the hotel and be very visible. Go talk to that journalist friend of yours—"

"He's not our friend," I said. If Gray could stand up for me, I'd return the favor by standing up for him.

"Make him your friend," József instructed. "Use him. Tell him what you learned at the embassy today. You want to expose Miner, don't you?"

My brother gave a pained smile. "A scoop like this will make Ames's career. Just what I wanted: a friend for life."

Ames, as usual, was delighted to see us. We'd spotted him in the lobby as we left the dining room after our meal.

"Here goes," said Gray, grim-faced but determined.

"Ah, the travelers have returned." Hurriedly excusing himself from the sofa where he'd been gabbing with one of his colleagues, the tabloid journalist led the way to the bar and eased his bulk onto a stool. "What will it be, dearies?" The bartender had set a pink gin in front of him without being asked and now stood by, awaiting our orders. They were no longer making a pretense of enforcing the alcohol ban at the Duna and, looking around the room, I noticed a number of the patrons drinking hard liquor, doubtless fortifying themselves for what lay ahead.

We ordered beers—the pilsner was more than acceptable, according to Ames—and launched into an account of our visit to the embassy. The British journalist heard us out, his interest sharpening as Jakub detailed his suspicions regarding Nicholas's prior activities in Spain and France.

"Hold on, I'd like the Reuters chap to hear this. It's really his purview. He covers the diplomatic beat, might have run into this Miner character."

The Reuters chap, a bearded, red-headed Scotsman named Ian, proved rather cagey. When pressed by Ames, he admitted to having been inside the American embassy once or twice, but that was as far as he'd go.

"A dinnae ken him."

"What did he say?" my husband whispered.

"He claims he doesn't know Nicholas," I whispered back.

Ames, however, was doggedly making the case for investigating our story. "You know the Yanks. Would they knowingly put a man with Communist ties in a sensitive position?"

"A hae nae thochtie," Ian replied unintelligibly, rising from his barstool. He offered the seat to Gray, who'd vacated it when the Scotsman joined us, taking himself and his glass of whiskey off to the nether regions of the bar.

Just then, a group Ames's compatriots entered the room. "He's done it!" one of them proclaimed. "Nagy is pulling out of the Warsaw pact."

"Bloody hell!" said Ames. He hastily downed his drink and followed the other newsmen to an empty table in the back corner. We dragged a few chairs over and joined them. Someone had brought along a radio and tuned it to the BBC. After the pips marking the top of the eight o'clock hour, we all strained to hear the news on Hungary, but the majority of the broadcast was taken up with the Suez Crisis.

"Gyppos asked for it, closing the canal," Ames opined to general agreement. "Nasser has to be taught a lesson."

Toward the end of the program, the announcer mentioned unconfirmed reports that Soviet forces had surrounded the Budapest airport. There were also rumors of armored battalions crossing from Ukraine into eastern Hungary and making their way toward the city.

"Rumors, my foot," complained the *Times* reporter. "My photographer risked his life to bring back solid evidence of a troop build-up. Don't they know what's going on?"

"Oh, they know all right," said Jakub. He then surprised me by informing the entire group about the convoy. "We'll be on it, and I wouldn't linger too long in Budapest if I were you," he told the assembled newsmen. I realized he was doing exactly as József had instructed, making us the center of attention. My husband's ability to converse in French, Italian, and Polish guaranteed him a good-sized audience of foreign correspondents, all wanting to learn more about the American view of the uprising, and he was soon at the center of a lively conversation being conducted in several languages simultaneously.

Gray, meanwhile, was discoursing with the English speakers around the table on the upcoming presidential election in the United States. Eisenhower was expected to win a second term, but my brother let it be known that he supported Stevenson.

"What, are you an egghead, too, then?" said someone with an Irish accent.

"Not really." My brother admired Stevenson chiefly for his stance against McCarthyism, as he proceeded to explain—a lecture I'd sat through more than once. His listeners grew outraged when he got to the part about how Richard Nixon had accused Stevenson of spreading Communist propaganda while governor of Illinois.

"The vice president said that? He's as good as charging Stevenson with treason, according to the Fourteenth Amendment: giving aid or comfort to the enemy." The *Times* man had evidently studied our Constitution.

"Damn straight," agreed Gray, whose loathing of Nixon knew no bounds. "That lying red-baiter will use every trick in the book to smear his opponent. He's angling for the presidency and heaven help us if he manages to get himself elected."

The conversation turned to the country's new prime minister, Imre Nagy. Pulling out of the Warsaw Pact and proclaiming Hungarian neutrality was a desperate move, evidence that the new prime minister realized the revolution would fail. Austria may have gotten away with declaring its neutrality a year earlier, but Austria had never been a Soviet satellite.

"Mark my words, mates," predicted an Australian photographer, "this game will be over in no time." There was unanimous agreement around the table, which wasn't surprising. We'd been given the same prognosis by everyone, from Dr. Keller to the embassy official who'd told us about the convoy to the couple we met in Republic Square.

My gaze wandered to the doorway. A man in a dark overcoat had just entered the bar. Was it my imagination, or was he watching us? Jakub squeezed my hand under the table to let me know he was also aware of our observer. I sipped my beer, sneaking glances at the worrisome man every few minutes. He'd moved out of the doorway but remained standing, crossing and uncrossing his arms, checking his watch. He appeared to be waiting for someone and as time passed without his pal showing up, his fidgeting increased. Then a familiar figure entered the bar: Frankie. I recognized him by his physique—he was easily the tallest person in the room. Nodding to the man in the overcoat, the stringer positioned himself at a center table, where we couldn't avoid passing him, were we to leave. Gray stood up and went around to Ames's side of the table. Putting a hand on the journalist's shoulder, he leaned down to speak to him.

"Do you see that man who just sat down?" He jerked his head in Frankie's direction.

"Aye, laddie."

Ian had materialized out of nowhere. Did he also suspect Frankie of not being what he said he was? He must have, for he pulled up a chair at the journalists' table and stayed close by, silently sipping his whiskey. There was something gnome-like about him, a combination of the beard and his gruff demeanor, but I found his presence reassuring—I think we all did—and as the evening wore on he seemed to mellow toward us.

Heeding József's warning, our suitcases were packed and stowed with the bellman. All that remained was to settle our bill in the morning, but getting through the night was going to be a challenge. I could barely keep my eyes open, and it was only 10 p.m. Jakub was drowsy too, and even Gray was slowing down.

"If yer tired, try fer a kip," said Ian.

"A kip?" Another word my husband had never encountered.

Ames explained that "kip" was Scottish for "lie-down," the British expression for a nap. "Go on then, up to bed with the three of you," he prodded. "You'll want to have your wits about you for the drive tomorrow."

We weren't about to admit in front of the others that we were afraid to go up to our rooms. Not with Frankie there, nursing his single glass of pálinka and watching our every move. But Ian solved the problem by offering us the use of his suite. He had a story to file and would be working in the living room; the three of us could kip in the bedroom if we didn't mind the noise of his typewriter clattering away on the other side of the wall. I assured him that I could think of no more comforting a sound. In fact, I'd grown used to falling asleep to the plinks of Gray typing in the next room when we were sharing a flat in London.

"He's an insomniac," Ames confided as the Scotsman went to pay his tab. He himself wasn't ready to call it a night, however. There might be more to learn from his fellow newsmen. "What time did you say that convoy was leaving?"

"Seven o'clock," said Jakub. "We'll be getting an early start in the morning." Of course we had no intention of joining the convoy. József would direct us to the outskirts of the city once we'd picked up the tire. He'd promised the mechanic a hefty bonus if it was ready for us first thing.

"Oh, my. Much too early for me, dearies. I'll just say goodbye now."

"Goodbye, Mr. Ames." I reached across the table to shake his hand. He'd grown on me. In his own way, he'd been looking out for us, and I realized that I wouldn't mind one bit if our paths were to cross again. Beneath the bluster was a good heart and I thought that even my brother had warmed toward him.

We took the elevator up to the third floor with Ian. When the doors opened, he insisted upon getting out first, motioning for us to stay a few paces behind as we followed him down the hall to his suite. Once inside, the Scotsman put a finger to his lips and went straight to the typewriter: *What kind of trouble have you gotten yourselves into?* In print, he expressed himself in plain English, I was glad to see.

Gray took Ian's seat and pecked out a response. *We may have uncovered a spy at the American embassy. We were trying to tell you in the bar.*

The bar is no place for that kind of conversation. Tell me now.

His name is Nicholas Miner. We think he was with Comintern in Spain—

Ian nudged him aside. *Wait a second.* He put a clean sheet of paper in the typewriter and put a series of questions to Gray, beginning with how we'd met Nicholas, then moving on to our suspicions regarding the man's Communist affiliations. The two of them went back and forth, with Jakub occasionally taking a turn at the keys to offer his insight into Nicholas's activities. Ian collected the pages as they came out of the typewriter, numbering and dating each one before placing it inside a folder he'd pulled from his briefcase. By midnight, he'd compiled a full report on the alleged Soviet agent.

I will make sure that this information gets into the right hands. Now tell me about tomorrow. You don't want to go anywhere near the American embassy.

We know. That was just to throw them off the scent. My brother typed out our plan to pick up the tire and leave directly from the garage. *By the time Miner realizes that we're not with the convoy, we'll be well on our way to Vienna.*

Ian wasn't satisfied. *For your own safety, you must pay very close attention in case you're followed. Take a roundabout route to the garage, double back, and make a note of any vehicles that stay with you for any length of time. Avoid narrow streets where you could get blocked in. Do you understand?*

We will be careful.

I hope so. Now get some sleep.

I didn't expect to sleep, lying fully clothed beside Jakub on top of one twin bed, while Gray occupied the other, but I drifted off almost instantly in my husband's arms. It would be my last untroubled night. Early the next morning, as we left the hotel, we found József lying face down on the sidewalk in a pool of blood.

CHAPTER NINE

November 2, 1956

I might have screamed, but Jakub, who had seen the body first, quickly put down our suitcase and pulled me into his arms. "Shhh, it's all right. I'm here."

Gray was kneeling by József with his back to us, searching for a pulse. "His throat's been cut," he said, straightening up and stepping away from the corpse.

"Oh, God. No." I buried my head against Jakub's chest, sobbing into his camel hair overcoat. József was our friend. No, he was more than that: he was our compass, our light, guiding us through the morass.

I'd been entertaining a little fantasy about rescuing him and his family. The idea had come to me the night before, while killing time in the bar. I was thinking about József's despair over Péti—his terror, really, that his son might end up in prison. He'd refused my offer to bring Péti out of Hungary and seemed resigned to a dire future, but there had to be a solution. We couldn't turn our backs on him and his family. What if we called Lázár as soon as we reached Vienna? The puppeteer would be on the next train, I was quite sure of it, and we'd be waiting for him with the Romanian playwright's car in good running order. Lázár could drive back across the border and bring out his relatives as soon as it was feasible while the three of us proceeded to Paris by train, arriving in plenty of time to welcome them when they arrived. I imagined them stepping into the café. József, impeccable in his tweeds, ever the British gentleman. Would he eventually make his way back to England, I wondered? With his command of the language, he'd be happier there, and Péti no doubt could continue his studies at one of the British universities, once he'd mastered English. Gray would do what he could to help the family, and Jakub and I would be frequent visitors, in between gigs.

Crazy thinking, but I was replaying this far-fetched scenario in one corner of my mind as I stood there crying over József's body. Some part of me knew he was dead. I would never see him again, in Paris or anywhere else. Oh, but I did see him. Even with my eyes closed, the image of his body on the sidewalk was all too vivid. Gray was still kneeling, telling us that József's throat had been cut. There was blood all around.

Stop it, I told myself.

Now I was imagining a different scenario, one that involved turning back time. We woke up in Ian's suite, tiptoeing past the Scotsman, who was snoring on the sofa. So far, we were keeping to the morning's script, but instead of wasting precious minutes with Attila, who'd insisted on providing us with a bag of freshly-baked rolls for the journey, what if we'd arrived outside in time to stop the murder from happening? József's assailants would have fled at our approach. Or maybe they wouldn't have fled. Maybe they'd have turned on us because we were the intended victims, weren't we? József might have been trying to warn us. He might have discovered them, lying in wait. He'd walked into an ambush intended for us.

So many alternatives, but we'd done nothing. It was our fault he was dead.

"*Najdroższa*," said my husband, gently extricating himself from my grip. "We cannot stay here. It isn't safe." Taking my elbow, he steered me down the sidewalk, turning every so often to look over his shoulder. I heard my brother behind us, panting to keep up. "Quickly, quickly," urged Jakub, hurrying us away from the Duna.

It was barely light, and our side of the avenue was engulfed by shadows. Were József's killers hiding among those shadows? I stumbled along, vision blurred by tears. *Please keep us safe. Please keep us safe.* I didn't know who I was praying to. Father had cast aside his own religion long before I was born. I'd grown up without any particular faith, but actors are superstitious, seeking portents wherever we can. As we rounded the corner of the side street where we'd left the Škoda, I realized I'd been addressing my prayers to our missing brother. Zoltán utca was the name of the street where we'd parked. I'd remarked on the coincidence the evening before: was it a sign of some sort? Now, as we walked briskly toward the car, I couldn't shake the feeling that Zoltán was working mysteriously behind the scenes, shepherding us in a direction as yet unknown.

We reached the Škoda. Gray opened the trunk and put his and our bags inside, then handed the keys to Jakub and went around to check the tire. My husband slid behind the wheel and reached across to unlock the doors on the passenger side.

"It's down from where it was when I filled it," said Gray, climbing into the back seat, "but we're okay for now."

"Now is good enough for me. Let's go!" Jakub turned the key in the ignition. I barely had time to slam the door shut before he took off, pulling out of the parking space and careening down the narrow street with a screech of tires as if we were in the Indy 500. Weaving around the rubble at such speed, I was sure we'd smash into something, or run over a piece of shrapnel. We couldn't afford another flat.

"Be careful, darling," I said, my voice quavery. The heater was struggling to warm things up inside, but my shivering had little to do with the cold. I knew enough about Budapest's geography to realize we weren't going in the right direction for the service station. Instead of driving further east into Pest's labyrinth of streets, Jakub had us heading off in the opposite direction, across the river to Buda on the Chain Bridge. We passed a pair of massive stone lions on either side of the long span and went under an arch, through which I could just make out the majestic castle perched high on the opposite bank. My husband's eyes kept darting to the rearview mirror, checking to see if anyone was on our tail. We made it across the Danube without being followed, I was glad to observe. The next thing I knew, we were winding our way up a series of steep curves to the summit of Castle Hill.

Buda was older and quainter than Pest, its cobblestone streets miraculously untouched by the strife below. Here were trees, and stately buildings ranged along a promenade with a vista overlooking the western hills. Jakub eased the Škoda onto a pull-out in front of a small park and turned off the engine. Above us loomed the spires of an ancient church. It was so quiet that when I rolled down my window for a breath of fresh air, I could hear birdsong.

I was trying to recall every encounter we'd ever had with József in chronological order, to fix him in my memory forever. His voice on the telephone saying, "Yes, Zoltán is your brother," his excitement carrying across the wires. After three years of sharing a cell, there wasn't much the two of them didn't know about one another, he'd told us, delighted to be of service. All the fineness of József's character was already revealed in that first conversation, I realized. He'd set aside his troubles to help us track our brother down, putting our needs ahead of his own. It's easy to notice a man like Zoltán, the standard-bearer who dashes headlong into the fray, but in his modest way, József had been no less noble. We'd never stopped to consider how much we were asking of him. He should have been with his family, making plans to keep Péti safe, not looking after us.

It occurred to me that Jakub was equally selfless when it came to me. Now, for example, he'd started the car and was watching a black sedan as it drove up the hill toward us, his hand poised over the gearshift in readiness for a quick getaway. The car went past without slowing but he didn't relax. He couldn't. For my sake, he'd pushed his grief aside.

I resolved to do the same. My beloved had enough on his mind without having to hold me together. We'd take care of one other, once we were safely back in Paris, but for now I needed to be strong. Scooting closer, I gave Jakub a peck on the cheek, letting him know I would be okay.

"Hey, take a look at this." Gray held up the Dante snippet we'd found in Zoltán's typewriter. The English translation had been penciled in beneath the Hungarian stanza. Craning my neck to see over the back of the front seat, I could just make out the words. *And the frost bound the tears between those orbs, and held them there.*

Jakub was puzzled. "What are we supposed to be looking at?"

"This was sticking out of József's pocket. He must have been intending to show it to us before we left, although damned if I can figure out why. I do know the place where it comes from."

"Go ahead," I said, "tell us." I'd encountered the *Divine*

Comedy in boarding school, although it had left no mark on me. "Maybe we can figure it out together."

My brother needed no further prompting. "Dante comes upon a group of sinners, frozen in ice up to their necks. He describes them as blue-pinched, and there's a lovely bit about the chattering of their teeth sounding like the cry of a stork. Two brothers, Alessandro and Napoleone Alberti, are stuck together, chest to chest, pressed so tightly against one another that the hair on their heads is intermingled. Dante stumbles upon them, literally. He practically steps on their heads. They both raise their faces to look at him and as they do, tears, unshed until that very moment, flow from their eyes and freeze, locking the brothers even more firmly together. The only way they can break the seal of those frozen tears is to butt heads, like goats."

"What did they do to land in Hell?" Despite myself, I was drawn in. I could actually picture the two brothers in the frozen lake, locked in ice for all eternity.

"That's what's so interesting," said Gray. "This section of the *Inferno* is known as the Caïna, named after Cain in the Bible, who killed his brother Abel, as I'm sure you both know."

Jakub nodded impatiently. "Yes, of course." He'd been drawn in as well.

"We've arrived in the ninth circle of Hell, where Dante's theme is betrayal. Canto 33 introduces a number of traitors who betrayed their country, but Zoltán's stanza comes a bit earlier, toward the end of Canto 32. Alessandro and Napoleone killed their father, Alberto, and then fought over who would inherit his wealth. They ended up killing one another—"

"What did you say?" I interrupted him. "They betrayed their father and then they killed each other? That's horrible!"

"Things were pretty nasty, back in Dante's day," Gray agreed, gratified by the vehemence of my reaction. "Betrayal was commonplace. Take the Borgias: fratricide was the least of it. No telling how many murders were committed by members of that depraved family, not to mention adultery and incest. Would you believe it, a couple of them were even popes!"

"I don't care about the Borgias." Was I the only one who realized what Zoltán must have been thinking, when he'd typed out those lines of Dante's up there in his bullet-spattered office? "He hid those surveillance reports in the very section of the *Inferno* that's about family betrayal. Doesn't that tell you something?"

"It tells me he was paranoid," said my brother, miffed over my dismissal of the Borgias. "Not that he didn't have reason, mind you."

"Look what he did!" My voice sounded shrill to my own ears. I made an effort to modulate it. "He read the reports. He must have figured out who betrayed him, back then. There were only three of them in that living room. So what does he do next?"

"He went and tried to get himself killed? That's taking things awfully literally," said Gray skeptically.

"I don't know why he got involved in a gun battle," I admitted, "but we know he typed out those lines for us to find after he got wounded. There's blood on the page."

Quick as usual, Jakub saw what I was getting at. "He wanted us to know that his betrayer was still out there."

"Yes. He meant for us to find the clue the next morning, when we got to the office."

"Would it have changed anything if we had?" mused my husband.

"I think so. He was trying to tell us that his home wasn't

safe, to warn us off going there. We knew something was wrong when we showed up there with József. He said it, remember: Dr. Szabó was scared to death. We should never have gone there. We've led Zoltán's enemy straight to his front door."

"It's his own fault for not keeping his head down," my brother insisted self-righteously. "If he hadn't gotten himself shot at in that office of his, we wouldn't have had to go bumbling around, trying to pick up his traces. We'd all be eating wiener schnitzel in the Sacher by now, safe and sound."

"Is that all you care about?" I was shouting now. "Everyone we've met here in Budapest is in danger, thanks to our bumbling around, and you're talking about wiener schnitzel?"

"I'm sorry, Cara. I didn't mean to be callous."

"I know you didn't." I stopped, aware of the tears flowing from my own eyes, which were not frozen. They were hot with remorse. So much for holding myself together. "József would still be alive, if it weren't for us. We set the hounds on him."

Jakub slid across the seat and took me into his arms. "You shouldn't blame yourself," he murmured into my hair. "This thing is much bigger than us, you know."

"Of course I blame myself." I swiped at my eyes with a sleeve, refusing to accept the way out he was offering. "This was our problem, not his. We had no right to drag him into this mess. What will his wife and son do without him?"

"I imagine they'll do the same thing they did when he was in prison," said my husband. "People in this country are experts at survival. But you're right: his death is on our hands."

I appreciated his frankness, cold as it was. This was a side to Jakub that I'd rarely seen, and under ordinary conditions, I might have found it off-putting, his ability to appraise a situation bluntly and move forward, setting his feelings aside. But he too was an expert at survival, and now was the time for action, not regrets.

"There's still time to warn her, isn't there?" I said.

My husband nodded. "If we hurry, yes."

"Warn who?" said Gray.

"Dr. Szabó could be in danger," I told him. "Whoever killed József might come after her next."

"You don't seriously intend to go back and talk to that woman, not after she made it plain that she wanted nothing whatsoever to do with us."

"After what happened to József, I refuse to leave the country without seeing Zoltán's wife and, at the very least, putting her on her guard."

"I agree with Cara," said Jakub.

"Oh, very well." I heard the hesitation in my brother's voice. "But how're we going to find that place again? It was pretty complicated, getting there from the hospital and the Budapest map doesn't go out that far."

"Pesterzsébet," said Jakub. "That's the name of the district." He opened the map to the Hungary side and located it. "The home was near a church, as I recall. And we took Üllői út to get there."

"How do you remember these things?" I marveled, although I was fairly certain that this skill was another vestige of his time in the Resistance. The ability to commit various details to memory—names, addresses, landmarks—may well have meant the difference between life and death during the war.

My husband brushed off the compliment. "My memory

won't be enough. What we really need is a Hungarian speaker. Someone who can handle our negotiations with the garage to start with. Then, when we get to Dr. Szabó's, someone's got to be able to explain coherently why we've returned. Otherwise, we'll only have made things worse."

Gray sighed dramatically and asked for the car keys. He got out and went around to open the trunk. We couldn't see what he was doing through the back window with it up, but when he returned, he was holding a fancy bottle of pálinka, one of the Duna's best.

"I was bringing it home as a souvenir," he said sheepishly. "The stuff grows on you."

I remembered the rolls that Attila had provided. Fetching the bag from my suitcase, I discovered the waiter had thoughtfully packed hard-boiled eggs, salami, and a hunk of cheese to go along with the rolls, all of which we hungrily consumed in the parked car while Gray got to work on the pálinka.

"Would you care for a swallow, a chaser to help wash breakfast down?" He proffered the bottle. "No? Cheers, then," he said, raising it to his lips.

"Cheers," we repeated.

Getting to the garage shouldn't have been difficult. Even I remembered the name of the street it was on, Rákóczi út, having confused it with the name of the recently deposed dictator. But winding our way back down Castle Hill took us through some damaged areas that rivaled those in Pest, necessitating a series of detours. After crossing the river again, this time on the Liberty Bridge, we passed the first of six upended trolley cars (I counted), followed by a stewed tank abandoned in front of what looked like an army barracks. I tried not to look at the charred remains of the Russian soldiers who had been inside the tank when it blew up, but the smell of their burned and rotting flesh carried with us for several blocks. I wished I possessed Jakub's ability to remain focused on the way forward, but I couldn't get past the horror of it all.

Gray, on the other hand, had found refuge in drink. We could hear him singing softly to himself in the back seat.

"He sounds pretty jolly," my husband commented. "How much has he had?"

I turned around to check the level of the bottle. "About a third, I'd say."

"When he gets to the halfway mark, better take it away from him. We should save the rest. It might prove necessary on the way to the border."

"Did you hear that?" I asked my brother.

"*Ne aggódj. Minden csodálatos!*" came the reply.

"On second thought, he's probably had enough already," said Jakub.

Eventually, after much detouring, we reached the garage where we'd left the tire. The spare was nearly flat by the time we arrived, and Jakub was concerned we might have damaged the rim. He wanted Gray to ask the mechanic to change the tire, a straightforward enough request and one hard to misinterpret, I'd have thought. The man was clearly expecting us. He'd come out of his office, rolling the tire across the lot, the moment he spotted the Škoda.

"*Szépjóreggelt!*" My brother rolled down his window and beckoned the mechanic over. He spoke a sentence or two in Hungarian and motioned to the tire, presumably conveying Jakub's request, but the mechanic seemed to take his words as a personal affront and showed no inclination whatsoever to comply. Hands on his hips, he regarded the three of us with no small amount of animosity. Had we not needed the tire replaced immediately, I'd have urged Jakub to drive away, fast. I could tell that the mechanic's attitude was making him nervous too.

"Maybe a bribe would help," he said, reaching into the pocket of his trousers and peeling off a few bills from the bundle of forints in his wallet. But it turned out that my brother had not mentioned the flat tire. He'd quoted a line from Marx, something to do with the wage slavery of the laborer.

I stared at him in disbelief. "Why'd you do that?"

"We may be representatives of a capitalist society, but we aren't here to exploit him," he announced pedantically. "The Hungarian people aren't looking to overturn the Communist system, you know. They just want to reform it, to make it more humane, which is what Marx had in mind in the first place, I'll have you know. Stalinism is a perversion of Marxist principles." He sounded quite pleased with himself after this little speech. Then he slapped his forehead.

"Uh oh."

"What's wrong?"

An embarrassed look came over Gray's face. "I'm afraid I made a boo-boo. I may have called him a stinky slave instead of a wage slave."

"Please tell me you're kidding."

"It was an honest mistake," he protested. "Don't look at me like that, Cara. I just got *bérszolga* and *büdös szolga* confused. Could have happened to anyone. Awfully inappropriate, though. I should probably say I'm sorry."

"Oh, for goodness sake!" I got out of the car and approached the fellow. Employing a combination of gestures, smiles, and apologetic grimaces, I communicated our desire to have him replace the flat tire with the one he'd repaired while simultaneously indicating that the man in the back seat was unhinged.

The job took less than ten minutes, during which time the mechanic insisted we wait in the heated office. Fortunately, he made no mention of József; I didn't know what Gray would have told him. He'd recovered himself after the stinky slave remark and was still in full propaganda mode as we set off for Pesterzsébet, regaling us with snippets of Marx hauled out from some limitless storehouse in his mind. Alcohol opened many doors, it seemed.

"Capital is dead labor that, vampire-like, only lives by sucking living labor, and lives the more the more labor it sucks."

"Marx wrote that? How fascinating," said Jakub. "Do you think he read *Dracula*?"

"Don't humor him," I warned. Too late.

"Marx had been dead for fourteen years by the time Bram Stoker wrote *Dracula*," my brother informed us. "But he and Stoker had a common source: Vlad the Impaler. I'm sure you can guess Vlad's favorite form of execution. Do you know, he once killed a pair of Turkish emissaries by nailing their turbans to their heads? Not what you'd call a welcoming guy. Needless to say, this angered the Sultan, but he was no match for Vlad, of course."

The drive went on like this, Gray prattling away and showing no signs of flagging. We'd reached the industrial zone on the outskirts of the city, the last familiar landmark. We were already off the Budapest inset on the map.

"There's the factory where the workers took over." I recognized the site by its graffiti-covered walls. Two days earlier, the building had looked deserted. Now groups of men milled around out front, taking turns warming their hands over a fire in a metal barrel.

Jakub pulled over. "Maybe we should ask for directions?" he suggested.

Gray was keen to approach the workers. "Let me handle this," he said, rolling down the window. "Brothers!" he shouted. "*Testvérek!*" Two or three of the workers turned to look and he gave them a friendly wave. The next thing we knew, he was bounding out of the car, pálinka in hand, to join the group by the barrel. The bottle began making the rounds, more workers drifting over as they saw what was going on. Soon he was at the center of a boisterous throng and we lost sight of him entirely. The gathering appeared friendly enough. We could hear laughter, and bursts of song, including one melody that sounded vaguely familiar.

"Is that 'Waltzing Matilda?'" I strained to hear the singing over the carousing.

"Waltzing Matilda?" my husband echoed. I explained it was a ballad about a hobo in the Australian bush, which somehow led me into a lengthy digression about hobos hopping freight trains during the Great Depression and Woody Guthrie's folk songs of the Dust Bowl era. Jakub knew next to nothing about the American folk tradition and, being a musician, begged me to sing one of Guthrie's anthems. I'd dredged up the first verse of "This Land is Your Land" and was just about to launch into the chorus when Gray came staggering back, supported by a pair of burly working men, one on either side. My brother's muffler had come loose from around his neck and was flapping uselessly about his shoulders. After assisting him into the back seat of the Škoda, one of his new friends undid the top button of his overcoat, tenderly tucking the ends of his muffler beneath the lapel. The other spoke to Gray, patiently and at length, pausing after every sentence so he could translate for us—a painstaking process—and watching our faces to be sure his message was getting across.

We were looking for Pesterzsébet, was that right?

"Yes," I said. "Pesterzsébet. And there's a great big church in the center, isn't there?"

Gray somehow succeeded in conveying my question and both men smiled and nodded. "*Igen-igen, a nagy templom.*"

"They want to show you something on the map," I understood my brother to say. I told him to tell them that the Budapest side of the map didn't show Pesterzsébet, and the Hungary side wasn't detailed enough to indicate streets, but the men insisted on seeing it anyhow. I passed it back to them.

"*Ez az,*" said the older of the two, pointing to a street that ran parallel to Üllői út for a short distance before diverging sharply away in the direction of the Danube.

"He's telling you that this street will take you to the church," Gray translated, making a valiant effort not to slur his words.

"That's all we need to know," said Jakub. This little escapade had cost us precious time. He turned the key in the ignition, signaling to Gray's pals that we meant to be off.

"Goodbye, goodbye. *Köszönöm, testvérek!*"

"*Szóra sem érdemes,*" they replied.

"Such sweet guys," said Gray, smiling to himself as we pulled away.

CHAPTER TEN

Lights burned within the children's home but all was quiet outside. The early morning mist had turned to midmorning drizzle as we made our way into Pesterzsébet, and the few passersby we glimpsed were either huddled under umbrellas or else they had their heads down and were in too much of a hurry to notice us stationed out front in the Škoda.

"I could go into that shop on the corner and see if anyone there speaks another language," said Jakub. He and I were weighing our options. We didn't have a plan for approaching Dr. Szabó, but sending Gray to the door in his inebriated state, even if one of us accompanied him, seemed like a very bad idea. He may have gotten along fine with the workers, but after the imbroglio with the garage mechanic, we didn't dare trust him with the sensitive matter of warning Zoltán's wife that she and her daughter were in danger.

"We don't want to involve a stranger in this, do we?"

"No, I suppose not," he conceded. "They might make things worse for the family later on. If only there were someone we could rely on."

My brother gave a shout from the back seat. "Cara! Jakub! Look over there, at the church."

"Not now." I was thinking about priests. How close were Italian and Latin? Could a priest, who presumably knew

Latin, understand Jakub's Italian well enough to serve as a go-between with the doctor? Surely we could trust a priest not to betray her.

"Isn't that the girl?" interrupted Gray. "The one we saw the other day?"

"Shhh!" I turned around to quiet him down.

Gray was pointing at a small figure who was making her way toward us. "I'm sure it's her. She's on crutches."

He was right; I recognized the girl. A satchel containing two loaves of bread was slung across her chest, leaving her hands free to maneuver the crutches. She was quite proficient on the wooden sticks, her pace steady as she swung one arm forward and then the other, dragging her left leg, which was considerably shorter than the right one, her small feet encased in clunky black shoes that must have taken considerable effort to lift.

"Come on," said Jakub, getting out of the car. Gray and I followed, crossing the street to meet her.

The girl beamed when she saw me. Talking a mile a minute, she allowed me to relieve her of the satchel, which was heavier than I expected because it contained not only bread, I realized, but also a cabbage along with some unlabeled canned goods.

"What's she saying?" I asked my brother.

"Her name is Juicy. No, that can't be right, can it? Juicy?"

The girl laughed. "Zsuzsi (jiu-gie)," she corrected, pronouncing the z's like half-swallowed g's.

"Hello, Zsuzsi. I'm Cara," I said, tapping my chest and repeating my name for good measure. "Cara."

"Carrra," she repeated, rolling the r in a pleasant way, like a cat's purr.

Gray was struggling to make sense of what she said next. "She's our niece?" He turned to face her and repeated the

125

word she'd just used. "*Unokahúgunk?*" Zsuzsi nodded vigorously.

So I was right! I pulled the framed family photograph out of my purse and showed it to her. Excitedly Zsuzsi pointed to the little girl and then to herself. Regarding her more closely, I could see the resemblance to her younger self, although her hair was loose now, her face no longer the round-cheeked toddler's, and of course the girl in the picture was not on crutches.

"*Apám,*" she said, indicating Zoltán. Then she tugged my hand and looked beseechingly up into my eyes, her own eyes brimming with tears. I put the satchel on the ground, bent down, and hugged her. The furious way she hugged me back brought to mind her adoring expression in the photo. So much had changed since that sunlit day. Her father's arrest and imprisonment, his years-long absence, her own bout with polio (I could think of no other explanation for the crutches). Now the revolution had upended her life once again.

"The daughter," said Jakub. "But she seemed to know who we were even before you showed her the picture. How is that possible?"

"Zoltán must have told her about us," I speculated, although this wouldn't explain why her mother had driven us away. Unless our brother was hiding in the house? Was he still there? I allowed myself a glimmer of hope, but I couldn't sustain it for long. If that were the case, why the tears? Had he taken a turn for the worse since checking himself out of the hospital? He might be inside dying. Poor Zsuzsi! Maybe the girl had been praying in the church for her father's recovery.

"Cara." My brother's voice pulled me back to the present moment. The rain was picking up, and we all moved into the shelter of the car, Jakub and I in back with the child sitting between us, her crutches and the satchel of food on the front seat next to Gray.

"Ask her about her father, find out if he's okay," I said, once we were settled.

"*Hogy van az apád? Hogy érzi magát?*"

"*Nem tudom,*" Zsuzsi sobbed. "*Eltünt.*"

"Oh, sweetie." I put an arm around her and patted her back.

"Zoltán's gone missing," my brother translated. He was doing very well, I thought, our niece's tender age keeping him focused on the here and now. "The reason she was so happy to see you the other day, Cara, is because she thought you'd been sent by her father. She says they were expecting you, she and her mother."

This was news. "They were?" my husband and I said in unison.

A look of doubt crossed my brother's face. "Well, I'm pretty sure that's what she said. She talks fast, and I might have gotten it wrong."

"Ask her again," Jakub said. "And see if you can't pin her down on exactly when she last saw her father."

"Are you sure that's a good idea, darling?" I objected. "She might not know that he was shot. We don't want to upset her unnecessarily."

"Good point. Don't ask her directly, but listen carefully to what she says."

"Oh, boy." Gray steeled himself for the ordeal. A series of questions, each answered at length by our garrulous niece, served merely to add a new wrinkle to the story. Not only had Zoltán informed his wife and daughter that we were coming, but he'd promised them that we would take them out of Hungary.

"She wants to see America," my brother reported.

Zsuzsi nodded enthusiastically, picking up on the word. "*Amerika*," she parroted. "*Elvisztek engem oda veletek*"

"She's asking if we'll take her there."

"Why not?" said Jakub. "You'd like that, wouldn't you, *najdroższa?*"

I smiled at him over the top of Zsuzsi's head. Why not indeed? It was the perfect solution: to bring the girl and her mother with us now and hope that Zoltán would find a way to join them later. We'd left the visa where he was sure to find it, and there had to be someone Dr. Szabó trusted enough to pass along the information of where they'd gone. She and Zoltán had to have established some way of communicating. We'd phone Father from Vienna. I was sure he'd welcome them at the lodge —he could invite them himself, in Hungarian. I was already picturing his delight, when he met his granddaughter.

"Cara," said Gray, once again disrupting my train of thought. "Are you listening? There's more. Zsuzsi told me that her parents were arguing a lot in the days leading up to his disappearance. Her mother didn't want to leave Hungary—"

I finished his sentence. "Because of the home." I wasn't really surprised. Dr. Szabó's devotion to the abandoned children under her care had been obvious from our first visit.

"That might have been part of it, but I got the impression that it had more to do with us."

"How so?" asked my husband.

"Her mother was furious with him—and she hasn't mentioned anything about Zoltán being wounded, by the way—so I'm guessing that he didn't go home after he checked himself out of the hospital. He must have gone right into hiding."

"Either that, or he went right back out and got himself killed," I said with a sinking heart. "Zoltán had it in him. If he'd come across another battle on his way home, I could see him launching himself right into the thick of it, couldn't you?"

Zsuzsi pulled on my arm, alarmed by our repeated use of her father's name, combined with the worried tone of my voice.

"*Valami baj van?*"

"*Az apádról beszéltünk,*" Gray said soothingly. "*Szeretnénk tudni hol van.*"

"*Anya tudja.*"

"*Anyád tudja?*"

"*Igen. Anya tudja, de nem árulja el.*"

"*Miert nem?*"

Our niece succumbed to a fresh bout of tears. Pulling her onto my lap, I gave Gray a dirty look over Zsuzsi's shoulder as I rubbed her back. "Shhh, it's okay. Don't cry."

"Jeez, I'm sorry," he apologized.

"What did you say to upset her?" I demanded in a loud whisper.

"I didn't mean to upset her. Really, I was just trying to figure things out. It's not easy talking to a kid in a situation like this. You want the job, go ahead. I resign."

Jakub stepped in to calm things down. "What did she say that confused you?"

"She thinks that her mother knows where Zoltán is. She knows—I should say—but she won't tell Zsuzsi."

"Why not?"

"That's the question I asked her when she fell apart."

"Oh."

I was getting a bad feeling about all this. Did Dr. Szabó suspect that her husband was dead? She might have been waiting for confirmation before she broke the news to her daughter, but the girl was perceptive enough to have sensed the truth. I looked at Zsuzsi, who was just then blowing her nose on the handkerchief I'd given her. Gray had a point: it was wrong of us to pump her for information. The person we should be talking to was her mother, and we needed to do it soon, before the effects of the pálinka wore off. At the very least, we'd warn her that she might be in danger, but maybe once she heard about József, she'd realize we were on her side and trust us enough to share her suspicions regarding her husband.

Saying goodbye to Zsuzsi was hard. As I was handing the child back her crutches and helping her on with the satchel, I wished I had the words to tell her we wanted to take her with us. But even if I'd spoken her language, I wouldn't have dared to get her hopes up when her mother was so set against us.

"*Ne hagyjatok itt!*" Our niece's face expressed her unwillingness to part from us so eloquently, I didn't need Gray to decipher her words.

I had an inspiration. "Ask her how many children live in the home." The answer came back: *kilenc*. Nine. I got out of the Škoda and went around to the trunk, removed ten bars of French chocolate from the stash of luxury goods, and put them in the satchel with the food. Zsuzsi smiled despite herself.

Dr. Szabó ran a clinic in the church basement on Fridays. It was free, but people brought what they could to compensate the doctor for her time; our niece's satchel had contained food donations the cook would use to make lunch.

There must have been thirty patients waiting their turn to be examined when I entered the clinic, and more sick people kept wandering in. Dr. Szabó and an assistant, a rosy-cheeked young woman no older than me, were managing the entire operation by themselves. They'd set up some portable screens in one corner of the basement, creating two makeshift examining rooms separated by a narrow "corridor" to provide patients with a modicum of privacy. The assistant kept things moving, ushering a new patient into one of the "examining rooms" the minute the doctor had finished with the previous patient and had stepped across the "corridor" to the other "room."

I watched her for quite some time. As was true in our earlier encounter, Dr. Szabó projected a formidable presence. Babies cried, small children darted through the waiting area, chased after by older siblings. Some of the patients seemed quite sick; I heard coughing and wheezing, but the clinic remained orderly with only the two women running it. Every so often, the assistant would fetch a pan of water from some offstage source—the operation in the church basement was so well-choreographed, I felt as if I were watching a performance—and the doctor would break away from her back-to-back consultations to wash her hands.

It was during one of these intervals that she finally noticed me standing a bit to the side of the doorway, inside the room but out of the flow of traffic. She'd taken a towel from the rosy-cheeked young woman and I saw her pause in the middle of drying her hands, distracted, as she tried to place me. A moment later she was conferring with her assistant and hanging up her white smock on a rack by the radiators. She was not exactly smiling as she approached, but I imagined she was not someone who smiled much.

At least she was willing to talk to me on this occasion. I indicated that I wished for her to follow me outside and she complied.

Jakub was drumming his fingers on the steering wheel while Gray drowsed in the Škoda's passenger seat. Between carousing with the working class outside the factory and keeping up with Zsuzsi, he'd expended most of his pálinka-fueled energy. I opened the door to the back seat and invited Dr. Szabó to get in out of the rain, then went around to the other side and joined her. The doctor accepted a cigarette and a light, but made it clear she could only talk to us for as long as it took to smoke it, looking pointedly at her watch after every few puffs.

"*Miért vannak itt?*"

"She wants to know why we're here," my brother translated.

"*Már megmondtam, hogy menjenek el.*"

"She told us to go away once already." Poor Gray was perspiring.

"*Nem fogok beszélni, mert maguk amerikai kémek!*"

"This is too much! Now she's accusing us of being American spies. What should I tell her?"

Jakub shrugged. "How about the truth? Her husband was supposed to meet us in his office, but when we got there, the place was all shot up and he was nowhere in sight. We came here with József the first time because we were worried about him."

"And now we're worried about her and Zsuzsi," I added. "Because of what happened to József. They're in grave danger. Make sure you tell her that too."

"You ought to tell her about József right away," my husband agreed. "She'll remember him, and it will explain why we came back a second time."

Gray sighed dramatically. "You expect me to say all that in Hungarian? We might be here all day."

"Just do the best you can," said Jakub. "She'll get the general idea, I'm sure."

"I wish I hadn't shared all my pálinka with the working class."

Jakub and I watched the cross-examination. Dr. Szabó looked angry at first, firing questions at my brother that left him flustered and stammering, half in English, half in a language that I wasn't sure was Hungarian, but he soldiered valiantly on and gradually her hostility dissipated. She must have decided we were innocent of whatever subterfuge she suspected us of. When Gray mentioned József's name, the doctor had been momentarily at a loss for words. Remembering the cigarette in her hand, she took a long drag, allowing the smoke to seep slowly out of her nostrils. She smoked it down to the filter, then stubbed it out in the ashtray.

"*Tudom, hogy hol van,*" she said finally.

"*Ki?*"

"*A báttya.*"

"*Tényleg tudja?*"

"*Igen.*"

"Zsuzsi was right. She does know where he is!" my brother announced.

"So he's alive." I breathed a sigh of relief.

Dr. Szabó snapped her fingers. "*Adjanak egy térképet..*"

"She's going to show us on the map!" He handed it to her, but she waved it away.

"*Nem a Budapestit. Magyarország térképét!*" With her index finger, she sketched a jagged, vaguely circular outline in the air.

Jakub realized what she wanted. "She wants to see the Hungary side."

133

Gray flipped the map over and attempted to smooth out the creases, flattening the paper against his thigh as he unfolded it, panel by panel. Impatiently, the doctor reached over the back of the seat and took the map from him. Holding it up against the side window so we could all see where she was pointing, she indicated a spot in the northeastern region of the country.

"*Itt,*" she proclaimed, stabbing at the place with her index finger. "*Zoltán Mádon van*"

We all squinted at the spot where she was pointing. It was a tiny town and the print was pretty small. "Mad," I read, amused. "It must not mean the same thing in Hungarian."

"Mád," she repeated. She pronounced it mard, adding an r to the middle of the word and opening her mouth to lengthen the sound.

My brother was astonished. "Jesus Christ! What was he thinking? Look at where he's gone. Mad's practically in the Soviet Union! He really must be mad."

"Mád," Dr. Szabó repeated. A strand of hair had come loose from her bun and I watched her pin it back in place with a practiced gesture. "*Biztonságos utazást.*" She reached for the door handle. Satisfied that we'd understood where our brother had gone, she was now eager to get back to her clinic.

"She wishes us a safe journey," translated Gray. "If you want to say 'thank you,' the word is *Köszönöm.*"

"*Köszönöm,*" I repeated, trying to get the intonation right. The stress was on the first syllable in Hungarian. I wished I knew how to say more, but 'thank you' would have to suffice. Seeing how far we had to travel, I too was eager to be on our way.

Gray was visibly relieved when she'd gone. "Whew! Am I glad that's over."

I allowed Jakub to get back behind the wheel before I spoke. "Can we make it there and back by nightfall, do you think?"

"I'd imagine so. It's still early," he said.

"You two can't be serious," my brother protested. "Mád must be hours away, and in the completely wrong direction to boot."

Knowing I had Jakub's support made it easier to argue with him. "We can't leave without Zoltán, now that we know where he is. He's the whole reason we came. We've got to help him and his family."

"Cara, you're not suggesting that we bring them all with us to Vienna."

"Yes, I am." Daringly, I played my last card. "Why do you think she told us where he is? It's obvious she wants us to find him. She realizes she's in trouble and she has nowhere else to turn. How can we say no?"

Gray made an appeal to Jakub. "Are you on board with this cockamamie scheme? Driving all the way to Mád— when the tanks come, that's the direction they'll be coming from—you know that, right? You don't seriously believe we can outrun them."

"I'm hoping it won't come to that,' my husband replied, "but if need be, I'm sure we can find an alternate route to the border. Zoltán asked for our help, and it looks to me as if he needs it more than ever. He and his family." He turned the key in the ignition. "I agree with Cara: it would be wrong to abandon them."

"Oh, very well." My brother pulled his hat down over his eyes and settled his limbs as best he could across the seat. "Wake me when we get there. I feel the beginning of a massive headache coming on."

CHAPTER ELEVEN

En Route to Mád

"What are those clumps?" I asked my husband, pointing to a mass of dark green vegetation clustered high in the branches of a leafless tree.

"Clumps? What is a clump?" Every so often, I used a word he did not know.

"That's a clump. We've seen a lot of them. What are they, some kind of bird's nest?"

"Those clumps," said Jakub with a mischievous smile, "are mistletoe."

"Are they really? So that's how it grows."

We were driving along a two-lane highway, a flat expanse of road bordered by muddy fields, stone houses abutting the edges. In summer I imagined it would be quite lush, green stretching all the way to the horizon, but our view that day was unrelentingly bleak. Once we'd gone beyond the city's outskirts, the few towns we passed through seemed deserted. I imagined their inhabitants were all huddled indoors behind drawn curtains, bracing for the Soviet onslaught.

At Aszód, where the train line paralleled our route for several miles, we stopped at a railroad station for a bite to eat. Gray was sleeping soundly in the back seat and I was not eager to wake him. In his semi-inebriated state, he hadn't thought to question the particulars of our cockamamie scheme, as he termed it, but finding Zoltán wouldn't be easy. Once we reached Mád, we could hardly go around knocking on strangers' doors. I'd broached this problem with my husband, who'd assured me there were other ways of finding someone, although he'd declined to elaborate on what those 'other ways' might be, saying only that he'd figure something out, once he saw the town and got the lay of the land.

The station's café wasn't much to write home about. Located at one end of the battered stone building, it consisted of two or three flimsy tables and a bar manned by a rough-looking fellow with an impressive mustache, like you'd see on a hussar. The place was bustling with railroad workers taking a midmorning break. After gulping down some coffee, we managed to communicate that we too would like to order some of the thick slices of bread heaped with bacon and onions that we saw our fellow patrons enjoying.

"*Trzy*," said Jakub, holding up three fingers.

The hussar mimicked the gesture. "*Három*," he said, holding up three fingers of his own. Then he looked more closely at Jakub. "*Lengyel?*"

My husband repeated the question, carefully imitating the man's intonation in the hopes that he would elaborate. Instead, the hussar chose simply to restate it more emphatically, several times, raising his voice with each repetition as if dealing with a person who was hard of hearing.

"*Polski*," called out a wizened railroad worker sitting at the table behind us.

An expression of pure delight came to my husband's face as he turned around to face the worker. "*Tak, jestem polskim.*"

"*Jestem polskim zbyt*," came the reply.

The hussar frowned. He seemed to disapprove of patrons who spoke languages other than Hungarian, perhaps with good reason. No doubt he'd be serving a fair number of Russians in the coming days and weeks. For all he knew, we were with the invaders.

"Cara, that gentleman's Polish." Jakub was like a kid who'd just made a new friend. He was so good at languages, it hadn't occurred to me that he might miss speaking his native tongue, but I could see he was itching for a conversation.

"Go ahead, talk to him," I urged. "See what you can learn."

He needed no further encouragement. Picking up his coffee cup, he walked over to join his countryman, who was patting the empty chair beside him. An instant later they were engaged in an animated exchange.

I left them to it and went to freshen up. The restroom in the train station was unheated, but it had running water. Traveling in southern Italy two summers ago, I'd come across so-called bathrooms that were nothing more than a hole in the ground that you squatted over. Here there was a toilet and a sink, with separate facilities for men and women. I relieved myself and washed my hands, then pulled out my compact and powdered my nose, fluffed my short hair with my fingertips, and reapplied my pink lipstick. I wanted to look presentable for Zoltán.

Jakub was bidding his new friend goodbye as I returned to the café. We all shook hands before going our separate ways, the railwayman to his job, the two of us to the Škoda, where we found Gray sprawled across the back seat exactly as we'd left him. In addition to the food, Jakub had purchased a fresh bottle of pálinka "for emergencies," as he put it. I tucked the bottle alongside the packet containing our sandwiches by my feet, hoping fervently that an occasion to use it would not arise.

The Polish railwayman had given Jakub a crucial piece of information. The Soviets might have pulled out of Budapest, but elsewhere they were firmly entrenched, occupying key junctions throughout the country. Forewarned, we were not unprepared when we encountered a battalion of soldiers and a fleet of armored vehicles in the very next town. Hatvan stood at the intersection of two major routes. The road we were traveling on, from Budapest, continued eastward to the border with the USSR, but another artery branched off to the north, heading into Czechoslovakia. The Soviets had set up a roadblock at the crossroads, flanked on either side by soldiers equipped with machine guns. We had no choice but to stop and endure their scrutiny.

"Let me handle this," my husband said.

A young recruit in a fur cap stepped up to the driver's side and indicated that Jakub should roll down the window. His Asiatic features confused me. The only Russians I'd ever met were a pair of émigrés from Moscow, the European part of the Soviet Union. It hadn't occurred to me that people from the eastern reaches of that vast empire would look Chinese.

"*Vy Nemetskiy?*"

Jakub shook his head. "*Polski.*" I recognized the word he used because it was the same word I'd heard the railwayman use in the café to identify himself as a fellow Pole. He must have been trying to defuse a potentially dangerous situation—a carload of Americans confronting an armed company of Soviet troops sent sub rosa to quash a revolution—by passing the three of us off as Polish. But how had he deciphered the soldier's question? I couldn't believe he'd made a lucky guess.

"*Oni Polskiy,*" announced the sentry. The others greeted this statement of our nationality with hoots of laughter. A series of what appeared to be wisecracks ensued, accompanied by rude gestures impugning my husband's manhood. I'd seen a good deal of this sort of thing in Italy and paid them scant attention, and was glad to see that Jakub too remained unfazed. We had a moment of uneasiness when several of the soldiers approached the Škoda to get a closer look at us, but the sight of Gray conked out in the back seat sent them into another round of hilarity.

"Could you give me that bottle of pálinka?" said Jakub.

The gift was accepted. "*Do svidaniya, Polyaki.*" Still snickering, the soldier waved us through, calls of *domoy Polyaki* erupting from the group behind him.

"*Do widzenia,*" said Jakub quietly, rolling up the window. He put the car in gear and slowly pulled away.

"Don't let it bother you. Those men were cretins." I thought he must have felt insulted after all, but he ignored my reassurances and continued to ponder the encounter. "What are you thinking about?" I asked.

"He assumed we were German. Must have been the Austrian license plate."

"Wait a minute. You understood him?" My husband spoke French and Italian in addition to Polish and English, but this was the first indication that he knew Russian.

"Not really. I picked up a bit of it during the war. The words for 'German' and 'Polish' sound pretty much the same in Russian. Goodbye, too."

Some of his fellow Communists in the French Resistance must have been Russian, I realized, but this phase of Jakub's life was not one he dwelled upon. He'd left the Party several years before I met him; the show trials in Eastern Europe had turned his stomach, he'd told me. "They went after the Jews." At the time, I hadn't asked him to elaborate—it embarrassed me, how little I knew about politics—but I was getting an education on this trip, learning firsthand what Communism meant. Gray's lectures and the debates among his blacklisted fellow travelers in London did not pertain to the lives of the people we'd met in Hungary. Nor did they help me understand the role the Party had played in my husband's life. I wanted to know more, not simply from piecing together aspects of his wartime experiences from chance encounters with his former confederates in Paris or the random snippets he let drop from time to time. The risk-taking side of Jakub derived from those years and I couldn't love him completely until I accepted all of him.

We'd driven a few miles without encountering any more Russian soldiers. Jakub pulled over to the side of the road and studied the map, tracing our route with his forefinger as it wound northward to the city of Miskolc, another major junction. South of Miskolc, near the town of Nyékládháza, a spur road veered east, bypassing the city.

"Do you see his road here?" he said. "It may add a little time to our journey, but I think we'd be wise to take it."

I nodded in assent. "I'd just as soon avoid any more Russian roadblocks. The next contingent might not find us as amusing."

"Exactly. And we're out of pálinka."

The map indicated that we'd have to backtrack a bit when we reached the town of Tokaj. Then I made the connection: Father hailed from the Tokaj region. Proud of the area's winemaking traditions, he never tired of educating his guests on the virtues of the Tokaji Aszú, the most esteemed variety of Tokaji. Popes and czars, emperors, kings, and queens all prized the wine, which was being produced to exacting standards for centuries, well before Port and Bordeaux. He might have taken an American name, but Father honored his Hungarian heritage in his own way.

If Zoltán had gone back to the town where he was born, there might be a way of locating him after all. I turned and reached over the seat back to nudge Gray awake.

"What? Are we there?" He sat up groggily and peered out the window.

"Do you know where Father was born? The specific place, I mean."

"You roused me out of a drunken stupor to ask me that?"

"Yes," I said. "I'm sorry, but it's important."

Yawning, my brother ran a hand through his hair. He stretched and rolled his shoulders, rotating his head in circles, first to the left, then around to the right. He seemed to be working out a crick in his neck.

"The town?" I prompted, eager to get his attention before he could launch into the next exercise in the series of seated calisthenics that generally followed the head rotation sequence. As a writer, he spent a lot of time in his chair and had developed an elaborate ritual to loosen up.

"Excuse me while I answer the call of nature," he said, opening the car door. We watched him pick his way along the ruts of an adjacent field until he reached the cover of a stand of trees.

"He must be freezing out there," Jakub commented, turning up the heat in the Škoda. I noticed bits of ice in the rivulets that flowed down the windshield. Gray returned, shaking his head like a wet dog as he got back in, droplets scattering everywhere. Belatedly, I raised my forearm in an effort to shield myself from the spray.

"Why didn't you wear your hat?"

"My hat!" He reached down and pulled the crumpled

fedora from the floor, brushed it off with his sleeve and plunked it on his head. "Much better," he said. "Now, what were you wanting to know about Father?"

I showed him the map. "Look at where we're going: Tokaj. Father grew up somewhere in the region; you know how he was always going on and on about the wine. Could he have come from Mád?"

"He always seemed a little mad," said Gray.

"Mard," I corrected him automatically. Then I shared my thinking. "We know that Father met your mother when Zoltán was small, right? By the time you were born, he was already in America. I'm guessing that his wife and son stayed in Mád. Where else could she have gone? A woman without a husband in those days would have had no option but to rely on her family. Maybe that's how Dr. Szabó knew where he was. I mean, it makes sense that he'd go back to the place where he grew up, not to some random town in the middle of nowhere. Some of his relatives on his mother's side might still be alive. He could be hiding with someone he knows."

True to form, Gray threw cold water on my hopeful speculations. "It's still going to be like trying to find a needle in a haystack. We don't know the slightest thing about Zoltán's mother, beginning with her maiden name. How are we supposed to find her family?"

"Someone ought to know," I persisted. "Look at the map. Mád's a teensy-weensy village. I'm sure everybody knows everybody else. If we ask around, I bet someone will be able to direct us to their house."

My husband interrupted me. "You don't want to do that, *najdroższa,* believe me."

"I don't?"

"These little villages have complicated pasts. The last

thing people want is to be reminded of the Jews who lived there before the war. Some of them may have benefited, you see, taking over Jewish property when they realized that the owners weren't coming back. They might think we've come to reclaim it." He stopped and a haunted look came to his eyes. When he resumed speaking, his voice was low and uneven, the words tumbling out of his mouth as if by speaking in a rush, he could rid himself of the memories they evoked.

"I heard about it in Warsaw when I went back afterward to look for my family, in '45. The handful of survivors who returned from the camps found Polish families living in their homes. It happened in Kielce and Kraków and in some of the smaller villages too. There were pogroms, just like in the old days. Mobs hunting Jews down in the streets, beatings and lynchings. Hundreds were murdered."

Hundreds. I felt cold, profoundly cold, as if I had been thrust naked into the frigid landscape outside. The death camps, I had thought, were the worst thing human beings could do to one another.

Six months earlier I'd seen *Night and Fog*. Images of the skeletal inmates behind barbed wire, the mounds of corpses being shoveled by bulldozers into mass graves, the small detail of fingernail scratches in the cement ceilings of the crematoria still haunted my dreams: none of this would I allow myself to forget. Now I was learning that the survivors' suffering didn't end with their liberation. Imagine coming back from that hell and being set upon by your former neighbors. I could hardly bear to think about it and, from the look on Gray's face, it was plain that he was equally appalled, but he was fortunate in having an excellent memory for poetry. Once more, he sought refuge in Dante:

"Three dispositions adverse to heaven's will,
"Incontinence, malice, and mad brutishness."

Jakub bowed his head in mute acknowledgment of the poet's acuity. "These sins were common all across Europe after the war," he said. "I knew Jews in France who had to petition through the courts to get their apartments back when they returned from the camps, and it took months. Many people helped Jews, or kept quiet about their neighbors who were hiding them, but there were some who betrayed them, and from what I witnessed, the French authorities were only too willing to hand Jews over to the Gestapo. It will be years before the full story is known, and I have no doubt that it's the same here in Hungary. We're outsiders, don't forget. It'll be hard enough to earn the trust of the villagers as it is. We'd be making a serious mistake if we were to dredge up incidents that most, I'm sure, would prefer to forget."

"I understand." If Jakub was having second thoughts, it was time to concede the battle. "You think we should turn around?"

"Certainly not! There are other ways of tracking your brother down, as I said." A half smile lit his face. "God's on our side, you know."

Gray and I looked at one another, uncertain whether we'd heard him properly. My husband had never once mentioned God in all the time we'd been together. Granted we hadn't been together all that long, but he'd led me to assume that music was his religion. Indeed, to hear him play the violin was to enter some higher realm.

"Today is Friday," he explained. "If there are any Jews left in Mád, they'll be gathering at sundown to pray."

CHAPTER TWELVE

If any Jews remained in Mád, they were keeping a very low profile, and yet the place once teemed with Jewish life. A ruined synagogue perched on a hill near the village center attested to the fact, as did the old cemetery at the far edge of town, its weathered tombstones etched with Hebrew inscriptions. Some of these dated back to the eighteenth century, but none of the graves appeared to have been tended in a long time.

"Nobody came back? Not a single soul?" I said, unnerved by the air of desolation that hung about the site. The graves were crowded together in disorderly rows, a good many of them tilting at precarious angles or toppled over completely.

Jakub's response was matter-of-fact. "They had nothing to come back for, *najdroższa*."

It wasn't only the Jewish sites that were neglected; the entire village was in shambles. Nestled amid terraced hills planted with rows and rows of grapevines, Mád appeared quite picturesque from a distance, its red tile roofs with their dusting of snow reminding me somehow of Italy, or of how I imagined Italy would look in winter. As we drew closer, however, the signs of deterioration were impossible to miss. Driving the town's rutted roads, we passed stately buildings in disrepair, crumbling stucco walls revealing the rotten wooden structure underneath.

Weed-filled courtyards could be glimpsed through rusty gates fronting the few sizable homes in town—vestiges of a more prosperous era, clearly, as was the shuttered bank, a majestic two-story building that took up half a block.

Time had not stood still in this remote part of Hungary, it had moved backward.

I tried to imagine how Mád might have appeared in Father's day. The dilapidated cottages we saw would have been new then, their walls freshly painted. The mule-drawn carts wouldn't have had to contend with automobiles and trucks on the narrow streets, and somehow I thought that the faces of the town's inhabitants would not have been so dour in the early part of the twentieth century, when Franz Joseph reigned and Hungary flourished.

Our roundabout route had added more than an hour onto our journey, and the light was already fading as we pulled into town. Dark clouds smudged the sky, but the sleet was tapering off, which made exploring the place on foot feasible, although hardly pleasant in such raw weather. The cemetery was located at the end of a steep dirt track too treacherous to drive. We'd had to leave the Škoda at the bottom and walk around the perimeter through the slush until we found the opening in the wall, and by the time we got inside the graveyard, our shoes were soaked through.

"Look, I've found them!" Gray hailed us from midway down the hill, where he'd wandered in search of the family plot. Treading carefully to avoid slipping on the icy slope, Jakub and I picked our way down to where he was standing. "Szabó Mozes, Szabó Dávid, Szabó Eszter, Szabó Izsak, Szabó Judit, Szabó Zsófia," he read from the clustered tombstones.

"Zsófia?" I peered at the gravestones. "Which one's hers?"

My brother gave me a quizzical look and pointed to one of the more upright markers. "Why are you asking?"

"Father mentioned a sister named Zsófia. I'm wondering if it could be her. Look, she was born in 1896, three years after him." I noted that she'd died in 1937, at the relatively young age of forty-one. Perhaps this was fortunate, dying before the war and the deportations. Had Father known that his younger sister had died back in Hungary? I'd have been around four at the time, too young to have remembered if he'd grieved a loss, but he was so private where his past was concerned that I rather doubted he'd shared the news with anyone, apart from my mother. And perhaps not even her; Vivien was considerably younger than Father, her experience of the world quite limited. In 1937, she'd have been twenty-one.

Gray hadn't known the names of any of Father's siblings. Like me, he hadn't been curious enough to ask.

"You know, it's hard to believe that Father could have expunged his entire history. I mean, he didn't just cut out on his wife and son—which was bad enough, don't get me wrong—he walked away from all of this," he said, making a sweeping gesture with his arm.

"He closed the door and never looked back," I agreed. "But that's Hollywood, isn't it? People moved there to reinvent themselves, changing their names, their nationality, their life stories, as easily as they changed their hair color. If Father was trying to forget his past, I'd say he picked the perfect place to go and do it."

"Yeah," said Gray, "but don't you think it's strange that he never mentioned any of this, not even privately to us? Two sisters and a brother, parents, and grandparents. Aunts and uncles and cousins too, I'd imagine. His entire childhood spent in this town and we never knew a thing about it."

"We never asked," I pointed out.

My brother considered this. "Maybe he felt guilty about leaving his wife for another woman. Everyone in town must've sided with her."

"That would explain why he didn't go back before the war, when his relatives were still alive."

"There was no going back, after what he did," said Jakub. "Not in a traditional Jewish community like this one."

We both stared at him, appalled. "That's pretty extreme punishment for adultery, isn't it?" Gray commented.

"Your mother wasn't Jewish, was she?" Jakub asked my brother.

"No, she was Roman Catholic." He gave a wry smile. "Lapsed, obviously."

"Lapsed or not, by marrying her, your father violated Jewish law. A Jew who marries outside his faith is as good as dead. His children will not be Jewish, you see, because their mother isn't Jewish. The status passes through the mother."

A worrying thought occurred to me. "Would your parents have objected to our marriage?"

Jakub reached for my hand and gave it a reassuring squeeze. "My family was not observant. We ate pork and celebrated Christmas, like ordinary Poles, and rarely went to synagogue. My parents would have loved you, *najdroższa*."

"I wish I could have met them." I stood on tiptoes and kissed him. As I did, another thought occurred to me. "But how do you know so much about Jewish tradition if you weren't raised in a religious household?"

"Hitler made me Jewish. Since the war, I've taken it upon myself to learn what that means."

"Do you know what this means?" asked Gray. He was crouched by one of the half-toppled tombstones in the

Szabó family plot, examining a small mound of pebbles resting in its lee. It was obvious they'd been placed there deliberately, and scanning the neighboring graves with their light covering of snow, I saw that a fair number of them, including Zsófia's, exhibited similar mounds: small cairns either balanced on top of the headstone if it was standing upright, or piled on the ground in front of the ones that had tilted precariously or fallen over entirely.

Jakub was elated. "It tells me that not all of Mád's Jews are gone," he said. "Someone's been visiting these graves. They've left the stones to honor the memory of the dead and, from the looks of it, they've been coming regularly. I wonder if they've visited anyone else besides your family. I'm just going to have another look around." His voice trailed off as he ambled away to scrutinize the next row of tombstones, pausing to read the inscriptions and standing, lost in thought for a moment or two, in front of each one before moving on.

I was wearing slacks, a wool hat, and gloves. I'd pulled my coat's beaver collar up around my ears in an effort to keep out the wind, but I was still chilled to the bone. Jakub was making very slow progress. I tried stamping my feet to keep my circulation going, but after watching him for several minutes and growing progressively more frozen, I told my brother I'd be waiting for them back in the car. It would soon be dark and we needed to think about where we'd be spending the night. There was nothing remotely resembling a hotel in Mád.

"Are you looking for someone in particular?" An old tramp accosted me at the cemetery entrance. Taken aback by his sudden appearance, it didn't even register, the fact that he'd addressed me in English, and with a British accent, no less.

"Um, well, yes, we are. Or, we were, but we found them. My father's family."

The tramp's features were difficult to discern beneath his grizzled beard. Lacking a hat, he'd wrapped a wool scarf, mummy fashion, around his head. Only his eyes peeked out, dark and penetrating. Yet for all his shabbiness, the tattered overcoat, the threadbare trousers patched in multiple places, giving him a harlequin air, the ancient rucksack slung on his back, he conveyed a gentleness that put me instantly at ease.

"And who am I speaking to?" he said. Then he paused and put a hand to his forehead. "Excuse me, my English has grown rusty from disuse. I ought to have said 'to whom.'"

Only now did the incongruity strike me: coming upon a beggar in this tiny town in a remote part of Hungary who not only spoke English, but who primly corrected his own grammar.

"I'm Cara. Cara Walden. To whom do I have the pleasure of speaking?" I couldn't resist adding. I don't think I imagined the twinkle in his eye.

"György." He held out a gloved hand. "Fleischmann György. Although you'd put it in the reverse order, wouldn't you?" Here he paused. "Walden? Do I know a Walden?"

"Sorry, I should have explained. My father changed his name. It used to be. . ."

"Szabó," he said in quiet amazement. "Szabó Robi!" Tears sprung to my companion's eyes. "Szabó Robi," he repeated, overcome with emotion. "Please forgive me."

I waited for him to collect himself. "You knew my father?" It was almost too much for me to take in, and I fought back the urge to throw my arms around him and hug him.

"I did indeed. We grew up together." He drew an old-fashioned pair of eyeglasses from some hidden pocket and attached them to his ears. I saw his eyes widen in surprise as I came into focus.

"Your father, did you say? That can't be right. Robi's an old man, like me. He couldn't possibly have a daughter your age. His son would be over forty by now."

His son. He must have meant Zoltán. Did he know our brother? It sounded as if he had at one time, but "would be" suggested that he hadn't seen Zoltán for a while. My brain was flooded with questions, beyond the simple curiosity of what had brought this poor man out to the graveyard on such a miserable day. But before I could pose them, we were joined by Gray and Jakub and my questions were lost in the flurry of introducing them to György.

"Children," he said in a shaky voice as he fought once more to regain his composure. "Please, we should not be standing out here in the cold. I invite you to come back with me, to my home. There is room for you to stay the night. Plenty of room. And I will give you something to eat. But first we must stop at the shul. It won't take long, I promise."

We bundled ourselves into the Škoda and drove the short distance from the cemetery to Mád's synagogue. Jakub parked in front, as instructed, and György led the way around to a double door on the east side of the building. Pulling a set of keys from his pocket, he fumbled in the half light until he found the one he wanted, then went to insert it in the lock, but the doors swung open of their own accord the moment he touched them.

"*Ó, ne. Már megint?*" He turned to face us, distraught. "Not again."

"What is it? What's wrong?" we asked in alarm.

"Vandals," he said.

Worriedly, I asked if it was safe to go inside and Jakub

offered to take a look around, just in case they were still on the premises, but György assured us that we had nothing to fear.

"They're always breaking in, the boys from the town. I don't know what they expect to find. There's nothing left to steal."

He entered the building and beckoned for the three of us to come along. We found ourselves in a kind of antechamber that opened onto the main sanctuary. György urged us forward and pulled the door closed behind us. Reaching into a small recess by the doorway, he brought out two dusty black skullcaps, brushed them off as best he could, and gave them to Gray and Jakub. Fastidious to a fault, my brother grimaced as he realized that he was expected to wear the yarmulke. Our companion noticed his hesitation. "You may keep your own hat on, if you prefer," he said as he proceeded to unwind the scarf from around his head, revealing a skullcap of his own, a colorful one festooned with a yellow star of David embroidered on a field of red, white, and green.

"A Bar Mitzvah gift," he said with a slight smile. The three of us must have been staring. "One of my aunts made it for me. She was quite nationalistic, Aunt Edit. It's embroidered in the colors of the Hungarian flag. The old flag, that is."

"You kept it all these years?"

"Nothing could induce me to wear it at the time, but I was too afraid of Aunt Edit to get rid of it. She used to ask me to show it to her when she visited, which wasn't often, fortunately. I found it in the back of my bureau drawer. The Russians must have missed it."

"I gather they didn't miss much," said Gray.

György acknowledged the comment with a nod, but he said nothing. Shrugging off the canvas rucksack, he stuffed his scarf inside the front pouch. From the main compartment, he extracted a flashlight and shone it into the sanctuary. The beam illuminated a scene of utter desecration. Busted wooden pews were strewn about like broken playthings, and these were no flimsy benches. It must have taken several men to pry the massive rows of seats with their carved backs and solid armrests from their fixtures and drag them across the floor. Nor was this the worst of it. Arched windows spaced at intervals along the high-ceilinged room, their glass missing, threw dusky light upon an even greater sacrilege. The temple's ark, which had once held Torahs, was now nothing more than a gaping hole. It looked as if someone had taken a sledgehammer to the marble encasement and laid waste to the entire structure after burning the scrolls within. The surrounding masonry was scorched all the way up to the high arched ceiling. Next to me, Jakub gave a sharp intake of breath.

"Ah, yes," György acknowledged with a sigh. "I'm so accustomed to the shul, I forget how shocking it is to see the sanctuary for the first time." He glanced at his watch. "We can talk more afterward, children, but it's nearly Shabbas and we have an obligation to fulfill."

Moving purposefully, he now made for the dais in the center of the room, the three of us following more cautiously in his wake to avoid stumbling on the debris. Setting the rucksack down on the floor, György handed Gray the flashlight to hold while he reached inside to extract a pair of silver candlesticks from the bag's depths. These he placed close together on a white linen tablecloth he spread out on the top step leading up to the marble platform, smoothing the wrinkles almost lovingly, as if setting a banquet table for royal guests.

"There used to be a stand on the bima," he explained

as he stuck short white candles into the holders, "but I'm afraid this is the best I can do." Next came a loaf of bread wrapped in a clean towel, followed by a bottle of wine. From its shape, I knew it to be a very fine Tokaji, the long, thin neck characteristic of the sweet Aszú that Father and his friends used to enjoy at the lodge. Uncorking the bottle, he poured a generous measure of wine into an ornate metal cup, which he set in front of the candlesticks. The final item in the rucksack was a woven shawl with long tassels knotted at each of the four corners. Reverently, he unfolded the woven cloth and kissed one of the tassels before draping the shawl around his shoulders.

"Do you know the blessing over the candles?" he asked me. I shook my head no. "Never mind." He gave me a box of matches. "You may still light them. I'll say it for you."

"Now?"

He nodded. I struck a match and as the wicks caught flame, György extended his arms out over the candles and drew his hands in toward himself three times, gathering the light as if to insulate us from the encroaching gloom. Covering his eyes, he began to recite the Hebrew prayer.

"Baruch ata Adonay, Eloheinu melech haolam . . ."

A whispering echo came from my husband's direction. Eyes closed, head bowed slightly, he was absorbed in the ancient words in the same way I'd seen him absorbed in the notes when he played the violin, lost in a private space I could not enter.

". . . *asher kidishanu bimitzvotav vitzivanoo, lihadleek ner shel Shabat kodesh.*"

The two of them finished the prayer in unison. György made the blessing over the wine, passing around the cup for the rest of us to drink from after he'd taken a sip. Gray and I exchanged smiles as we savored the honey-like sweetness of the Aszú. Such a distance we'd traveled to end up here, but our travels were insignificant compared to the journey Father had made. He'd spent his boyhood in this simple village, separated by more than an ocean from the luxurious life he lived in Hollywood. He'd bridged two worlds in one lifetime. The two worlds had nothing in common, but drinking his favorite wine in the town where it was produced, enveloped in the welcoming glow of the sabbath candles, I felt connected to Father in a profound way. A vital piece of the puzzle of who he was had been given to me—one that I hadn't even realized was missing until the revelation of Zoltán's existence a mere ten days before. Here were his origins, the place where he'd been formed, and I was eager to learn more about him from his oldest friend.

"Good Shabbos, children." The cup had come back around and György refilled it before reciting the blessing over the bread. He seemed perfectly content, in that moment, to have us there with him. Who knew how long he had been performing this ritual in the desecrated synagogue all by himself? Had he alone survived the cataclysm that had destroyed his entire community? To tell the truth, I was no less curious to learn why György had stayed in Mád as I was to understand our Father's reasons for having left.

The wine was soon gone, the bread consumed, and we stood huddled around the dais in the dark synagogue watching the candles burn. It seemed as good a time as any to broach the subject of Zoltán.

"Outside the cemetery, when we first started talking, you mentioned our brother. He's the reason we're in Mád."

"Zoli? I'm so glad you know him!"

"I'm afraid we don't know him. We don't even know where he is." I proceeded to explain about our fruitless efforts to track Zoltán down in Budapest, starting with our visit to his office and the dismaying evidence that he'd been wounded in the fighting by the university district.

György interrupted me before I could tell him about our latest encounter with Zoltán's wife. "He's here," said the old man.

"Do you mean to tell us he's staying with you? Thank goodness!"

"Not with me, no. He's in the balcony, if I'm not mistaken. I sensed someone's presence the minute we entered the shul." György turned back toward the doorway through which we'd entered the sanctuary and shone the flashlight upward, illuminating the second-floor railing. "*Zoli, ha ott fenn rejtőzöl, gyere le azonnal!*" he called into the emptiness.

We heard a rustling noise from up above, succeeded by the sound of a heavy item being dragged across the floor. Footsteps descending a staircase heralded our brother's approach, but the gait was slow, uneven. A haggard figure emerged from the shadows by the back wall of the sanctuary. His left arm was in a sling and he was using his right arm, with only partial success, to pull a wool blanket around his body. Blinking behind his tortoiseshell glasses, our brother stood unsteadily before us. He swallowed hard, opened his mouth to speak, but the words came out with difficulty.

"I'm sorry for making you come all this way for nothing," he croaked, "but I've decided to stay and fight." The blanket slipped off his shoulders as he reached out with his good arm to brace himself against the edge of the dais.

György made a tsking sound and moved to lend him an arm for support. "Still the romantic, I see. Ah, Zoli. Let's get you home."

CHAPTER THIRTEEN

György lived in one of the decaying mansions along
Mád's main street. We'd passed by it on our way
through town, but the bulk of the property was concealed
behind a fortress-like wall constructed of limestone blocks
and I'd only gotten a peek through the metal gate. During the
war, the house had been occupied by the German army, and
then by the Russians. The downstairs rooms had evidently
been used as barracks and in the cold winter of '44, nearly
everything had been burned: furniture, drapes, doors. The
wainscoting had been ripped from the walls, floor boards
pried up, window molding stripped away, and twelve years
later the rooms remained in this ravaged condition. Only the
kitchen had come through unscathed. In return for keeping
the soldiers fed, the family's cook had been allowed to live
there and had somehow managed to keep the marauders at
bay.

"Magda also preserved my father's wine cellar," said
György, uncorking a bottle of wine.

Gray asked if he might look at the label. "Tokaji Fordítás.
The aszú berries are pressed twice, aren't they?"

"Your father taught you a few things about wine, I see.
I'm not surprised. Robi was quite the connoisseur."

We were all in the kitchen, sitting around a long wooden
table and being served steaming bowls of goulash—
all except for Zoltán, who was taking a bath at Magda's

insistence. One look at his filthy state and the old woman had sent him straight upstairs. The second floor of György's house was in decent shape; the officers had been billeted in the family's bedrooms. Jakub and I were given the master bedroom, and while we settled in, Magda had conjured up dinner.

Our host poured a small amount of wine into my brother's wineglass and watched approvingly as Gray swirled the topaz liquid around in the bowl before passing the glass under his nose and inhaling the bouquet. His first swallow was ecstasy, I could tell. He closed his eyes and his face assumed an angelic expression. György nodded to himself, poured glasses for the rest of us, and refilled Gray's. He raised his glass to eye level and made a toast, looking at each of us in turn before putting the glass to his lips.

"*Egészségetekre*. To your health, children."

"To your health," I repeated.

"Cheers!" said Gray.

"*Na zdrowie!*" said Jakub.

I'm positive that this was the best wine I've ever drunk and am ever likely to drink in my lifetime. Sweet without being cloying, it brought me back to an afternoon Jakub and I had spent walking along the Boulevard de la Croisette in Cannes, oblivious to everything but one another. It was that perfect. I snuck a look at him, sitting on my right, to all appearances focused on the hearty meal in front of him, but sensing my gaze he shifted ever so slightly in his chair, until our legs were touching underneath the table. We'd been attuned like that since the day we met, communicating without needing to use words, and seeing that we were still able to reclaim that connection gave me hope that we would survive this ordeal.

No small part of my well-being at that moment had to do with feeling safe, for the first time since we'd arrived in Hungary. A cozy room, Magda fussing over us like a mother hen, urging us to take second helpings of her delicious goulash, and the promise of a night in the arms of my beloved, far from Nicholas and his minions. Was it only that morning we'd found József's body on the sidewalk in front of our hotel? Had we really skirted roadblocks and advancing Soviet troops to arrive in this backwater, where we'd actually succeeded in finding our brother, along with our father's boyhood friend?

We'd found Zoltán! Quite a feat, considering the hiding place he'd chosen. Mád was a small town, to be sure, but minus the chance encounter with György we'd never have thought to look for him in the deserted synagogue.

"How did you know that Zoltán was in the balcony?" I asked our host. Upon reflection, he'd been awfully nonchalant when he'd called our brother out of hiding.

György made a dismissive motion with his hand. "It was more wishful thinking than anything else," he admitted. "Zoli is like a son to me. When you told me that he was in trouble, I dared to hope. As a boy, and even as a young man, he knew he was always welcome, either here, or at my apartment in Budapest, no matter what the hour or what condition he was in." His face grew soft with remembrance. "Your brother was quite a rabble-rouser in his university days. Communism was illegal under Horthy and they came looking for him at his mother's home. We had to hide him here and smuggle him out through the cellars, or he'd have been arrested. Magda gave him a proper dressing down on that occasion."

The lesson must have sunk in. Half a lifetime later, Zoltán was not about to cross the old servant. She'd ordered him around as if he were still a boy, and he'd obeyed her without a moment's hesitation.

"But why was he hiding in the synagogue?" I said.

György looked so stricken, I regretted having asked the question. "We parted on bad terms, the last time he was here. That was after the liberation of Hungary, years ago. A difficult time, for both of us."

"He might also have been afraid to approach you directly," said Jakub, deftly steering the conversation in a different direction. "In case you were being watched."

"His fears were well-founded." György sighed. "The entire country has become a penitentiary. Someone is always watching."

Gray was incredulous. "Even here? In the middle of nowhere?"

"Especially here. Do you think it was an accident, our meeting outside the graveyard? Your arrival in town was noted, your movements tracked. I received a call telling me that three strangers had been seen entering the Jewish cemetery, and I can assure you that we were observed earlier going into the shul together. People will know that you are here with me now. They'll be wondering who you are and why you've come to Mád, driving a car with foreign plates. Tomorrow morning we're bound to have visitors, inquisitive neighbors and very likely an official visit from the mayor. We'll have to think of a good story, to protect Zoli. It's possible that he made his way back to Mád undetected, and it was dark by the time we got home."

I remembered the way György had hopped out of the Škoda, the minute we'd driven into the courtyard of his stately residence and were out of view from prying eyes on the street. Declining Gray's and Jakub's offers of assistance, he'd had the front door open and was escorting Zoltán inside the house before the rest of us had so much as gotten ourselves out of the car. Now a new stratagem must have occurred to him. He rattled off a set of orders in Hungarian to Magda, who grabbed her coat from its hook in the pantry and hastened off to do his bidding.

"I sent her to borrow some eggs from a woman on the street, a notorious gossip. She'll mention three unexpected guests from America. With luck, that will be interesting enough to distract the curious from our other guest." He glanced over at the doorway through which the cook had just departed, and burst out laughing.

Zoltán stood in the hallway, half wrapped in a paisley silk dressing gown that barely covered his body. "It was hanging in the bathroom," he apologized. "Magda seems to have taken my clothes. It was either this or coming down in a towel." He was, in fact, holding a towel to a wound on the upper portion of his left arm, and blood was beginning to seep through the terrycloth.

György was still chuckling as he accompanied him back upstairs to find something more suitable to wear. "I want to take a look at that arm, too. What happened to you Zoli?" I heard him say. Our brother's response was in Hungarian, and the two continued their conversation in that language. While I couldn't understand the words, from György's gentle, chiding tone and Zoltán's bantering responses, the depth of the affection between them was plainly evident. I'd never have guessed that they hadn't seen one another since the end of the war, or that they'd parted on angry terms. All I noticed was an unnatural brightness in both sets of eyes when the two came back into the kitchen.

Zoltán now sported a black velvet smoking jacket with a green satin lapel over a white dress shirt. A pair of high-waisted trousers completed the ensemble, the sort of elegant evening ensemble favored by Fred Astaire in his heyday. Cleaned up and freshly shaven, his sparse hair combed flat against his head, he might have been mistaken for Astaire were it not for the Harold Lloyd eyeglasses. He had the same reedy build as the actor, another trait he had inherited from Father.

Gray did a double take. "Nice duds!"

"They were made by your father's family business," said our host. "I'm afraid I've run through the more practical items of my former wardrobe."

Zoltán struck a pose. "Uncle György lived the high life in the twenties and thirties. A suite in the Hotel Astoria. A front table when he dined at the Gundel. Summer weekends at Lake Balaton, always with a different woman on his arm." He winked at György. "They were all beautiful, although you had a distinct preference for blondes, isn't that right, *Gyuri bácsi?*"

"Those days are gone for good." Our host gave a rueful smile and patted his pot belly. Indeed, it was hard to reconcile the raggedly dressed man who stood before us with the dapper playboy he'd evidently been in younger days. Still, I reminded myself, he had been Father's friend, and our father was nothing if not debonair. The smoking jacket looked like something he might have worn in the thirties, when he met my mother. I had a scrapbook full of pictures of the two of them, publicity stills culled from gossip magazines and the like. Despite the difference in their ages, they'd made a handsome couple.

"Uncle?" said Gray, picking up on the term of endearment that Zoltán had used. "Are the two of you related?"

György explained that "uncle"— *bácsi*—applied to any older person with whom one is on familiar terms. "I was the sandek at your brother's bris. I held him still on my lap while the mohel circumcised him."

"I hardly think this is the time to bring up my bris," said Zoltán, turning beet red. He was spared further embarrassment by Magda's return. She bustled into the room, took stock of the fancy dress, and nodded her approval.

"*Ez már jobban tetszik.*" She made our brother sit down and set a bowl of goulash in front of him. "*Most ehetsz!*"

"Finally, she says I can eat," he translated.

György poured him some of the wine and refilled our glasses as well. He'd brought out three bottles when we arrived and evidently intended for us to drink them all. Excusing himself from the table, he beckoned to Magda, and the two of them stepped into the hallway, where they conferred in low voices before going their separate ways. We heard the old woman's footsteps as she trudged upstairs, but Gyögy seemed to be busying himself elsewhere in the house and did not return immediately.

It was awkward in the kitchen without him there. I was sure that Gray and Jakub were bursting with questions for Zoltán—I couldn't have been the only one—but where to begin? After his dramatic announcement in the synagogue, I didn't think any of us were ready to challenge him on his reasons for wanting to remain in Hungary, but he had to know his wife had sent us out here. How else would we have found our way to this remote town?

Come to think of it, he'd been remarkably incurious about how we'd managed to locate him on the basis of the scant clues he'd provided. He wasn't the least bit surprised that we'd turned up in the Mád synagogue; it was almost as if he'd been expecting us. How could this be? I worked backward, from the present moment all the way through to the day we arrived at the Duna, searching for something we'd missed, something obvious that might have prompted us to look for him here, but nothing occurred to me. Then I tried viewing those same events from our brother's perspective, and that's when it hit me: Zoltán wasn't aware that Father had been so circumspect about his past. He probably thought Gray and I knew all about the town where he'd grown up, making it a logical place to go if we were trying to pick up our brother's traces. That could explain why he wasn't surprised to see us; for all he knew, Father had been in contact with his old friend.

Zoltán had no idea that we'd met his wife, and that she was the one who sent us out to bring him back. He'd tried to keep us away from his house, and yet we'd ended up going there not once, but twice, putting the people he loved in danger. This paled, however, in comparison to József's murder. József, his companion in hell. I dreaded telling our brother the news of how he'd died. How long could we put off breaking it to him? Watching him and György, the warmth of their reunion, was almost unbearably moving. Each of them had lost so much, but now they'd revived their connection and I just thought they deserved time, the consolation of shared memories and shared tears unencumbered by the ugliness of reality. We could dole out reality in small doses, couldn't we? Save the worst for morning, allow the two of them their sweet reminiscences. It soothed me to think that this one gift was within our power, that we could do something to stave off pain for a little while, provided we kept away from dangerous topics.

Jakub and Gray had their heads together, talking over our route to the border, leaving me to make conversation with our brother. I cast about for an innocuous opening.

"Where did you learn to speak English so well? Did you spend time in London?" Father spoke English fluently, almost like an American, with just a trace of a Hungarian accent, but he'd lived in Hollywood for close to forty years. Jakub had picked up English from the US soldiers he'd befriended in Italy after the war and spoke a delightfully French- and Polish-inflected American English. Zoltán and György both spoke proper British English, but unlike József, neither displayed a Hungarian accent.

"I was sent to the Calvinist college in the neighboring town, Sárospatak," Zoltán answered between spoonfuls of goulash. "An old, old school, it's been around for centuries. Uncle György went there."

Our host was just coming back into the kitchen. "Yes, centuries ago." He laughed. "All the best Jewish families sent their sons to Sárospatak. Your father went there too."

"He did?" said Gray. This was news to me as well, first because Father sounded like an American, but also because, as far as I knew, he hadn't gone to college.

György explained that Sárospatak was a college in the British sense, a prep school for academically talented high school students who would proceed from there to university. "But it's closed now," he added.

"Closed?" Zoltán paused in his eating. "Since when?"

"The government shut it down in '52. You hadn't heard?"

"I was in prison at the time. We didn't get news of the outside world."

"In prison! Zoli, I had no idea. Where?"

"Recsk." Our brother's tone was matter-of-fact, dismissive. I had the impression he regretted having brought the subject up, but it was too late.

"Recsk!" György was devastated. "Why? No, it doesn't matter. They didn't need a reason, did they?"

"It was my own fault, *Gyuri bácsi*. You told me I'd end up paying for my allegiances."

166

"I spoke in anger. I wouldn't have wished that punishment on my worst enemy."

Zoltán smiled. "You called me Stalin's henchman, if I remember correctly."

"So many times, I've regretted those words of mine."

Seeing the dreadful look on his face, I felt his agony as if it were my own. It was because I cared about him already, as well as Zoltán, and it caused me torment to observe the grave wounds they'd inflicted on one another. All I could do was watch as they worked through it.

"I was a fool, blind to the evidence in front of my own eyes. Sanctimonious and ungrateful besides," said our brother vehemently. "I'm ashamed of the way I behaved. You were kind enough to take me in when I returned from France. There I was, lecturing you, singing the praises of the brave Russian soldiers who'd liberated Hungary when they'd taken everything you had."

"No," said György quietly. "The Germans did that. The Russians just took what was left."

Our brother hung his head. "Yes, of course. *Gyuri bácsi*, will you forgive me?"

György went over to where he was sitting and placed a hand on his shoulder. "You had good reason to despise me. I sacrificed nothing in the war. Believe me, if I could go back and relive those years, I would have stayed here with my loved ones."

Beside me, I felt Jakub flinch. My poor darling. The others had no idea of his history, he hid his sorrow so well.

"Then you'd have died along with them," Zoltán said.

"I might have preferred that," murmured György, taking a seat at the table. He poured himself a glass of wine and drank it, looking straight at our brother the entire time. The two of them seemed to be carrying on a silent exchange;

the rest of us might as well not have been in the room. I almost wished we weren't. I felt like an intruder, watching a private drama unfold between these men, and had it been possible, I would have left the room with Jakub and Gray, to give them space. Such pain, on both sides—pain over the traumas each had suffered in the long years they'd been apart—but what really hurt me was seeing how much they still cared for one another. They were like father and son, they were that close, and yet their political differences had prevented them from finding solace together until this very moment. What a waste of years.

Now the stories emerged of how each had spent the war, and of their painful reunion in its aftermath. Survivors had begun trickling back to the village in the spring of '45. Some, like György, had been living in Budapest and were spared the fate of Hungary's rural Jews. Others, notably the Communists, had gone into exile, driven out by Horthy's right-wing policies or motivated (as in Zoltán's case) by their political convictions to fight the fascists in Spain and elsewhere. They came home at last, expecting to be reunited with the families they'd left behind, but very few Jews returned from the death camps. Not Zoltán's mother, Zsuzsanna, who had been sent directly to the gas chambers upon arrival, nor György's elderly parents. They'd been locked in the synagogue with the rest of Mád's Jewish community for three days without food or water, then herded into a cattle car, where they reportedly perished on the way to Auschwitz. One nephew had simply vanished, drafted into a labor detail and sent into Ukraine to clear minefields, while the boy's parents, György's sister and her husband, were thought to have died in Lippstadt, a Buchenwald sub-camp. Uncles, aunts, cousins—the Fleischmann clan had been quite large, as was György's mother's family, the Teitelbaums—none survived the cataclysm. The only relatives he'd succeeded in locating were some cousins who had emigrated to Palestine before the war.

"Stragglers" was the word György used when referring to himself and his fellow returnees. "We stragglers were not fit company in those days. We kept to our homes, those of us who still had homes"—here he nodded solemnly toward Zoltán—"and we nursed our grief in private."

"Why did you stay here, *Gyuri bácsi*? You had a good life in Budapest. You could have gone back to your job in the museum, surrounded yourself with beautiful things."

"I lost my taste for beautiful things," said our host. Looking at György's sorrowful expression, I understood that the clothes he wore, the state of his house, were outward manifestations of the terrible shame he felt inside, the wretchedness of his soul. Such a long time to be repenting for having survived. I couldn't imagine how he'd borne this burden, but in some small way, I believed, his lonely Friday night ritual in the ruined synagogue must have helped.

I'd met a good number of Italians when I was in Sicily who'd survived the war. Not all of them had resisted fascism or fought with the partisans to retake their country from the Germans, but so much work was required to rebuild Italy that people managed to put their grudges aside. The nation had come together and, in the postwar spirit of reconciliation, Italians partook of the illusion they had belonged to some collective effort. Nor had the Allies cared to disabuse them of this illusion. Aid poured in, and Mussolini's exploits were forgotten.

The spirit of reconciliation had quickly soured in Hungary, as we'd learned from József. The Soviets made Hungary pay in myriad ways, as a nation, for Horthy's wartime alliance with Germany, and once they'd installed their puppets, talk of a common effort was little more than hollow propaganda. Even those like Zoltán, who had been battling fascism for a decade, were isolated and excluded, and it was worse for Hungary's Jews.

Our brother had made his way back through war-torn Europe to find another family occupying the home where he and his mother had lived with her parents since Father abandoned them. Both grandparents had passed away while he was still at university in Budapest, his grandmother succumbing to cancer, his grandfather suffering a fatal heart attack later in the same year. To make ends meet, his mother had taken in borders, and the woman who opened the door was one of these. He even remembered her name: Vera. Newly married then, she and her husband had moved into his grandparents' room and in one of the letters he'd received from his mother while he was volunteering in Spain, she'd mentioned that they'd had a baby. He saw a couple of children in the house, and Vera was heavily pregnant, but there was another man living with her. The first husband had fought with the Hungarian Second Army in Voronezh and died on the battlefield, she informed him in hushed tones, all the while looking nervously over her shoulder. Zoltán sensed she would have invited him in, but the new husband barred his way, coming to stand menacingly at the door with his arms crossed.

"He claimed that they owned the house," said Zoltán. Peering around the man, he'd recognized several pieces of furniture in the living room. A mahogany sideboard and the gilded mirror that hung above it. A Chippendale sofa upholstered in a lemon-colored silk. His mother had been wild about the fabric, the pale yellow a pleasing contrast against the blue drapes that hung in the room, but the drapes hung in tatters and he identified the sofa mainly by its shape, it was so heavily soiled.

György made a face. "You could have taken it up with the town authorities, Zoli. I told you that before. Zsuzsanna owned the house outright. After her death, the property belonged to you. Nobody would have disputed your right to reclaim it."

"How could I stay here?"

That single glimpse into the living room of his grandparents' house had been enough to convince him that his future lay elsewhere. He'd cast his lot with the forces of progress ages ago. The Party would take care of him. He'd find work as a translator for one of the publishing houses in Budapest and write poetry on the side while working to rebuild Hungary. His country needed him! Such were his thoughts as he made his way on foot back to the train station.

Trains ran infrequently. Most of Hungary's rolling stock had been confiscated outright by the occupying forces and the main railroad lines had been severely damaged in the fighting that raged throughout the country during the final months of the war. Our brother was stuck in Mád for several days, sleeping rough in the ravaged fields and scrounging for food, until he happened to run into György on the street.

"He didn't recognize me. '*Gyuri bácsi!*' I said. He stared straight in front of him as if I were invisible."

"You looked like an anarchist! I had no idea who you were, underneath that beard."

Zoltán ran a hand over his smoothly shaven cheek. "You're one to talk. What happened to the dapper fellow who used to visit the barber in Andrássy út every single day? I'm surprised Magda lets you go about dressed as you are."

"She knows better than to argue with an old man."

We were, by this time, well into the second bottle of wine and I was growing drowsy. "Excuse me." I stifled a yawn.

"We should get some sleep, children," said György. "You'll be wanting to make an early start tomorrow."

"You seem to be under the impression that I'm leaving," said Zoltán.

"Of course you're leaving, Zoli. The fight is over."

"You're wrong. The struggle will continue even after the Russians come back. It continued under Rákosi. Even in Recsk it continued."

Jakub, Gray, and I looked at one another and I could tell we were all thinking the same thing. The moment had come to raise the question of Dr. Szabò and Zsuzsi. Whether or not Zoltán was aware that his wife had sent us to Mád, he ought to be thinking of their future and not only of his own.

"What about your wife? And your daughter?" said Gray. "Zsuzsi's worried sick about you."

"Zsuzsi," said Zoltán. He sounded confused. "You've spoken to Zsuzsi?"

Wife? Daughter? György mouthed the words, too astonished to speak. If I hadn't left my purse in the bedroom, I'd have fished out the photo to show him. I couldn't believe that Zoltán hadn't mentioned his family during the time they were upstairs. György, who was practically a relative, the sole link to his past? I'd have thought he'd have told him about Anna and Zsuzsi first thing, but even now he seemed reluctant to talk about them. Was he so angry that we'd ignored the clue he'd left and gone to his house that he didn't trust himself to speak?

Jakub took it upon himself to explain. "Dr. Szabó—that's Zoltán's wife—runs an orphanage in one of Budapest's outer districts. She told us we'd find him here."

"Anna sent you, did she?" Our brother folded his arms

across his chest and leaned back in his chair. He wasn't angry, I realized, he was dismayed by the news that his wife had given his hiding place away. Had he sworn her to secrecy?

"Well, not right away," I said, rushing to Dr. Szabó's defense. "It took two visits before she trusted us enough to tell us where you were, and even so, it was like pulling teeth. But I think she wanted us to find you and bring you back so we could get the three of you out of Hungary."

He pondered this for a moment. "Interesting, but highly unlikely," he said. "I didn't tell Anna I was coming here."

"You didn't tell your own wife?" I couldn't believe it.

"I didn't tell a soul."

Gray slammed his palm down on the table. "What the hell! How did you expect us to find you? Telepathy?"

"I was counting on good old American ingenuity." Zoltán looked him right in the eye and smiled condescendingly, as if addressing a bright but overeager pupil, the sort who could stand being taken down a peg or two.

"In other words, you expected us to ferret out your hiding place on our own," said Jakub.

Our brother clapped his hands slowly, in a parody of applause. "Bravo."

"But why?" my husband persisted. "Why lure us all the way to Mád if you never had any intention of leaving the country with us?"

"Oh, come now. You've made it this far. You're clever enough to figure out the rest."

"Stop taunting them, Zoli," said György, his voice quite stern. "You're behaving abominably. This isn't a game, you know. You've put them in danger."

"I'm well aware that this isn't a game." Impatiently, Zoltán got up from the table and went to stand by the stove. "I needed someone I could trust, and that meant someone from outside Hungary. This country is so byzantine, it's hard to tell your friends from your enemies. So often it turns out that they're the same people."

"Are you saying that you don't trust your wife?" asked Jakub.

György put up his hand to get our attention. "This conversation is moving much too quickly for an old man. Would someone please start from the beginning?"

"I'm sorry, *Gyuri bácsi*," said our brother. "Let me explain. These three contacted me last week through an acquaintance. They'd somehow learned who I was—I'm not clear on all the details—and wanted to meet me. Naturally, I was curious. As you know, my father left my mother and me when I was still an infant. We never heard a word from him, once he got to America. Now, here were my brother and sister, offering to come to Budapest, with a revolution raging all around, and bring me out with them if I chose to go. My first impulse was to avail myself of their help and get my family to safety. But Anna made it clear she would never leave her work. During the years I was in prison, it became quite important to her, which has baffled me, I will confess—but of course I didn't know everything."

Gray was still irritated. "Give us a hint: what do you know now that you didn't know then?"

"The day before we were supposed to meet, I got hold of my *kader*, the secret files the ÁVH was keeping on me, going back for years. I learned the names of the people who'd informed on me. Colleagues, neighbors. The editor at the newspaper I worked for, before he shot himself. There were dozens of names. People I'd trusted. People I loved. One of them was Anna."

"Anna! No, that's impossible." I didn't want to believe him, but even as I was voicing the denial, I could see from

Zoltán's face that it was true. He still loved her, and I realized he'd have given anything for his wife to have been innocent of the betrayal.

"Anna," he repeated. His voice was flat. "So, you see, I had nowhere else to turn. I needed your help."

"How exactly did we help you?" said Gray, unwilling to let him off the hook.

"By poking around, asking innocent questions, making people nervous. Americans are remarkably good at that kind of thing."

Jakub whispered something I didn't quite catch. It sounded like a phrase in French.

"What was that?" I whispered back.

"*La chèvre.*" This time he said the words loudly enough for the others to hear. "It means goat. From what I understand, they're sometimes used as bait. To attract wolves."

I was watching Zoltán. A flash of something—triumph?—appeared in his eyes, but before he could open his mouth, Gray had leapt up from the table and was grasping our brother with both hands by his elegant satin lapels.

"You bastard!"

"Technically, I'm afraid that you're the bastard," said Zoltán, calmly removing Gray's hands from his person. "You and your sister both." He took care smoothing down his jacket while my brother fumed. "Our father was still married to my mother when he left for America. To the best of my knowledge, he never asked for a divorce. My mother would have refused to grant it, in any event. He was her first love and I don't believe she ever got over him."

CHAPTER FOURTEEN

November 2-3, 1956

"Zoli, sit down." György pointed to a chair at one end of the long table. "You, sir," he ordered my brother, indicating a chair at the other end. "Over there, please." He waited until both men were settled as far apart from one another as possible before taking a seat himself.

Jakub had risen from the table, prepared to come between them to avert a fight. He remained standing, vigilantly dividing his attention between the two of them as they sat, stone-faced, in their respective chairs. Finally, Gray broke the impasse. From his jacket pocket, he extracted a familiar-looking sheaf of notebook pages and waved them in Zoltán's direction.

"I believe these belong to you," he said. "Some of your secret files, no doubt. So very clever of you, leaving them inside the *Inferno* for us to find."

Zoltán refused to be baited. "I didn't leave them for you. I meant for József to have them."

József. I covered my mouth with my hand, a gesture that did not go unnoticed by our Hungarian brother. He looked all huddled in upon himself, as if someone had punched him in the chest. He'd guessed the truth, but he still needed to hear it from one of us.

"Your friend József—" I started to say, but there was no

gentle way to put it. From across the room, where he was standing, Jakub watched me with concern.

"What happened to him?" said Zoltán.

"He's dead." Gray wasn't concerned with the niceties.

A sharp intake of breath. "How?"

"Someone slit his throat. That's what came of your little game. Setting us up like decoys to flush out your enemies. We flushed them out, all right. I hope you're satisfied."

Zoltán put his head down on the table and wept, great wrenching sobs coming from deep inside. The sight of him torn open like that, so raw, terrified me. It was rage I was seeing, scorching rage turned inward, and it was consuming him the way fire consumes dry timber. This very same rage, turned outward, had impelled him to get hold of a gun and join the insurgents, not caring whether he survived the battle. He'd lost everything: faith in his wife, belief in the power of words to change things, trust in the shared struggle, in comradeship. Everything that sustained him, suddenly gone. The life he was struggling to rebuild after Recsk. All that remained was his tie to József. Now József was gone too.

"*Kedves gyermekem.*" György got up from the table and came to stand behind him, resting a hand on his shoulder. "You're not alone, dear child."

"*Gyuri bácsi!*"

Long past midnight, after we'd finished the third bottle of wine, we sat in the warm kitchen and Zoltán talked about his friend. "His father had a post in Károlyi's cabinet after World War I," he told us. "One of those liberal aristocrats, like Károlyi himself. Kún's people murdered him, and the entire family suffered during the Red Terror. József was taken in by relatives who'd emigrated to Britain. He read law at Cambridge, but there was never any question of his remaining in England, once the war ended." Here our brother paused, to clear his throat. "He would have made a superb statesman if they'd given him a chance."

"He thought quite highly of you," said Jakub.

"I'm afraid his confidence was misplaced." Zoltán's voice cracked and he could say no more. I saw that he would never forgive himself for József's death, and it would be useless to point out that we all shared in the blame. I remembered what József had said in the car on the way to the hospital. A small comfort, perhaps, but I offered it up regardless.

"He told us your poetry saved his life."

"Not my poetry. Dante's. He described the dark wastes so elegiacally in the *Inferno*, one felt he was there with us, in Recsk. A companion whose words made us feel less alone."

Gray was moved by this short speech. "József was right," he said. "You are a poet." I knew he regretted his harshness. They were so alike, he and Zoltán, that he'd known instinctively where to aim his words to cause the maximum damage.

Our brother looked away. "I once thought so," he murmured.

"And you'll think so again in the morning," said György briskly. "He was so morose as an adolescent," he confided in the three of us. "I couldn't fathom it, how the sunny boy who used to make everyone laugh with his silly jokes had turned into a dour creature who went about dressed in black, reciting lines from Edgar Allan Poe's *Fleurs du mal*."

"You're confusing Poe with Baudelaire, *Gyuri bácsi.*"

"Poe, Baudelaire, and that other one you liked. The German philosopher who went mad. What was his name?"

"Nietzsche."

"Nietzsche! What on earth did you see in him? The man was a Nazi."

Zoltán couldn't let this ride. "You've got him wrong. Nietzsche would have hated the Nazis and everything they stood for. He was deliberately misread."

"Misread? Him and his talk of blond supermen, a master race. Don't fool yourself. Hitler found the prophet he was looking for in your friend Nietzsche."

"Ha!" Our brother had a smug look on his face. "You read it, didn't you? I win after all."

"Win what?" said Jakub, who had been following the conversation with amusement.

Zoltán explained, "Years ago, when I was a morose adolescent, I used to slip books into Uncle György's shelves, in an effort to enlighten him."

"Indoctrinate is more like it," said our host. "What use did I have for Marx and Lenin, I ask you? And that lunatic Leon Trotsky. Stalin was right to have him assassinated."

"Wait a minute. Did I just hear you defending Stalin?" He looked to us for support. "You heard it too, didn't you? Since when is assassinating one's rivals justifiable?"

György broke out laughing, and an instant later, our brother was laughing too.

"Damn it, *Gyuri bácsi!*"

It was an old strategy of György's, apparently, to lift Zoltán out of his dark moods by provoking him into an argument, and it had worked on all of us. Spirits lifted, we bid our host goodnight and went upstairs to bed, where my husband promptly fell asleep. I'd gone down the hall to use the bathroom and returned to find him conked out, still fully dressed, and with the lights in the bedroom blazing. He must have stayed awake the entire night in Ian's suite, keeping watch over me as I dozed in his arms. Such devotion, and I hadn't even known. Carefully, to avoid waking him, I got him undressed and under the covers, turned out the lights, and slipped in beside him. Brushing the back of his neck with my lips, I spooned against his body and tried to match my breathing to his.

I myself could not sleep, thinking about Zsuzsi. It felt so wrong, leaving her behind, like giving up my son all over again. Worse. Although I regretted my decision, I still believed my son was being raised in a loving home. He would have opportunities, growing up in America, but what kind of future could our niece look forward to, with her parents estranged and her country returning to dictatorship? All night I fretted, but it was like the popular folk song about the old lady who swallowed the spider to catch the fly, and on and on. We needed György if we were to get Zoltán to come with us, we needed Zoltán and Anna to reconcile in order to get Zsuzsi. But György wasn't about to leave Mád, and Zoltán wouldn't abandon György to come with us. Even if we miraculously persuaded both of them to go, Zoltán wasn't ready to forgive Anna for betraying him, although I thought there had to be more to the story than he was seeing.

Why had Dr. Szabó told us where to look for our brother? She had to know that if we succeeded in tracking him down, he would know she'd sent us. She'd given herself away as surely as if she'd signed a confession, and she was not a stupid woman. It baffled me: watching her at work in the basement clinic, I'd been impressed by her skill and efficiency. She thought things through. So, what had she been thinking when she pointed to Mád on the map? After Zoltán's revelations, I could only come up with one answer. She wanted us to take both him and her daughter with us out of Hungary while she remained behind to tend to the children in the home. Honestly, it was the only explanation that made sense, but could I get our brother to see it? He'd been tight-lipped about Zsuzsi when we brought her up, displaying not a trace of fatherly pride or curiosity as to what we'd thought of his daughter. Well, I intended to let him know how I felt, the first opportunity I got. The child adored him, and I had no doubt that, were she asked to choose between her two parents, knowing she might never see one of them again, she'd go with her father without a second's hesitation.

Gray was sitting at the kitchen table when Jakub and I came downstairs for breakfast the next morning, a cup of tea growing cold in front of him. Magda poured tea for each of us as well, and offered to make eggs, holding one up and miming the action of breaking it into a frying pan. Sausage? She held up a string of them. Onions? Peppers? We smiled and nodded enthusiastically after each ingredient and she set to work at the stove. The woman looked ancient, thinning white hair scraped back into a bun, stooped posture, wrinkled skin, but she possessed remarkable vigor, doing the work of half a dozen people without a hint of complaint. I hadn't seen her sit down for so much as a minute since we'd entered the house.

"Don't go overboard on the ingredients," cautioned my brother. "You'll offend her if you don't eat every last bite." He may have managed to clean his plate, but on closer inspection, he did look rather bilious. Gray had never been one for breakfast, apart from coffee. When he was working on a play, he required copious amounts to get his day started, but seemed to get through the morning otherwise on little more than dry toast and the occasional banana.

"No coffee?" I teased. "How will you survive?"

"I didn't have the nerve to ask. I think she assumes we drink this stuff the way the Brits do because we speak English, but I happen to remember the Hungarian word for coffee, if either of you is feeling daring. It's *kávé*."

Jakub raised a hand in demurral. "Tea's fine. I wouldn't want to put her to any more trouble. It looks to me as if she's eager to get back to whatever she was doing before we interrupted her."

What Magda had been doing was mending and ironing Zoltán's clothes, which she'd apparently washed and left to dry overnight by the stove after we went to bed.

"Any word?" I asked Gray, stirring sugar into my tea.

He passed me the milk. "I haven't seen either one of them this morning."

I tried to decide whether that was a good sign or not. At György's insistence, Zoltán would be accompanying us as far as the Austrian border. "You brought them here, and it's your obligation to lead them safely out of Hungary," the old man had commanded, adding direly, "and if you have any sense, you'll go with them."

"Not without you," our brother had replied.

Magda set two plates of scrambled eggs with sausage, onions, and red pepper on the table and stood watching as the two of us dug in. She hovered long enough to refill our teacups from the pot, then returned to her ironing. The eggs were delicious, and I was hungrier than I'd realized.

"Good morning, children. I trust you slept well." György entered the kitchen, followed by Zoltán, who was carrying a large wooden crate, the kind used for packing fruit. Through the slats, I could see an assortment of odds and ends—keepsakes from his grandparents' house, our host informed us, delivered by Vera years ago, presumably on a day when her husband was not around.

"Thank you, yes," said Gray, answering for the three of us.

Our brother set the crate down on the floor by the far end of the table and began sorting through the contents, inspecting each item before placing it into one of two piles: keep and discard. He unwrapped a bone china figurine of a shepherdess, her costume hand-painted in painstaking detail. You could see the sprigs of flowers decorating the lace bodice of her dress and the frill of her petticoat peeking out beneath. In one delicate hand, she held a crook, which showed signs of repair work at the bend.

"My mother's favorite possession," said Zoltán, noting my interest. "She'd had it since she was a little girl. I'm the one who broke it, and believe me, I suffered for that careless act of mine."

"She must have been very angry." His willingness to impart such an intimate memory heartened me. Something had caused him to lower his defenses. Perhaps György had persuaded him to join us after all and he was trying to make himself agreeable, anticipating the long journey ahead.

"I might have preferred it, if she'd been angry," he said. "No, it was the first time I made her cry and I felt quite dreadful about it afterward." He gave a small shake of his head as the memory came flooding back. "I often tested her, but she had a blind spot where I was concerned. She refused to believe a single bad thing about me, not even when it was true."

György looked up from the task he'd begun, unknotting a length of butcher's twine he evidently intended to reuse for some purpose. At home, we'd have thrown the tangled mess away, but Europeans were not so profligate. Here in Hungary, scrimping was probably necessary. There were shortages of nearly everything under the Communists, but even the well-to-do British and Italians I knew tended to save things like string, rubber bands, and paper bags.

"She was very proud of you, Zoli."

"I know that." Zoltán's voice was so soft, he was practically speaking to himself. The figurine went into the "keep" pile on the right-hand side of the table. I watched him unpack a set of marbles in a leather bag with a drawstring, some toy soldiers, a model airplane, these boyhood mementos all consigned to the pile on the left, with the exception of a small pen knife, which he opened, testing the blade against his thumb before placing it in the pocket of his trousers. Next came a small collection of books, identically bound in Morocco leather, whose titles I could not read because they were all in Hungarian. He paged idly through the topmost volume, then pushed it across the table toward us.

"Here's something," he said. "Our father might like to have it as a memento." There it was. He'd made up his mind to stay. I fought my impulse to bring up Zsuzsi, clenching my hands so tightly together in my lap that I could feel my wedding ring cutting into the skin. The memory of the child swinging her way down the street on her crutches, her face brightening as she recognized me, came into my mind. I struggled to return to the conversation in György's kitchen.

Gray was reading aloud the author's name of the book, which was stamped on the spine in gold letters. "Szabó, Z." He looked up in surprise. "Yours?"

"I'm afraid not. Look at the year of publication."

My brother opened the book to the title page. "1915. It's inscribed 'Zsuzsanna.' Wait, that was your mother's name, wasn't it?"

"Yes. My mother wrote poetry. Our father had a small edition of her poems printed and bound. He presented them to her on the day I was born."

Jakub laughed. "She gave birth twice, you might say."

"She saw it that way," said Zoltán. An indulgent tone had crept into his voice. "It was like having a rival, vying with her poetry for attention. When she was in the throes of inspiration, she'd be distracted for days, caught up in some line or other. My grandmother would complain that she was neglectful of her appearance. She couldn't be bothered to fix her hair and would wander about the house wearing an old jacket over a pair of man's trousers our father had left behind, repeating phrases to herself. My friends all thought she was rather . . ." He paused, hunting for the right word.

"Unconventional?" suggested Gray.

"For a mother, yes. Unconventional is a good word." He smiled as a private memory took hold of him. "I don't know where she got her ideas."

I envisioned Zoltán's mother as a tomboy, much like the character of Jo in *Little Women.* I'd seen the movie with June Allyson in the role of Jo more times than I could remember. Everyone raved about Elizabeth Taylor as Amy—Villi and Ilona would have loved her, I'm sure—but Amy bored me silly. Beth too, although I had friends who wept every time Margaret O'Brien appeared in a scene, anticipating her character's untimely demise.

No, I admired Jo's independence, and the message was not lost on me, that she found love with the forty-year-old German professor at the end of the picture. Maybe that's why I fell for an actor twice my age when I was sixteen. Serious people sought mature romantic partners. On some level, I must have been following in Jo's footsteps.

Zsuzsanna was a serious person, just like Jo. A figure in the background until now, Zoltán had succeeded in bringing his mother to life with just a few details and I couldn't help wanting to know more about her. Was it her mind that attracted Father? That would have made her unique among his wives. When it came to women, I'm afraid he was rather unenlightened, but here was evidence that he had supported one woman, at least initially, in her desire to create something for herself.

Zsuzsanna had probably been too much for him, in the end. He hadn't liked it when Vivien embarked on a course of self-improvement that led her to challenge his decisions over what was best for her career. And for all his encouragement of my efforts to launch myself as an actress, I knew he was relieved to have married me off. Not that he didn't respect Jakub. He admired his new son-in-law, and was genuinely happy with the life we proposed to lead, traveling and performing together throughout Europe, but the key thing in Father's mind was that I would be properly looked after when he was no longer around.

Magda cleared away the empty cups and plates and Zoltán returned to sorting through the crate. He removed a set of white linen napkins, each embroidered with the letter S, the monogram intricately worked inside a floral frame. The motif was repeated on a tablecloth, which he extracted with great care. I saw there was something wrapped inside, a light but fragile object, judging from the way he handled it. Pulling away the fabric, he revealed a violin and bow.

Jakub's eyes lit up. "Do you play?"

"I'm afraid not. It belonged to my grandfather."

"May I?" Barely waiting to receive permission, my husband reached for the instrument and began to appraise it. The next thing we knew, he was tuning the strings and sliding the bow across them, coaxing sound from the old violin. A familiar melody filled the room, bright and ominous at the same time, with its military rhythm. "The

Rákóczi March." I felt as if he were honoring József's wish to hear it again, and it was almost as if he were in the room with us, that fine, fine man. Jakub played for several minutes, and when he finished nobody spoke. In the corner by the stove, Magda was pressing Zoltán's shirt, the thumping of her heavy iron as she passed it across the fabric the only sound in the room.

György broke the silence. "You play so beautifully. You must have trained somewhere professionally."

"I studied in Paris." Jakub's formal training was cut short by the war and he was not inclined to talk about his career as a classical musician. For all the joy he took in performing with his trio, there were moments when I sensed his regret for what might have been.

Zoltán looked up from his unpacking. "At the Conservatoire?"

My husband nodded. "You know it?"

"I was living a stone's throw from the rue de Madrid at the end of the war."

"Really?" said Gray. "We heard you were in Marseille."

"Where did you hear that?" Our brother's tone was sharp with suspicion. The easy rapport we'd established that morning had evaporated in the space of a few seconds, but it was important for Zoltán to know about Nicholas.

"We met a man who knew you in France. He was running some kind of relief agency during the war," I said. "Jakub could tell you more about it." I felt a little guilty about delegating to Jakub the task of explaining how we'd come to learn of Zoltán's underground activities in France, but he knew that clandestine world intimately and was the only one of the three of us who understood fully the threat that Nicholas represented.

"Nicholas Miner!" Zoltán was clearly dismayed by the

news. "You met him here, you say? What's he doing in Hungary?"

My husband put down the violin and answered him bluntly. "Spying on the Americans for the Soviet Union, as near as I can tell."

"Shrewd of you to pick it up from a single encounter." Our brother eyed Jakub with new appreciation, the familiar moment of reckoning I'd come to expect, when people realized that my husband had a past in the shadow world of wartime resistance.

"I've encountered his sort before."

"Have you now? His ostensible employers in France hadn't a clue as to who he was actually working for."

"Who were his ostensible employers?" György wanted to know, alarmed to learn of the precarious existence that Zoltán had led during the war.

"He was hired by an American missionary organization to head up their refugee office in Paris. The women who worked with him were sturdy minister's wives who spent their time handing out clothing and canned goods. They couldn't have cared less who was in charge; they just went from one crisis to the next. From time to time, the church leadership sent someone over to check up on things."

Gray interrupted him. "Were they aware of the smuggling operation?"

"I presume so, in a vague way—they were funding it, after all—but they left Nicholas to his own devices, which suited his purposes. Then, when the Germans occupied the city, they moved the enterprise, lock, stock, and barrel, to the southern zone."

"How did you get into it?"

"I first met Nicholas in Spain. I was a volunteer with a Hungarian unit of the International Brigades. We were all Communists and he was our liaison, the officer who conveyed Moscow's orders. After the Republic fell and we were forced to leave Spain, I ran into him in Marseille. A number of us from the battalion had ended up living there illegally: the French wanted to deport us, but we couldn't go back to Hungary. Horthy would have put us in jail. Nicholas offered us work, and false papers. A chance to reenlist in the cause and do some good."

"Comrade to comrade?" said my brother with smirk.

Zoltán acknowledged the smirk with a slight inclination of his head. "Comrade to comrade, yes. Nicholas had a list of foreign nationals and it was our job to get them out of France through Spain and into Portugal, using routes known to the *brigadistas* among us. By the end of '42, every one of our escape routes had been closed down. Every last one. We'd lost operatives, good men and women. Maybe we'd been infiltrated, or maybe the French police were getting better at tracking us down."

"They had the Gestapo helping them by that time, don't forget," said Jakub.

"How could I forget? The Gestapo gave them the incentive to do their job properly."

"Yes, that was my experience as well," said my husband drily. "Miner seemed surprised to learn that you'd survived the war and made it back to Hungary. Was your unit compromised in some way?"

Zoltán shook his head sadly. "It was, but I was no longer part of it when that happened. It reached the point where I decided the risk wasn't worth it any longer. I wanted to serve the cause, but I wasn't suicidal. The chances of surviving a mission were growing slimmer by the day. Nicholas knew it; how could he not? Of the fourteen original couriers, only three of us remained. But he showed little concern for our safety and kept sending us out. 'Just this one last mission, and then we'll dissolve the unit,' he'd promise. One mission, and then another, and then another one after that. All he cared about was pleasing his Soviet masters. In the overall scheme of things, our lives mattered not a whit. Moscow would add more names to the list, but we could only transport so many without drawing attention to ourselves. One route would be sabotaged and we'd need to find another, or the Gestapo would raid a safe house and arrest everyone, so we'd have to start over, build a new network, find people we could trust. Some of us realized that we couldn't trust Nicholas."

I recalled Nicholas's words in the corridor of the embassy. "You disappeared, didn't you?"

"How did you guess?"

"I didn't have to guess. He told me: 'Icarus knows how to disappear.'"

Zoltán absorbed this piece of information. "So he knows," he said, frowning.

"What does he know?"

"He knows I deceived him." Absentmindedly, our brother picked up one of the lead soldiers from the discard pile.

"He sounds quite ruthless," commented György. "You did well to be rid of him, Zoli."

Jakub nodded in agreement. "I'd like to know how you managed it, though."

"It took some conniving, I'll admit, and a good deal of luck. I started stockpiling a few necessities in a room I'd rented under a different name. I had a set of false documents made for me in yet another name. One day I failed to show up at a designated meeting place. I went to ground instead, avoided my old apartment, just left my things there hoping he would assume I'd been killed or arrested. I laid low for a week, then I made my way to Paris. A big city offers many places to hide, if you're not particular about your bedfellows."

Gray raised an eyebrow. "Bedfellows?"

"You may have noticed that a certain type of establishment is found in the vicinity of train stations." Zoltán paused, and glanced in my direction, measuring his words. "The neighborhood behind the Gare Saint-Lazare was ideal. Any Germans I encountered were there for, er, recreational purposes, and unlikely to look too closely at my papers."

"You hid out in a brothel," I said, unruffled. If there was one thing I couldn't tolerate, it was being treated as a fragile young lady. I knew all about prostitutes from Italy, and plenty more besides. I knew about the poverty that drove girls and women into selling their bodies for money. I'd seen it up close in Sicily, people still living in the ruins of towns and cities damaged during the war, hungry children begging in the streets, their arms and legs covered in scabs. What wouldn't a mother do to help them survive?

György was troubled by our brother's story. "It would appear that you trusted your own side no more than you trusted the Germans."

"With good reason, *Gyuri bácsi*." Zoltán set the lead soldier to stand on the table in front of him. A flick of his finger sent it toppling over, face down. His meaning was plain: they'd have killed him just like that.

"You're still dangerous to Miner," warned Jakub. "You may be the only person alive who can link him to the Soviets. You see that, don't you? Miner knows you survived, thanks to us. If you stay in Hungary, sooner or later he'll find you."

"Not if I find him first," said Zoltán.

"Zoli!"

"I'm sorry, but it's a lesson one learns early on, when

191

fighting a war: don't wait for the enemy to attack. Surprise him when he thinks he has the advantage. Your best chance is to strike fast, when his guard is down."

Our host absorbed this. "Where did you say you ran into this awful man?" he asked us.

"He works in the American embassy, processing visas to the United States," said Gray. "We were trying to figure out how to get Zoltán his visa, in case he turned up after we left Hungary."

"We didn't want to leave the country without him," I hastened to add, "but we were warned not to stay."

"You'd have been wise to heed the warning," said György. "The noose is drawing tighter. This morning there were tanks on the road to Miskolc. They were talking about it in town when I went out to get bread. Go with them, Zoli. Please, for my sake."

To my surprise, our brother put up no fight. All he asked was to visit the synagogue one last time, to say a prayer for his loved ones. Magda gave him his clothes and he went upstairs to change out of György's smoking jacket. Our host urged the three of us to pack our suitcases and put them in the trunk of the car. We'd only stop back at the house long enough to drop him off before proceeding to the border. Keeping to the smaller roads and avoiding the cities, we'd be lucky to make it out of Hungary by nightfall, and there remained the perpetual problem of finding gas, although we were fortunate in that Mád's one gas station was open for business that morning. We'd stop there to fill up on the way to the synagogue.

Jakub drove, with György directing. Sitting between my two brothers in the back seat of the Škoda, I tried not to think about Zsuzsi. Of course there was no question of going back for her. I knew that, and yet I was determined to press Zoltán about his daughter, once we were underway on our journey to the border. She was his only child and he should want the best for her. That meant getting her to the West.

CHAPTER FIFTEEN

By night, the ruined synagogue had been tragic enough. By day it was heartbreaking. You could see how exquisite the sanctuary had been, a baroque jewel box. The vaulted ceiling was once brightly painted, repeating patterns picked out in crimson, turquoise, ochre, and rose. Stars and flowers, clusters of leaves, fleur-de-lis designs painstakingly carved into the cornices. Above the ark, a sculpted tablet bearing the Ten Commandments was flanked on either side by golden lions, and above these flew fantastic winged creatures, also golden.

"Those are the seraphim that grace the throne of God," said György. "You can't see it now, the soot has blackened everything, but they're holding a crown and written upon it is the word *Adonai*, which is God's name. 'Holy, holy, holy,' they proclaim."

I think it was his casual mention of the scouring fire that was intended to destroy every last trace of Mád's Jewish community, when the members of that community had already been sent to their deaths—suddenly, I was having trouble breathing. All of these people were murdered, my ancestors among them. Standing in this sacred place where they'd come together to pray, I was overwhelmed by sadness. Soot and ash might obscure the building's splendor, but the embers of the congregation's beliefs glowed through. There'd been joy in the fanciful adornments; pleasure and wonder and delight in the world outside the temple walls had carried into the celebrations that took place inside the sanctuary. Our father had married Zoltán's mother in this room, I realized. His parents, and their parents before them, would have gathered to mark both happy and solemn occasions. Looking around at the charred remains of more than a century of religious observance, I glimpsed vestiges of my own history, and Gray's. Some part of us had died along with the Jews of Mád.

Jakub had brought the violin into the sanctuary and asked if he might play a short piece of music, something to console us. The piece he had in mind was the Kol Nidre.

"The Max Bruch arrangement?" said György. "Please do. It has been too long since that prayer was heard within these walls."

The Kol Nidre was a prayer of mourning recited on the eve of Yom Kippur, the Day of Atonement, when Jews reflect on their conduct over the previous year and ask God to forgive their sins. Set to music at the end of the nineteenth century by a German composer, György told us that its poignancy was said to make the heart weep. Persecution, exile, and suffering were all woven into the ancient elegy, which penetrated where words could not go, reminding me of every loss I'd ever experienced. And yet the resolution of the piece was like a new dawn. How could one find hope after so much sorrow?

When the last note had faded away, Jakub bowed his head over the instrument. He had given us the precious gift of peace, momentary but healing all the same.

"Amen," said György, the tears still wet on his cheeks.

"Amen," we echoed.

195

A black sedan was parked across the street from György's house. Inside, we could see the driver, smoking a cigarette.

"Are you expecting someone?" asked Zoltán. "The mayor?"

"Nobody in town drives a car like that."

Gray wanted to keep going. "We could try sneaking in some other way, surprise whoever's inside."

"There's no time for sneaking around," said György. "Magda's alone in the house." He was quite anxious about her and refused to consider any tactics that might cost us time, leaving us no option but to drive in through the gate and walk into an obvious trap.

Zoltán insisted on going first. "The rest of you stay here."

"I'll come with you," said Jakub, carefully avoiding looking at me.

"Don't be an ass," snapped Zoltán. If there were people waiting inside György's house who intended to harm us, we shouldn't make it easy for them by sending in the best trained members of our group at once. Gray was to turn the Škoda around in the courtyard so that we were facing out, for a quick getaway. We were to keep the motor running. He would try and send Magda out, in which case we shouldn't wait for him. We should drive away.

"Zoli, be careful—"

Our brother already had his door open. "*Gyuri bácsi.*" A tender look passed between them. Then Zoltán set off across the courtyard, shoulders squared. We watched him approach the house. He paused on the doorstep before entering, looked our way as if reminding us one last time of his instructions, then disappeared inside. I was gripping Jakub's hand, my desire to prevent him from rushing in overriding every other instinct, but it didn't matter because Zoltán came out again almost immediately.

"I'm sorry, but he wants all of us."

"He?" said Gray. "It's just one man we're dealing with in there?"

Zoltán grimaced. "One man with a gun. And a hostage."

"We still outnumber him," said my husband, his eagerness to sacrifice himself unnerving. "We should watch for an opportunity."

"I agree. Leave the keys in the ignition," he told my brother. "We may need to leave fast."

Jakub put a protective arm around me as we entered the house, but as we approached the kitchen, he was forced to let go. A voice barked out a series of commands, first in Hungarian, then in English.

"*Lassan. Egyszerre csak egy!* Slowly. One at a time!"

Even had we not seen the black sedan out front, if we'd come in without being warned that all was not right, I would have known instantly that something was off because the first thing I saw was Magda sitting idle at the kitchen table. The gunman had positioned her close to the door, so that she, not he, would be the target, had we attempted an ambush. Stoically she sat, staring down her assailant, who stood with his back against the wall, pointing his gun at her chest.

"Sit down, all of you," said Frankie. He motioned to the empty chairs. "Hands on the table where I can see them." We took our seats and did as we were told. "I'm happy to see that you found your brother," he added maliciously, pulling out a chair for himself.

"Why don't you tell us what you want?" said Zoltán. But Frankie refused to be drawn out, perhaps fearing he might lose his focus and allow the men an opening. Really, I was surprised that he'd come alone, with just a driver for backup. I'd assumed the other man was watching for us and would have come in after us with his own weapon, but it appeared he was watching for reinforcements. Frankie must have been dispatched to hold us until they arrived. Every so often, he glanced at the kitchen clock, which sat on the ledge over the stove. Fifteen minutes passed and, during that time, every effort on our part to find out what we had in store for us met with silence.

Finally, after half an hour, Frankie spoke. "I'd like the girl to get me one of my cigarettes. There's a pack of them in the right pocket of my coat. The rest of you are to sit still. The girl may get up now. That's right, do it slowly."

I did as he asked, conscious all the while that he was now pointing his pistol at Jakub, who was seated immediately to his right. *Just breathe*, I told myself. *Stand tall. No stopping you now.* I used to whisper these words as a little pep talk before stepping onstage, and it calmed me to think that I was simply acting a part.

"Good. Now come closer—that's close enough," he said when I was within arm's reach of him. "Get my cigarettes out of my pocket."

I felt around until my hand closed around the packet. Lifting it out, I recognized the green label with its black-and-white emblem, a drawing of the hero of the 1848 revolution, Sándor Kossuth. József's brand, they were unfiltered and quite strong.

"Are you sure you wouldn't like one of my Marlboros?" quipped Gray. I'm sure he was trying to lighten the mood, for my sake, but the effort backfired.

"Shut up, you faggot," said Frankie, turning in his seat so the gun was now pointed at Gray. Eyes on my brother, he now directed me to remove a cigarette from the pack and place it between his lips. As I did so, he grasped my wrist with his free hand and stroked it, causing me to drop the cigarette on the floor.

Jakub shifted in his chair. I kept my eyes on Frankie, whose lips parted in a cruel smile as he observed the effect his attentions were having on my husband.

"Sexy little wife you have, my friend. I enjoyed watching her move on the dance floor, but you need to be rough with a woman." Tightening his grip, he began to twist my wrist, pulling me toward him at the same time. I winced at the pain, but refused to give him the satisfaction of crying out. Frankie wasn't interested in my reaction anyway; he was looking to get a rise out of Jakub.

"Pick up the cigarette and let's try again," he said, releasing my wrist and pushing me away. I stumbled, but steadied myself on the edge of the table. Frankie gave a grunt of satisfaction. Jakub had risen from his chair and was coming to my aid, just as my tormenter wanted. Pointing the pistol at me now, he cocked it and dared my husband to take another step. Jakub had no choice but to sit back down and watch, seething in frustration, as I stooped to retrieve the cigarette and put it in Frankie's mouth.

While this drama was taking place, I saw Magda sliding her fingers inch by inch along the table until they reached the piece of twine that György had been working on earlier. Before anyone else noticed, she'd gathered the length of it into her hand and moved her hand to her lap. I wasn't sure what she intended to do with it, but I wanted to be ready, should she need assistance.

Frankie now wanted a light. He had me go into his pocket again, to fish out his lighter. I'd seen the model before, a metal briquet lighter, quite utilitarian and probably indestructible. I flicked open the lid and was just about to snap the wheel to ignite the flint, my thumb poised to strike, when I observed Magda, out of the corner of my eye, give a nearly imperceptible shake of her head. She didn't want me to light Frankie's cigarette? But he'd ordered me to do it. Was she trying to get me shot? I moved my thumb to the wheel. Again the cautionary shake. Her meaning was clear: *don't do it.*

I pretended to slide my thumb downward once, twice, three times. "I can't make it work," I whined, like a helpless female. "Is it out of fluid?" My hands were actually trembling, I was so nervous, which probably made the act more convincing, but inside I was cool, focused. Waiting for my opportunity.

"*A lány hülye. Hadd csináljam én,*" Magda said. I learned from Zoltán later on that she'd called me stupid. I didn't mind, given what she did next.

Frankie laughed nastily. "*Rendben.*"

Cautiously, the old servant got up from her chair and made her way around the table. She moved like a feeble creature, which was not at all the way she'd appeared to us, but I realized she was trying to convey that she was not a threat as she crept up to our captor and reached to take the lighter from my hand.

In a flash it was over. Magda wrapped the twine around Frankie's neck and pulled it tight, her strong arms gripping it until welts formed around her bulging knuckles. Frankie struggled, jerking convulsively as he fought for breath, but the old woman was in control. I kept my eyes on her knuckles as opposed to watching Frankie's face, but I couldn't close my ears to the horrible gurgling sounds he was making as she choked him to death. His body pitched forward as she released him, the gun falling from his hand and clattering to the floor. Someone told me to pick it up and I obeyed automatically, putting the weapon into Magda's outstretched hand. Then Jakub had an arm around me and Zoltán was praising me for my self-possession.

"I couldn't have done what you did," he said, "enduring the attentions of that thug. You played him perfectly."

"My sister is a superb actress," bragged Gray.

György smiled at me. "You were quite brave."

Was I? I didn't feel particularly brave, and as for my skill as an actress, it was surprising how little effort was required to get a man killed. I'd worked harder at memorizing Cole Porter lyrics before a gig with the trio. But the worst of it was that I didn't care. Frankie lay slumped on the kitchen table not two feet from Jakub and me, his face a horrible violet color, eyes bulging out of their sockets. The way he'd tormented us, the sadistic pleasure he took in flaunting his power: there was nothing human in him, no decency or compassion. He'd have killed us without a moment's hesitation, just for fun, and I had no regrets about the part I'd played in his death. But it was a small part, going along with the game of the cigarettes and the lighter, distracting him long enough for Magda to make her move. She was the star performer, Magda, who was looking at me with maternal pride. I'd entered her realm, the realm of women who took matters into their own hands and did what needed to be done. This I would cherish, Magda's respect, because it gave me confidence in my own strength.

The men were busy making plans. "Nicholas is behind this, I'm sure of it," said Zoltán.

"He could be arriving any minute, too," added Gray.

"How do we get out of here without alerting the driver out front?" My husband turned to György. "You mentioned an escape route, didn't you? A tunnel of some sort?"

"The cellars! Of course."

"Eugène won't be happy about the Škoda," Gray fretted.

"I know," said Jakub, "but it can't be helped."

I imagined that we could find another car for the Romanian

playwright, once we were back in Paris. Getting out of the kitchen and away from the sight of Frankie's face was my top priority, but how would we get to the border without a car?

In fact, Zoltán was debating this very question with György. They switched to Hungarian, bringing Magda into the conversation, but something in her posture suggested impatience, as if she already knew what the two of them were going to decide and was eager to be about her business.

"*Igen*," I heard the old woman say, satisfied and with finality, when the men at long last arrived at the proper conclusion. Nodding to me, her newfound ally, she went into the front hallway to use the telephone.

"This way, children." György led us into the pantry, a tight little room with floor-to-ceiling shelves along three walls. Jars of preserved fruits and vegetables crammed the shelves, enough to last out another siege, if need be. There was a trapdoor in the floor. Zoltán stooped to pull it open, revealing a steep wooden staircase.

"Is there a flashlight, *Gyuri bácsi?*"

"Magda's bringing one. Ah, here she is." He handed me the flashlight and told me to go down first. "You'll find candles on the ledge on the right-hand side down by the bottom, along with some empty wine bottles, and there should be some matches with them." I was to light the candles, stick them in the neck of the empty wine bottles, and call up to them when I'd gotten the cellar illuminated. Then the others would carry down Frankie's body, to confuse Nicholas into thinking that we'd all gone off with him somewhere, buying us time.

"It won't be the first corpse down there," said Zoltán. Sensing Magda's eyes on me, I tried not to flinch. I would do what needed to be done like the strong woman I was.

Descending the staircase, I located the candles and the wine bottles, although I had to dig out my own lighter from my purse because there were no matches anywhere I could see.

"Ready!"

Gray and Jakub came down first, each shouldering one of Frankie's legs, followed by Magda and Zoltán, who were hefting him under the arms. Last came György with a lantern, lighting their way from behind. Carrying such a big man put considerable strain on all four of Frankie's bearers. They had to rest when they reached the bottom, propping his body against the staircase while they caught their breath. I turned to study the wall behind me to avoid looking at him. A gauzy black growth covered the earthen sides of the cellar, like cobwebs in a mummy's tomb. I half expected to see Lon Chaney come limping out of the darkness, moaning and trailing his rags.

"It's called 'noble rot,'" said Zoltán, noticing my attention. "It's a fungus."

Gray was skeptical. "A fungus? What's so noble about that?"

"It's what gives the Aszú its sweetness. Botrytis cinerea. Don't make that face—it's a benevolent fungus—Uncle György can explain how it works. He knows viticulture inside out, even if he chose not to enter the family business."

"And just as well," said György, who had paused midway down the stairs to close the trapdoor and was now descending the rest of the way. "The wines they've produced since the industry was nationalized hardly merit the label. Those were prewar bottles we were drinking. I'll be sorry to leave them behind."

I glanced over at Jakub, to confirm that I hadn't mistaken what György had said. Yes, my husband was smiling. I couldn't help but smile in return. György was coming with us! Of course, we were still in serious danger, but I somehow managed to push those fears aside. While the others took up Frankie's body once again and shambled off to deposit it in some out-of-the-way part of the cellar, I kept my mind occupied by imagining Father's reaction, when we brought both his long-lost son and his oldest friend to meet him in California. Would Magda be coming too? I didn't see how we could leave her behind to face the consequences of Frankie's murder and our escape. Although it was difficult to imagine the old housekeeper thriving outside of Hungary, I was sure there'd be a place for her at the lodge. She deserved to retire in a sunny place—and, of course, György would be close by.

But Magda had no intention of leaving Mád. "She's very well-liked in the town. People will protect her," Zoltán assured us. "She's survived two wars and countless changes of regime, don't forget."

György had gone on ahead, to procure us a vehicle for the journey to the border. The rest of us were making our way through a tunnel that led out to the street—the same tunnel our brother had used to escape arrest, two decades earlier. Eyes fixed on the wavering beam of Magda's flashlight, each holding a candle in a wine bottle to light our way, all we could do was to trust the plan they'd put together to get us safely to the border.

At last we reached the exit. Magda pulled a keyring from her coat pocket and opened an iron grating. We emerged onto a drainage ditch that stretched between two rows of houses in the lower part of town.

"*Siessetek!*" Magda pointed to a narrow board spanning the ditch, a makeshift bridge we needed to cross to reach the street side of the ditch. "*Óvatosan!*" She urged us forward, locking the grating behind.

A horn sounded as we came out onto the street. There, behind the wheel of a livestock truck, sat György, looking the part of a local farmer in his patched wool coat, bits of straw clinging to his clothing. The truck was used for transporting pigs to market and had high wooden sides and the bed was filled with straw.

"Don't worry, it's clean," he said, opening the slatted tailgate for us. "You'll find some blankets back there as well. Bundle up and keep your heads down."

Magda got in the cab with György while the rest of us clambered into the back. Avoiding the main roads would make for a cold and bumpy ride, but if all went well, we would still reach the border before nightfall. Jakub and I lay side by side in the middle of the truck bed, snuggled under a blanket, while Gray and Zoltán, each wrapped in his own blanket, took turns peering out through the wooden slats and describing what they saw.

"Attila the Hun is supposed to be buried near here," said our brother. We were driving across the Great Hungarian Plain, where the barbarian invader had set up headquarters, launching forays into Greece and the Balkans. After his defeat at Châlons, he returned here to lick his wounds and plan his next attack on the Eastern Roman Empire, but he died under mysterious circumstances on his wedding night. Legend had it that his grieving generals diverted the course of a river in order to bury their leader in its bed, releasing the damned-up waters after the burial ceremony so that Attila's tomb would be forever submerged. Indeed, it had never been found.

"Must have been some wedding night," murmured my husband, nuzzling his face against mine. He hadn't shaved for two days, and his cheek was scratchy, but his lips were soft and inviting, reminding me vividly of our own wedding night and our subsequent honeymoon weekend, when he also hadn't bothered to shave.

We'd been married by a justice of the peace in a private morning ceremony at the lodge, just Father, Gray, Jakub, and me. Afterward, we went out to lunch at the Polo Lounge in the Beverly Hills Hotel. We'd decided on lunch as opposed to dinner because the hard-drinking members of the Rat Pack commandeered the place in the evenings, but Father surprised us by inviting a few of my favorite stars to drop by our table for a glass of champagne. Fred Astaire was there, and Gregory Peck and Lauren Bacall, who both happened to be outside by the pool that day, filming the opening scenes of *Designing Women.* John Wayne was eating a steak at a neighboring table, but he and Father had never gotten along and we pretended not to notice him.

The best surprise arrived with dessert. Marlene Dietrich sashayed into the room wearing a man's suit that made her look anything but boyish.

"I hope you've saved me a piece of cake," she said in that alluring German accent of hers.

Father rose to pull out her chair. "Only you would upstage the groom at his own wedding party."

"What do you mean?" she pouted. "I wore this for you, Robbie."

Another bottle of champagne appeared. "To love," said Marlene, when our glasses had been filled.

"To love," we all repeated, clinking glasses.

Jakub drained his glass in one gulp, his eyes never leaving the actress's. I could see that he was completely smitten, but there was no point in being jealous; Marlene had that effect on everyone. John Wayne had stopped eating the moment she entered the room. They'd had a torrid affair in the forties and he seemed eager to pick up where they'd left off, but she was still carrying a torch for Yul Brynner.

After the champagne and the cake, Marlene handed Jakub and me the keys to her bungalow. "Number ten, darlings. You'll like the bed. It's custom-made, and you can just pick up the telephone and order room service—they'll bill it to me—that way you won't have to leave the room if you don't want to."

Attila the Hun probably didn't have room service, I was thinking. We'd stopped for gas at Szolnok, a crossroads town at the confluence of two rivers, the Tisza and the Zagyva. György sent Magda around to open the tailgate, allowing us to get out and stretch our legs. She'd purchased bread and sausages from a market in one of the towns we'd passed through earlier. While we consumed the food, György entered into a lengthy conversation with the filling station attendant. Zoltán was straining to overhear the exchange and, toward the end, he managed to pick up a snippet or two, which caused him to burst out laughing.

"What's so funny?" said Gray.

"Do you like pigs?" Our brother was still chuckling.

"As food?" I asked through a mouthful of sausage. It was seasoned with paprika and was pretty tasty.

"No," said Zoltán. "As company."

We assumed he was joking, but then we saw Magda go off with the attendant on the back of his motorcycle. Ten minutes later they returned, and when they dismounted, we saw that the old woman was clutching a pair of piglets to her chest.

I'd never held a baby pig. These were Mangalicas, a famous Hungarian breed that grow up to be wooly haired, like sheep. Our two were not very wooly; their coats were still coming in. To me, they resembled puppies, plump and floppy-eared. True, they had cloven hooves and snouts but, like puppies, they adored being tickled on their bellies.

We were embarking on the most difficult leg of our journey. Budapest was completely surrounded, Soviet forces stationed at various junctions all along the way to the border. The filling station attendant had been hearing reports of troop buildups all day. He thought our best chance of avoiding a military checkpoint was to head south, giving the capital a wide berth. Students from the university in Sopron had seized control of the municipal government and we'd be safest crossing there. The piglets were for distraction, in case we were stopped and searched. Daylight was fading, and if we covered ourselves with straw and kept to the back of the truck, we might not be spotted.

Once we were underway, I claimed the smaller of the two piglets for my own. "Her name is Princess," I informed the others, having checked to make sure that Princess was a girl. I lured her into my lap with a piece of bread; it didn't seem right to feed her sausage.

Jakub picked up the other piglet and ascertained he was a boy. "This one's ours. What should we call him?"

"How about Karamazov?" proposed Zoltán.

Gray, who admired Dostoyevsky, approved. His first play in London was an adaptation of *The Brothers Karamazov*. Yet again, I was struck by the similarities between my Hungarian and American brothers.

Princess and Karamazov liked playing fetch with my gloves. We'd toss one in the back corner of the truck bed and they'd both race off after it as fast as their stubby little trotters could carry them. Karamazov, being bigger and heavier, rarely reached it first, so we'd throw the other glove for him to retrieve, once Princess had hers. This game amused us for much of the trip, but it proved to be our undoing.

We'd gotten as far as Sárvár, a town in the northwest county of Vas, which bordered Austria. It had a sorry history, Zoltán told us. Sárvár's Jewish population had been persecuted by the Reds and the Whites in turn, and many fled the country, leaving behind their businesses and their property. Gradually, calm was restored, and the community rebuilt itself. On the eve of World War II, Sárvár had two synagogues and a religious school that enrolled over a hundred children. Between the town and the surrounding villages, close to a thousand Jews lived in the area. All were rounded up and interned in a sugar factory that was turned into a Jewish ghetto, from which they were deported to Auschwitz. Poles and Serbs were also interned in Sárvár under brutal conditions, and many died of disease and starvation.

"How do you know so much about this place?" said Gray.

"Sárvár was Anna's town."

Was there nobody in Hungary who hadn't suffered? I didn't know if Anna was Jewish, whether her family had vanished like Zoltán's and György's, but even if she weren't Jewish, simply enduring the war in such a place would have taken its toll. People you'd known, neighbors, friends, shopkeepers, taken away. A woman who devoted her life to caring for the abandoned children of the regime's victims could not have observed this with indifference. I wondered if Anna's experiences in Sárvár did not determine her subsequent choice of career. She might have been powerless to prevent wrongs from being committed, but she would do what she could to repair the damages.

"We seem to be stopping," said Jakub. Peering out through the slats of the tailgate, he reported seeing soldiers standing with automatic weapons, heavy artillery stationed nearby, along with tanks and armored carriers. A line of vehicles stretched behind us.

"Get away from there and lie down!" hissed Zoltán. He crawled from one of us to the next, covering us with straw. Burrowed inside my little cocoon, I heard the sound of him heaping straw on himself, then all was still. The piglets were both sleeping, exhausted after the game with the gloves. Our truck inched forward. I knew we'd reached the checkpoint when I heard voices shouting in Hungarian, followed by the sound of the door to the cab opening. Were they arresting György?

Now the voices had moved around to the back of the truck, and I recognized György's among them. He was still at liberty, thank goodness. I couldn't understand the conversation, but I heard him express a series of denials, and at one point Magda joined in, lending support to his case. Their answers seemed to do the trick; the soldiers' tone softened and I dared to hope we'd be let through. Perhaps they'd peeked in at the sleeping piglets.

Then a new voice entered the dialogue, a more commanding one. "*Otkroyte gruzovik!*" The tailgate opened with a bang, awakening the piglets, who began squealing. I heard laughter from the group, and someone must have picked Karamazov up, because now only Princess remained in the bed with us. Her squeal was higher-pitched than Karamazov's, and it was growing closer, accompanied by a snuffling sound just inches from my right hand. I felt her teeth biting my fingertips, and then she was tugging at my glove. The next thing I knew, she'd gotten it off, exposing my hand to the cold air.

"*Kifelé a kocsiból azonnal!*"

"They want you to get out of the truck, children," I heard

György say in a defeated voice.

Sitting up, I instinctively reached for Princess, but the sound of the shouting had terrified her, for she'd scurried away.

"Be brave, *najdroższa*," murmured Jakub as he helped me down. I took one last look at Princess, who was cowering silently in the corner with my glove in her mouth, and stepped out to join the others.

György and Magda were standing with their hands in the air, covered by a Hungarian soldier holding a submachine gun. He motioned for us to raise our hands as well. Another soldier was holding a squirming Karamazov, who continued to squeal, incurring the wrath of a Soviet officer who stood a few paces away.

"*Pomestite svin'yu obratno v gruzovik!*"

The soldier put Karamazov back in the truck. Gray, who was last to descend, realized what was coming before I did.

"Cara, don't watch."

The Soviet officer pulled his pistol out of its holster, cocked it, and fired a shot into the truck bed. The squealing stopped. He aimed again. Hands in the air, I squeezed my eyes shut, but I could not block out the sound of a second shot. Then I had to look, and when I saw the bloodied bodies of the two little piglets, I had to clench my teeth to keep from crying out. I knew that Jakub would have given anything to comfort me at that moment; I could feel his concern although he was not in my peripheral vision. The Hungarian soldier, whose face I could see quite clearly, had tears in his eyes, but my own eyes were dry.

I was enraged by this act of gratuitous cruelty, enraged but possessed at the same time with a cold awareness. I knew, for example, that I must not let the officer see the hatred burning in my eyes. Bowing my head, I looked fixedly at the ground, not daring to raise it until I'd regained mastery of myself. When I did so, I saw that we were now surrounded by Soviet soldiers, all of them armed.

"*Uvedite ikh!*" In response to this command of the officer's, the four of us were marched away under guard. From behind us came the sound of more shouting, and we all turned to look back. I was afraid that György and Magda might get shot next for having tried to hide us, but the shouting was not being directed at them. Rather, the Soviet officer was berating the two Hungarian soldiers, who hung their heads as a stream of abuse was directed toward them.

György and Magda remained standing motionless beside the truck as this harangue was taking place, no doubt expecting to be arrested the moment it ended, but that is not what happened. The shouting stopped, the Hungarians clicked their heels and saluted, were dismissed, and the officer indicated with a dismissive motion of his hand that György and Magda should get back in the cab. Then he waved the truck away.

Zoltán let out a sigh of relief. We were all glad to see them go. Magda's resourcefulness would keep them both safe. Whatever lay in store for Zoltán, Gray, Jakub, and me, at least somebody would know what had happened to us.

CHAPTER SIXTEEN

Sárvár, Hungary
November 4, 1956

Zoltán said, "I could have told you it would end like this."

"We risked our lives trying to get you out of Budapest," said Gray. "If you had any gratitude, you'd thank us."

Countless hours spent in the pitch black, four of us sharing a two-man cell, and tempers were fraying. I couldn't stop thinking about the piglets' deaths. The casual cruelty of the act was somehow more upsetting than Magda's cold-blooded murder of Frankie. Even József had been killed for a reason, whereas the Soviet officer had shot Princess and Karamazov for no reason whatsoever, simply because he could. And yet he'd chosen to be merciful toward György and Magda when he might just have easily shot them—and with justification. This is what it meant, I realized, to wield power over others. You were free to exercise your whims.

But we were not his to toy with, and thinking back, even Frankie's toying with me in György's kitchen had been halfhearted, a way of passing the time, nothing more. Someone who wielded power over both Frankie and the Soviet officer had sent orders to have us detained, not killed, and that someone could only have been Nicholas.

We'd been the target of an extensive search he'd set into motion from afar. They weren't arresting people en masse; we were the sole occupants of the Sárvár prison. I'd never have guessed that Nicholas had such clout, given his pedestrian role at the American embassy, but he'd deployed considerable resources to track us down. A Soviet army unit had been mobilized to find us—probably more than one unit—because we might have taken any of the multitude of routes to the border. We possessed something that Nicholas wanted. What was it, I wondered, and would it be enough to buy us our way out of Hungary?

Voices sounded in the corridor and the overhead light was switched on. The warden appeared, holding a ring of keys. He looked sleepy, and no wonder. According to my watch, it was two in the morning.

"*Valaki itt van önökért. Kövessenek.*"

"He wants us to follow him," Zoltán translated. "He says that someone has come for us."

So, Nicholas had arrived. Instinctively, I moved closer to my husband, who put an arm around my shoulders and drew me in for a kiss, a tender moment to fortify us for whatever lay ahead.

"*Jöjjenek,*" said the warden gently. He wasn't a bad man, but he had his orders.

The four of us made our way upstairs, passing through the main office of the police station on our way to the front door. The warden ushered us out and retreated back inside immediately, locking the door of the police station behind him, as if he wanted no part in what was about to transpire. We were left standing on the building's stone steps, looking down at the deserted town square.

"Isn't that your car?" said Zoltán, pointing across the street. It didn't seem possible, but there stood the Škoda.

Leaning against it, his white hair illuminated by the streetlight overhead, was Nicholas.

Gray made to descend the stairs. "Let's get this over with."

"Wait." Jakub held him back. "Let him come to us."

"What's the problem?"

"He's not alone."

We followed his gaze. Parked behind the Škoda was a black sedan, identical to the one we'd seen at György's. It must have been the standard-issue vehicle for the secret police. Through the glass, I could just make out the shadowy forms of two passengers in the back seat. They seemed to be slouching, heads down low as if they were trying not to be seen.

My husband squared his shoulders, anticipating a showdown. "*Najdroższa*, get behind me." I didn't budge. If there was to be a showdown, I was determined to face it by his side.

"What's he up to?" said Gray.

Once it became clear that we would not be coming down to join him on the street, Nicholas had gone over to the sedan and rapped on the window to get the driver's attention. The man got out of the car and went back to open the rear door of the vehicle, urging the passengers to come out. A small woman emerged first. She had a scarf tied around her head, and I didn't recognize her right away, but then she turned to help the other passenger, who was hindered by her crutches. Zsuzsi. The girl looked around confusedly. Then she recognized Zoltán and before anyone could stop her, she was half running, half limping across the street, crutches soon abandoned on the sidewalk in her rush up the steps.

"*Apa!*"

Zoltán stooped and gathered the child in his arms. "Zsuzsi,

az én kis Zsuzsim!" He was overcome with emotion and there were tears in my eyes too, I was so pleased to see the child again. Of course, I knew that Nicholas had brought her and Anna with him as hostages. The driver of the black sedan was pointing a revolver at Anna, who remained indifferent to the threat, her attention fixed on a shadow cast on the sidewalk by the streetlight. In the meantime, Nicholas had crossed the street and was now mounting the stairs.

"Icarus," he said, ignoring the three of us and focusing on our brother. "I'm delighted to see you alive."

Zoltán scowled at him. "What do you want?"

"Let's take a walk, shall we?"

I reached out my arms and Zoltàn transferred his daughter into my care.

"*Apa kérlek ne menj vele, rossz ember!*" Protesting, Zsuzsi grasped hold of her father's coat sleeve. I saw him wince; she must have been pulling at his wounded arm.

"*Ne aggódj, kicsim,*" he said. "*Cara nénéd vigyáz rád.*"

"*Nem, nem,*" she insisted, unwilling to let him go.

Nicholas grew impatient. "Leave the child and come along. We don't have all night."

"Shhh, shhh," I whispered, gently detaching Zsuzsi's fingers from her father's sleeve. Reluctantly, she gave up the fight, but her body remained stiff in my arms as she watched him and Nicholas stroll down the sidewalk. I leaned against the doorpost for support, not wanting to let go of her because I was afraid she'd run after them, crutches or no crutches. I knew she wouldn't catch up, but she might provoke action from the driver. He still had his sights trained on Anna but was keeping a wary eye on the rest of us while his boss conducted his business with our brother.

"Is she too heavy? Give her to me," offered Jakub.

"Thanks, but I can manage."

It wasn't long before our brother returned, an undecipherable expression on his face as he strode toward us and climbed the stairs, two at a time, leaving Nicholas below. He'd retrieved Zsuzsi's crutches and had me put her down on the step next to him. Keeping a reassuring hand on his daughter's shoulder, he told us the terms he'd agreed to: our freedom in exchange for his services to the new Soviet-backed regime.

Jakub was the first to raise an objection. "What kind of services?"

"He believes I might be useful to the Hungarian state, in the transition phase."

"After the revolution is crushed, do you mean?" said Gray.

Zoltán acknowledged the question with a curt nod. "The new government will need to rebuild the people's trust. Artists, poets, intellectuals. Hungarians have great respect for high culture. My support, he believes, will lend legitimacy to the regime. I'm to be rehabilitated."

"I suppose that's something," said my husband, digesting this information. "A reason to keep you alive at the outset. But surely there's more. What aren't you telling us?"

Our brother looked down at his feet. "There will be trials, eventually. I'm to testify against the others."

"Which others?"

"The other members of the Writer's Union."

"On what grounds?"

"Counterrevolutionary activity."

Gray had heard enough. "That's all he wants, is it? Betray your principles and send a bunch of your friends to the gallows. How will you live with yourself afterward?"

"That's my problem, not yours."

"No," said Jakub firmly. "It's our problem too. I'm not

sure how I feel about buying our freedom at such a steep price."

"It's her freedom too." Zoltán tilted his head toward his daughter. "Hers and Anna's. Miner has promised to let them both go with you."

I reached over and smoothed Zsuzsi's hair, mussed from having slept on it wrong. She'd probably drifted off on the car ride. How much was it worth, a clear conscience? This child's future, certainly. We were already complicit in József's death. If we had to make a deal with the devil to bring Zoltán's daughter out of Hungary, so be it.

"Take a look behind us and tell me what you see," said Gray. The four of us were in the Škoda, closely trailing the black sedan. Miner had kept Anna and Zsuzsi with him, as insurance. When we reached the crossing at Sopron, we'd make the trade. None of us trusted him to hold up his end of the bargain, but we didn't have much of a choice.

Zoltán, who was in the passenger seat next to my brother, adjusted the side mirror and scrutinized the traffic behind us. "What am I supposed to be looking for?"

"Two cars back," Gray told him. "A livestock truck. Watch how it moves."

Jakub and I turned to look out the rear window, but the truck was too distant for me to determine whether it was the same one we'd traveled in from Mád.

"See that?" Gray applied the brakes. "When I slowed down just now, the truck could've caught up with the car in front of it, but instead of closing the gap, it hung back."

Zoltán was displeased to know that György and Magda were following us. "I wish they'd gone home. They'll only end up complicating matters."

"Maybe so," said Jakub, "but they've been cautious so far, and we've got the benefit of surprise."

"How do you mean?"

"Miner doesn't know how we reached Sárvár. He's got no reason to suspect that we've got accomplices. If we can maneuver him away from your wife and daughter, we may be able to overpower him with their help."

Gray raised an objection. "What about the driver? He's got a gun, remember? Miner won't leave his hostages unguarded."

"I'm less worried about him than I am about Nicholas," said my husband. "I don't think he'll act without orders."

"His type never does," Zoltán agreed. "They're not trained to take the initiative."

"How much gas do we have?" asked Jakub.

Gray eyed the gauge. "Very little, actually."

"Good. That means he didn't bother to fill the tank." Zoltán rubbed his hands together as he worked out a strategy. "Start slowing down, let a car's length develop between you and them, then make it two. Or three. Wait for them to slow down—they won't want us falling too far behind—and beep the horn. Then pull over and turn off the engine."

We all grasped his plan without him having to spell it out any further: we'd pretend we were out of gas. Nicholas or the driver would have no choice but to stop and come back to find out what was going on, and in the time it took for them to get to us, György and Magda would have an opportunity to come to our aid. I had great confidence in Magda's cunning. If anyone could turn the tables on Nicholas, it was her. But I didn't intend to cower in the background and let the others take all the risks. I intended to fight back. Nobody would be expecting me to take the initiative; I too had the element of surprise on my side.

"Okay, here goes," said Gray. "I'm pulling over." He gave a few beeps of the horn and headed for the shoulder, steering around the groups of refugees who were making their way to the border on foot. While we were moving, they hadn't paid us much notice, but once we'd stopped we became a focus of attention. People peered in at us, curious. I was sitting on the right side, watching the onlookers' faces as they appeared in my window, briefly illuminated in the headlights of passing cars. A mother carrying a small child on her hip and leading another by the hand paused in front of me, shifting her burden. Our eyes met and a flicker of recognition passed between us. We were fellow travelers on this journey to freedom, her look seemed to say.

Zoltán alerted us to Nicholas's approach. "Here he comes. Get ready." The sedan had parked a short distance ahead and I could see the Soviet agent weaving through the stream of refugees. He was going against the current and by the time he reached the Škoda, he'd been forced out into the road. Approaching the driver's-side window, he motioned for my brother to roll it down.

"What do you think you're doing?" he hissed, all too aware of his audience of refugees.

"We've run out of gas." Our brother spoke across Gray, pointing to the gauge as if Nicholas could read it from outside the car.

The ploy worked. "Oh, for God's sake! Come out here so I can talk to you."

Zoltán got out and made his way around the front of the car to meet Nicholas by the driver's side.

"Change places with me, *najdroższa*." I wondered what Jakub had in mind, but I complied. Now seated behind Gray, I watched as the reflection of a set of headlights grew bright in the rearview mirror. I heard the rumbling of the truck's engine. Zoltán was facing in its direction, but Nicholas had his back to the oncoming traffic and didn't notice that the vehicle was slowing down. A squeal of brakes and it had come abreast of us, stopping in the middle of the road and corralling the two men, in effect, between the vehicles.

Magda was sitting in the passenger's seat. *"Bolondok! Blokkoljátok az utat!"* she said in an angry voice.

"Kuss, te vén kurva!" Our brother menaced her with his fist upraised.

Nicholas put a hand on his shoulder. "Ignore her. You're coming with me." He must have been intending to take Zoltán in his car, leaving the three of us to our fate. We couldn't let that happen. It was bad enough, leaving without our brother, but I refused to abandon Zsuzsi and her mother.

"Ne sértegesse a feleségemet?" György shouted from inside the cab. I heard the sound of a door slamming. He was coming around to have it out with Zoltán. Magda kept up a string of abuse, waving her arms and jabbing her finger through the open window. Meanwhile, Jakub took advantage of the distraction to slip out of the car. A small crowd had gathered to watch the drama, obscuring his escape. A glimpse of his back as he ran toward the sedan and he was gone.

"Please be careful, darling," I said under my breath. Gray turned around, his expression calm, reassuring. He had utter confidence in my husband.

"Senki sértéseket a feleségem!" György rounded the fender, making straight for Zoltán. Pushing past Nicholas, he shoved our brother into the side of the Škoda, thrusting himself between them. Now Magda was climbing down to stand beside György, further distancing Zoltán from the Soviet agent's reach. Nicholas was now aligned with

my door instead of Gray's, giving me a clear view of him through the window. His hand went to his waist. He was holding something in his palm, something small and metal. He raised his arm and I realized that he had a pistol. He aimed it at György, who was lunging at him, full tilt.

"No!" I screamed. Flinging open the passenger door, I clipped Nicholas in the back, knocking him off balance. A shot sounded and I heard screams from the some of the bystanders. György staggered, but continued to advance on his target, the two men falling together onto the ground. I scrambled out through the open door, desperate to save György, but Magda had already launched herself into the struggle, grabbing Nicholas's outstretched arm and twisting it until the pistol fell from his grip. Zoltán stooped to pick it up, unsure what to do with the weapon. The old woman seemed to have the situation well under control. She'd gotten the Soviet agent into a half nelson, pinning him with her body, one elbow locked around his neck.

Gray and I helped György to his feet. Blood was flowing down his face from a wound on his forehead. I attempted to staunch it with a handkerchief, but it was instantly soaked through. A woman came forward and handed me a piece of cloth, which turned out to be a baby's diaper. She smiled and made the sign of a cross as I took it from her.

"*Isten legyen veled.*"

Magda glanced up, momentarily loosening her hold on Nicholas. He sought to take advantage of this lapse of attention, thrashing his legs in an effort to free himself from her grip. In response, she drove her knee into his back, tightening her arm around his neck until he was still.

"Ugh," he said, fighting for breath.

I knew Magda had both the strength and the will to finish him off, but I didn't think she'd do it in front of a crowd of people. For one thing, Nicholas was disarmed; the threat he posed to any of us at this point was minimal. I was more worried about the driver of the sedan. What would he do, with Nicholas gone? Would he shoot his hostages? Would he shoot Jakub when he tried to rescue them? My husband would be cautious, but the man he was up against might be desperate, or ruthless. Or both.

To my relief, some of the refugees now came to Magda's aid. A pair of heavyset men tied Nicholas's wrists behind his back, using his own necktie. Another produced a piece of rope and proceeded to truss up his legs. Zoltán pressed the pistol to the Soviet agent's temple, for good measure.

"*Add ide!*" The old woman took the pistol away from him and pocketed it. She climbed back into the cab of the livestock truck and came down with a different gun— Frankie's gun—which she gave to him instead. "*Menj, és segítsd a családod.*" She pointed in the direction of the black sedan.

Our brother was itching to go, but still he hesitated. "*Gyuri bácsi*, will you be alright?"

"I'm fine. Go to your family, Zoli."

György didn't seem fine to me—he seemed dazed and weak—but he'd said what Zoltán needed to hear and I was glad he was going off to assist Jakub. Nearly fifteen minutes had elapsed since he'd snuck off—ample time to have accomplished his rescue mission, I would have thought. Why hadn't he returned with Anna and Zsuzsi? Any number of things could have gone wrong, and it was mostly to keep my imagination at bay that I suggested we move to the car, where György would be more comfortable. Magda nodded her assent as we eased him inside the Škoda, the determined set of her jaw a guarantee that she would guard Nicholas until the others returned.

"Bludy mess. Wha wallaped the auld codger?"

"Lay off the Scottish, that's a good man. Can't make sense of half the words that come out of your mouth."

"Sorry."

Ames and Ian were standing in the road, their voices carrying in through Gray's open window. The front of György's overcoat was drenched in blood. By putting pressure on the wound, I'd managed to stop the bleeding, but he did look pretty gruesome under the dome light.

"Do you know these gentlemen?" he said.

Gray introduced the two journalists—he used the word "journalists," but qualified it with "or so they claim."

"What? What? What do you mean?" sputtered Ames. "Of course we're journalists. I've got my press card right here." He pulled out his wallet, ready to produce the evidence, but Ian made him put it away.

"Gie it a break, Petey. He knows whit we ur."

"No Scottish, remember?" Ames scolded.

Remarkably, I was beginning to understand Ian. "What are you?"

Ames answered for both of them. "MI6, dearies."

"British intelligence!" My brother was outraged. "I thought you lot were professionals."

"We mucked up in Budapest," Ian admitted, nudging Ames with his elbow. "Petey here was supposed to be keeping an eye on that Frankie fellow."

"So, what happened?"

Ames looked at his feet. "I should have stuck to my own supply of gin. They slipped me a mickey."

"Yer wair oot yer nut," said the Scotsman, adding in English for our benefit, "sick as a dog afterward, he was."

I could tell from the look on his face that Gray was about to say something scathing, and I was angry too. József would

224

still be alive. None of the trials we'd undergone in the past twenty-four hours would have occurred. Zoltán and György would have reconciled without our being there to observe it, and György wouldn't be injured. Nicholas wouldn't have been in a position to endanger anyone if Ames had been doing his job. We'd have been fast asleep in our comfortable beds at the Hotel Sacher by this time and the various lives we'd disrupted by coming to Budapest would be returning to normal—or what passed for normal.

Which was the problem. Now that we'd made it through the ordeal and were poised to bring our brother and his family out of Budapest, I couldn't disown everything we'd been involved in. If someone had asked me whether I was willing to exchange one man's life for the liberty of three people—four, if you included György—of course I'd have said no, but the decision hadn't been in my hands, and here we were.

"Here's your husband!" announced Ames. "I was wondering where he'd gotten to. And that must be your brother, holding the child. Am I right?"

I rushed out of the car and embraced Jakub. "I'm so glad you're safe," I murmured, not caring that we were kissing in front of a crowd of strangers. It felt as if a month had passed since he went to rescue Zoltan's family.

"*Najdroższa.*" His kiss was more than perfunctory and it took me a moment to realize that something was off. Zoltán was right there behind us, as Ames had said, carrying Zsuzsi in his arms. The girl was weeping, and he was doing his best to comfort her.

Our brother answered my unspoken question. "Anna isn't coming. She won't leave the children."

Ames and Ian were loading Nicholas, trussed and gagged, into the back of their car. They'd be escorting us to the border, where "interested parties" would take him off their hands.

"Come along, dearies. Say your goodbyes and let's be off."

Anna would ride with Magda as far as Budapest. She took Zsuzsi aside and was crouched next to her by the truck, the two engaged in a somber conversation. She seemed to be extorting a promise from her daughter. We saw the girl nod, and then her mother straightened up, took her by the shoulders, and kissed her once on each cheek before sending her back to us and climbing up into the cab.

I was making an effort not to cry as I watched Zsuzsi approach on her crutches. Magda already had the engine running. The old woman was having difficulty turning around on the two-lane road, with so many people milling about, but Anna avoided looking at us. I thought that she was also trying not to cry.

József had said it first: heroes can be very hard to live with. Until the moment when Nicholas had forced him to choose between his family and his principles, Zoltán's moral purity was unsullied. He was like Icarus, heedless of those around him as he flew into the sun. Our brother was saving the world. Well before Anna betrayed him by turning informer, he'd betrayed her. The children's home was her way of saving the world—not the entire world, but a small piece of it. Zoltán had put all of that in jeopardy by engaging in his underground activities, subsuming her work, her ideals beneath his own.

I wasn't sure if anyone else saw Anna's dilemma as I did, but it made me think. Jakub had it too, that heroic instinct. No matter how tempting it was, to be taken care of, I wanted to be the author of my own life.

CHAPTER SEVENTEEN

Vienna, Austria
November 4, 1956

A pink mist was rising off the Danube as we arrived in Vienna. The city resembled Budapest so strongly, architecturally, that I was surprised to find it intact. It was too early on a Sunday morning for the trams to be running on the famous Ringstrasse; we had the vast boulevard practically to ourselves.

"There's the State Opera," said György, pointing to an elaborate building that filled an entire block, statues of men on horseback crowning its pillared facade. He'd traveled to Vienna frequently for his job as a curator at the Museum of Fine Arts, but it had been twenty years since his last visit.

Jakub had passed through the city after the war and remembered how much of it had been destroyed. "They've finished rebuilding it, I'm glad to see."

"Yes," said Zoltán, leaning forward to be heard by the others. "I was here as well. The building was a shell in '45 after you Americans bombed the place. This entire section of the city was in ruins."

Gray sighed in exasperation from behind the wheel. "The Germans were dug in, just like in Budapest. How else were we supposed to end the war? Hitler's orders were to stay or die."

"I suppose that explains Dresden as well?"

György turned in his seat and glared at our brother, admonishing him into silence, but Zsuzsi had already picked up on the tension in the car.

"*Mi a baj, apa?*" she said. "*Miért vagy ilyen mérges? Kérlek ne haragudj ránk.*"

Our brother looked stricken. "She already thinks I'm angry with her mother. Now she's afraid I'm angry with you." Pulling the child into his lap, he began speaking to her in a soft, reassuring voice, but his words did little to calm her fears. I wished I spoke Hungarian, so I could explain to Zsuzsi that her father wasn't angry with her mother or with any of us. He'd been carrying around that anger for most of his life, I wanted to tell her.

My own son might be harboring anger against me, and I would never know. At least there was a chance that Father and Zoltán might heal the breach between them, for Zsuzsi's sake. For my part, I pledged to remain in my niece's life. I could not take the place of her mother, but as she grew up, I hoped she might turn to me when she needed a woman's ear, a woman's understanding, to help her navigate the world. She would be the author of her own life. I would make sure of it.

Acknowledgments

Thanks to my readers, Dusty Miller and Bill Lucey. Your enthusiastic support kept me going, and I'm pleased that you laughed at most of my jokes.

Gabor Lukacs corrected my Hungarian and made many useful suggestions. *Köszönöm szépen* to Gergely Bárányos at Cityrama Budapest for leading my husband and me on a seven-hour walking tour around the sites of the 1956 revolution, with a few from 1848 thrown in at no extra charge, during a 2015 research trip to Hungary. The staff at Hotel Palazzo Zichy made our stay in Budapest special, and even managed to come up with a spare room when we were stranded for an additional two days, owing to the Lufthansa strike. Barnabás Fehér, the caretaker of the Mád synagogue, was kind enough to show us around.

Thanks also to my editors, Richard Marek and Lourdes Venard. *Burning Cold* is a better book as a result of your attentions. The team at Encircle Publications has been a pleasure to work with.

Finally, to Tim, my partner in publishing—along with everything else that matters: viva l'avventura!

About the Author

L isa Lieberman is the author of numerous works of postwar European history and the founder of the classic movie blog Deathless Prose. Trained as a modern European cultural and intellectual historian, she studied at the University of Pennsylvania and Yale University and taught for many years at Dickinson College. She now directs a nonprofit foundation dedicated to redressing racial and economic inequity in public elementary and secondary schools. In her spare time, she lectures on postwar efforts to come to terms with the trauma of the Holocaust in film and literature and works with young writers at the Paulo Freire Social Justice Charter School in Holyoke, Massachusetts. After dragging their three children all over Europe while they were growing up, Lisa and her husband are happily settled in Amherst, Massachusetts.

CPSIA information can be obtained
at www.ICGtesting.com
Printed in the USA
FFOW03n0217110917
39732FF

9 780998 983714